Praise for
FAUNA

'*Fauna* is the story of an experiment, as every relationship, every child, every hope we cling on to is an experiment—a leap into air. It is lush and corporeal and one of the most honest books I've ever read about what we carve away for our children from our hearts, our bodies, and our possible futures. I knew when I started that this book would end, yet every moment I hoped it wouldn't.' Amanda Niehaus, author of *The Breeding Season*

'*Fauna* lays bare an electrifying genetically re-coded future so real, so terrifying, so close, I can feel its baby breath soft against my cheek.' Robyn Mundy, author of *Wild Light*

'Mazza's novel asks hard questions, yet brims with compassion. A thrilling, unsettling read.' Paddy O'Reilly, author of *The Wonders*

FAUNA

DONNA MAZZA

ALLEN&UNWIN

SYDNEY·MELBOURNE·AUCKLAND·LONDON

Allen & Unwin
83 Alexander Street
Crows Nest NSW 2065
Australia
Phone: (61 2) 8425 0100
Email: info@allenandunwin.com
Web: www.allenandunwin.com

 A catalogue record for this book is available from the National Library of Australia

ISBN 978 1 76087 630 2

Internal design by Bookhouse, Sydney
Set in 13.2/18.9 pt Granjon LT Std by Bookhouse, Sydney
Printed and bound in Australia by Griffin Press, part of Ovato

10 9 8 7 6 5 4 3 2 1

FOR MY MOTHER, HER MOTHER, MY CHILDREN, THEIR FATHER AND MINE

IN UTERO

The longer I stare at the ring on the screen, the more it appears to shift. Cells are pinpoints, some surrounded by a thin halo, carrying the weight of life and all that it means. A concept so enormous I can't hold it in my mind. Its walls look thick, yet in reality it could drop on the floor and be impossible to find. It could blow away in the breeze or be sucked up a vacuum cleaner. The tiny things that make us who we are—smaller than a speck. Yet also everything. The totality of us written in strings and twists hidden inside each cell.

Isak sits beside me, our fingers interlocked while we watch the perfect circle magnified on the screen, already populated with a small collection of cells gathered in one hemisphere. The coagulation of being—sticking together. Re-made and made. This is a new experience for us. Our other children were conceived naturally, but no amount of acronyms or scientific terms can take away the magic of life and what makes it. They were all magical. This one is even more so.

The journey to this point hasn't been as complicated as I thought it would be. Not that far outside the realm of normal really. Lots of people go through IVF programs. A few blood tests. Harvesting some eggs and sperm. Laughing about the stupidity of it all. They took them off to the lab, did some snipping and pasting and now we have a successful blastocyst, with some germ-line modification—so they say. Testing has been done and it's still growing, cells dividing and forming, faster than usual and now ready for implantation. Heart and spine and brain and skin. There, under the microscope, are the beginnings of a new life.

.

In the toilets at the back of the clinic I pee into a plastic jar. Of course I also pee on my hand, I'm sure everyone does, but I wipe it dry with a piece of toilet paper and screw on the yellow lid. This is the test. Just an eye-dropper of urine on the stick and they know right away. Isak turns to me and smiles. I am shaking.

And so it begins. This journey I have travelled three times before, twice to a happy ending and once not. This time, I am reminded, the journey will not be the same.

A blood test confirms it—the wee did not lie.

LifeBLOOD® are very respectful and professional. They've explained the terms of our agreement in detail. Take it home, they said. Isak tried to read it but it was thirty-six pages of policy speak and clauses which all seemed quite straightforward. A lot of stuff about risk and indemnity, keeping informed, communication, mutual obligation. Isak read the financial support section in some detail, nodding to himself and interpreting it to me. What we expected, if we had given it that kind of thought. He signed it. There was nothing about love, but it was a legal contract and the two are repellent to each other. I signed it.

.

After the appointment we walk down the street for a coffee. At the florist Isak leads me through a heavy purple door and grabs a bunch of orange lilies from a bucket.

'Congratulations.' His arm around my shoulders. Kiss on the forehead. The dense scent of flowers and essences masks a note of green rot festering in the buckets.

I pull back a little, his grasp overly tight. 'It's a bit weird though. Not like our other kids.' I never saw their ingredients. Their codes and sequences remained veiled inside them.

He laughs, deepening the folds that crease his cheeks. 'I doubt it will be anything like our other kids.' Eyes shift. He pushes his hair back and we return to the street, traffic rippling the air.

This is the old part of Perth, buildings thick with paint, some restored to neat red bricks with tidy mortar. Constantly reinventing itself for each generation. New signs and styles of coffee, new specialists offering therapies, surgeries, enhancements and regeneration. Across the street, a row of pigeons perch on the rooftop of a bar, eyes firmly set on the tables below.

A cafe in one of the older buildings is carefully shabby, drawing on historic styles that never co-existed. We find a comfortable seat at a smoked glass table. Isak orders cake to share, coffee. He's already a bit buzzy from the appointment so coffee will make him talkative. I don't mind, it might stop the light from shining on that little seed that lurks at the edge of my thoughts, that truth. The one buried in the dark there—tangled in reasons.

When the cake comes, it has a tower of cream with it and Isak rakes a fork through the soft wedge, toppling it onto the table. I wipe it up with a serviette. 'We won't lose the house now, Stacey.' He talks through the cake about them paying our bills, details of the contract, which will make our lives much more secure. Education, clothes. He is boring when he gets stuck on money and I wither inside. I can make do with what we have, with op-shop clothes and simple things. I've never had much, or been much either. Bearing this child has a value beyond money.

'You've got more idea than me.' I hope this is the truth so I leave the administration of our lives to him. He finds ways to pay for things he wants but he works for it, not me. Not very empowering I know but I don't want to deal with our money. He would hate to think he is controlling, but it's me who surrendered.

'And when the child is an adult our job is done. That's the way with Emmy and Jake too.' He pushes the cake towards me but it's already collapsed. 'Want some?' Dark grains of it specked in the cream.

'You finish it,' I tell him, irritated. It's so rare that we eat out. 'When they're adults seems a long way off.'

He shrugs. More cake.

'It's pretty good.' I think he is talking about the cake but he goes on further about the money. 'We can give them all more of the things that are important. Music lessons. Holidays.'

'I can't even imagine what that'd be like.' We were both keen travellers but kids come first now and I haven't even bothered keeping my passport valid.

'We can take them back home.' I know he misses his mother, all the things he loves about the landscape and the wildlife, the lifestyle. I never had those roots and somehow this will help give it back to him, just a glimpse. I owe it to him now. He scrapes at the final smear of cream.

'We're not done yet though,' I try to bring it back to the pregnancy.

He holds my hand, realising there is a knot in me and why it is there. They talked in the clinic about the risk of miscarriage and the possibility it won't go to plan. He kisses my knuckles. 'We've been there too, Stacey, but LifeBLOOD® are investing in this baby and they'll look after you. They won't want that to happen.' But, of course, it is more than that.

.

Nobody really thought the first embryo would work but it did. In fact, as soon as the chance was there, that little life took it, growing in quick, definite arrangements. Unlike other pregnancies, I have not vomited. As my organs rearranged and things began settling into the nest of me I have had some cramps, which pin me to the couch for a few days, anxious not to bring on that unbearable loss.

The garden, such that it is, withers in the heat and I don't even rise to water the pots of scraggy basil. In the silence of school days I watch the breeze from the air-conditioner shift garlands of cobwebs across the ceiling. I wonder what this child will bring, to us and to the world. I bubble with the thrill of it, I swell and drop with anxiety. Nausea aggravated by my emotional tides. It's understandable, they say. As each day passes and the baby grows, I begin to understand it and the infinite possibilities it might bring and I wonder what I have done. So does Isak.

Mornings are the worst for nausea and afternoons for cramps. I turn in on myself and build a shell against Isak's growing uneasiness. He trawls through websites, shaking his head and sharing facts. I say I am sick and avoid the normal tasks of getting the kids ready for school, let Isak iron their uniforms and pack lunches. Emmy curls into bed beside me in her school clothes. 'Can't you make us lunch please, Mumma? I'm so sick of Dad's cheese and pickle sandwiches.' Her bony knee pokes into my abdomen and I flinch. She pulls back. Tomorrow, I tell her.

They kiss me goodbye. Isak leans over, 'Stop avoiding. The sooner we get to grips with it the better for all of us,' hands me the screen and a cup of ginger tea. 'Read it, you can't revoke your decision.'

'Our decision,' I call back and he rushes out the door, Jake's Spiderman schoolbag across his shoulder. Tension hangs in a silent wake that seems to hiss. A languid fly crawls across a convex mango skin scraped clean by small teeth.

The site on the screen is slick with graphics—*LifeBLOOD® Bringing Life Out of Darkness*. I scroll through the page, scan the promotional text.

LifeBLOOD® provides as normal a life as possible for all our parents and children. Raising any child is challenging and we understand how this will be different for parents of LifeBLOOD® children.

They refer to children. We're not the only ones doing this then. More spiel about qualified and inducted doctors and other allied health professionals. Occupational therapists, education experts, financial advisors and speech therapists are among the many staff available to support new parents. I have no patience and skip down the page—a non-disclosure clause that all parents must maintain complete discretion surrounding the genetic conditions under which LifeBLOOD® children are born. I skip sections. Can't focus on this language, have no discipline to read this kind of thing, it's no wonder I wasn't a good student. *Parents are required to*—something about counselling and I scroll down—*respond to all inquiries regarding the nature of appearance or developmental delays and behaviour in the LifeBLOOD® child according to postnatal direction.* My hand naturally drifts to below my navel and rests there. This child will be perfect and beautiful. This time.

I scroll down to the tabs for pages on diet, relationships, education, communication, stages of development and more. When I click on them, a notice for username and password pops up. The only ones that I can access are 'pregnancy' and 'policy and governance'. Isak will have read it all. The tea has gone cold but I finish the last of it. It spices my chest and quells the nausea. Scroll and stop—*LifeBLOOD® children must be sheltered from certain social situations and environments according to the direction of your practitioner. These may include avoiding exposure to stressful public events, large crowds, certain animals, excessive noise, technology in your home or an outbreak of virus. This area is under constant review to ensure safety and wellbeing.* Further down, another part of the page is illustrated by a photograph of a happy nuclear family playing in a park. They all have red hair. A toddler faces away from the camera, the action shot a little blurry—*Family units are vital to the development of any healthy child and LifeBLOOD® children require a peaceful home in which to flourish. Families entering into this program have already shown themselves to be excellent parents.*

In the silent air in this suburb of closed doors and faded greys I have planted myself somewhere without nourishment. The garden drags itself through the seasons; it is a victory for it to survive another year. Each grevillea, each aloe and cordyline clinging to the sandy soil, desperate for the fecundity buried somewhere under the fill sand of builders and subdividers. Their pale roots diving deep in search of lost swampland. The true land somewhere deep beneath us. In these long hours between the children's departure for school and their arrival home, sometimes I have been extinct. Now, though, even in stillness I am animate. Blood and cells and microbes, swirling into new life.

LifeBLOOD® children are an important part of new research that will bring benefits to human health and resilience. I push the screen to the end of the couch and try to sleep but that last phrase is burned on my internal view, the letters turning white on a black background, forming into a negative. Despite the humanity of this, we are now research. I try to push the thought of it away but it burns on, refusing to fade.

4 WEEKS

I cancel the first counselling session booked a fortnight after our conception is confirmed but when the second one comes around I can't find an excuse. Isak picks me up in the afternoon, a little later than he planned.

'They'll have to pardon the high-vis.' He dusts the front of the fluoro yellow and navy shirt. I spit-wash a dirty smear from his jaw as he drives the curves and roundabouts that lead from our suburb to the freeway. He smiles. 'That's unhygienic you know?'

'You love the attention.' A warm moment between us. The car smells of burgers and chips. 'I should clean out the car on the weekend.'

Isak slurps the last of his soft drink, rolls his eyes. He knows I never clean the car but he says nothing about it.

We cross the river, exit the freeway into affluent parts of old Perth where I au-paired for a while when I left home, in a nicer house with a nicer garden than my own. I have the urge to tell Isak about coming here with Alex, but he has heard it all before. Doing school again properly so we could go to uni. That window of freedom, just a couple of years really; it made Perth home, but it hasn't quite lived up to those memories this time.

In the waiting room, Isak smells slightly of perspiration and I suppress yawns. 'What do you think they want to talk to us about?' he whispers. I have no idea but I see he is anxious so I tell him they probably want to make sure I'm not depressed and that he's looking after me. I squeeze his hand. 'Which you are.' He smiles weakly. It's just us. Since we met it has always been just us. I think that's why they wanted us for this program—because just us has been enough for me and him. Just us and our children. Most of the time. There are no third parties to interfere.

The counsellor, named Fee, has spikey dyed hair and speaks in hushed tones, leading us into a room of frosted glass with a diffuser pushing a plume of lemongrass steam into a high column on a table between her two spare chairs. It masks Isak but the smell is far too tangy for a small room. My mother would object on health grounds during pregnancy but I don't want to sound like I'm into alternative medicine in here. I've tried to put it behind me. Deny my upbringing. I move the chair away slightly and inadvertently turn my back a little towards Isak.

After introducing herself, Fee leads with, 'So is everything okay between you two?' I twist the chair back. Breathe the toxic steam. He reaches for my hand and we both nod vigorously and giggle foolishly. She speaks for a while about parenthood in general terms and asks our philosophies on it. Isak tries to answer for us and goes on about taking the kids fishing, which he hasn't done for a very long time. It all sounds very wholesome but I know Jake's toddler-sized fishing rod is buried somewhere in the sand of the back garden. I cut off the hook so he wouldn't hurt himself. I shake my head but say nothing about it. Don't want to make Isak look stupid.

She refocuses the conversation back to us and aligns her gaze with mine. I hate counsellors, my hands sweat. She is picking something up, she says, from me. My heart is beating quickly, it's the kind of statement my mother would make during a tarot reading. 'I feel sick,' I lie. Do I need a glass of water? Her look of trained concern makes me panic. 'Can we turn off the diffuser?' Of course, she says and leans in between us with her broad back. The flowers of her shirt falling flat on the table like a dead bouquet.

'You okay, Stace?' Isak crouches in front of me, holds my eyes. She disappears for a moment and I calm.

'I hate the way they drill into stuff.' The scent makes me think of my mother.

'She's not really started yet.'

I nod.

'You don't have to speak much if you don't want to. I can talk to her.' He pats my arm. Fingernails always oily from working on machines.

She's back with water and soon settles into her chair to continue. Asks Isak about his work and if he can get time off from the refinery when the baby comes. He talks about his paternity leave arrangements and then she turns back to me.

'Feeling a bit better?' My eyes flick from her magenta glasses to the orange of her hair and I say nothing. There's a tight belt around my chest.

'Stacey? Are you feeling any better?' Isak glares at me.

'Yes, sorry. I'm a bit tired.'

'That's understandable,' she says. 'Most pregnant women get tired in the afternoon. Do you have a doctor's appointment coming up soon?'

Isak says we do. She nods a lot. My dislike for her is toxic and I burst.

'I'd rather see someone else for counselling next time.' They both look at me, I barely knew the words were coming when I said them. 'I'm not comfortable with you, sorry.' Her cheeks redden a little and Isak frowns. 'You remind me of my mother.' Fuck. Why did I say that?

'Your mother is a problem for you?' She looks at Isak and back to me. We'll never get out of here now. I feel trapped. Pushing down a panic attack. 'Sorting things out like this is important. You have big responsibilities to this child, and your other children.' I breathe deep, try to centre myself, rise above this feeling so we can go.

'We haven't spoken for a while.' I sit on my hands like a child. 'But I'll call her this week. She's very busy. I think it's just the smell of the lemongrass oil makes me think of her.' Breathe. I look over to Isak.

'Scent will do that.' She nods vigorously. 'We can talk it through next time. Attachment and detachment are important for us to work through together.' It's not just the scent.

•

In the car, Isak is prickly and annoyed with me for raising the issues with my mother. 'She's not that bad. There are much worse people around.' He puts some music on in the car. Ed Sheeran's old songs, which we used to sing along to when we met. We don't speak but the mood shifts and we drive to pick the children up from school. I wait in the car. His gaze back at me is long and a little sad.

6 WEEKS

LifeBLOOD's® digital imaging centre is on a busy corner and Isak throws the car into the last parking bay.

'Shit, Isak.' I hold the car door with stiff fingers to stop from slamming into it. 'Why so fast?'

He steams out a rush of breath. 'You said you'd call your mother. I won't come to appointments with you if you're going to lie to them, Stacey.' He turns in his seat, face red. 'I can't do it.' Tries to soften his tone but I see his anger, 'I'm worried.'

I don't know what to say. I'm worried too.

'Look, I don't want to look like a fool. She's your mother and you need to deal with it.'

I'm shaking inside. 'Forget about my mother. It's got nothing to do with her. Just let it go.'

'I'd love to see my mother. I'd give almost anything to; in fact, for me that's one of the big reasons for doing this in the first place.'

My hand goes to my abdomen. Instinct.

'That I can go back and pay the money I owe her,' he continues, 'and hold my head high.'

'We didn't need to buy a house.' He doesn't mention the baby.

'We did. We did absolutely. You want a childhood for Emmy and Jake where they move all the time? I don't think so.' His job is filthy, hard work. I know he hates it but he does it without complaining, day after day. For us. I have no qualifications to do anything. I could look after children, but I have my own. He is the only one who understands me.

'Why did you want this so bad, Stacey?'

I can't answer the question, not even in my own head.

'I can't explain it.' It was the lost baby and the zoo of brought-back animals. It just infested my thinking while the kids were at school; all that time when I lay in bed in the daytime, holding my empty belly and feeling the loss of the last baby like a small stone. The weight of it is always with me. All those new animals made from old ones and all that is lost. Lost and gone. Rhinoceros and the last specks of sea ice, polar bears and the worlds beneath the sea and great green forests filled with birds and orang-utans with souls in their eyes. I am carrying it now, all that has gone and is going. 'Maybe it was the mammoth,' I tell him.

'You aren't having a baby mammoth.' He looks at me with that expression he saves for the most stupid of situations.

'I can't explain it to you. It's too big; too complex.'

'I know you've been depressed, I understand.' He taps the steering wheel, staring out at the steaming line of cars. Heat slowly fills the silent car. 'But if you can't explain it to me, I really don't think I can come with you right now, Stacey.'

His disconnect hits me in the chest and I flinch, shrink from him. 'They'll ask me why you aren't there.'

He is a little teary and I feel it rise in my throat. 'It's still our baby,' these words crack into sharp points. Hot in my eyes.

He looks at me, flat. 'It's not the same as our babies.' He won't make eye contact with me, his jaw is hard and I can see his teeth clenched through his cheek. 'It's not. They sliced it up and made it into something else.'

I've never seen him so immovable.

'You agreed to it. You signed your consent, too. You read the stupid contract.' Anger winds up. Blame. 'I'm relying on you to understand what we are getting into.' What we're already into. I willed myself not to understand, just wanted it.

'Fuck—' Heat ticks outside. 'I know.' He picks at the sun-damaged plastic on the steering wheel. 'You were excited. It is exciting for fuck-sake.'

'You're scared and I get it. I am too.' I try to hold back the anxiety; it's a baby now and I'm not letting it go anywhere. It will be; I want it. 'We can do it though, Isak. We can be those people who do something amazing that's never been done before.'

He takes my hand, damp in my lap, and tries to be calm. 'Maybe we can.' He lets out a huff of hot breath. 'Look, I just need more time to think it through.'

I sniff back the tears. 'My appointment is in a few minutes. Please come with me.'

He stares at me with a hint of iciness. 'I don't think you hear me, Stacey. I need a bit of time. I'll be here when you come out.'

I throw open the door, my full bladder obstructing smooth movement, and belt the door shut with all my might. The car shakes. I can see his fingers on the steering wheel, tight and red on the cracked black plastic.

.

I sit gingerly in the reception area on the edge of my seat, foot tapping. The weight of our conversation makes my breath short. We never usually argue like this.

'Stacey?' I look up, furtive eye contact. Still caught in the emotion of argument. 'Come this way, please. Have you had all the water the doctor asked you to drink?'

I nod silently, collect myself and follow her down the dimmed hallway.

'Have you been to the toilet or is your bladder full?' She opens the door, *LifeBLOOD® Imaging—Private Facility.*

'Oh, no. My bladder is quite full.' An ironed sheet covers a low bed surrounded by various screens and equipment, cords, monitors, things hanging from the ceiling.

'I'll just get you up on the bed, shoes off and we'll have a quick look to check your dates.'

I close my eyes while she sets up the screen, taps on the keyboard and squirts gel on my belly. Try to focus on the baby.

.

Four years ago, when we were returning from Isak's sister's wedding in South Africa, we had a stopover for two nights in Singapore and took the kids to the 2033 Resurrection Exhibition, a travelling zoo from the Smithsonian's de-extinction program. Three enormous bio-domes were set up in a park—three environments decreasing in temperature. Tropical, temperate and tundra. The biosecurity was rigorous and we laughed at the white paper suits and plastic masks, but I was really overcome by the whole experience. It touched me deeply.

Briny water, warm damp air and huge fronded foliage created a primal scent. Interpretive signs with images of the dodo, specimens of eggs and models of skeletons and heads collected hundreds of years ago, left to die in European exhibitions as a curiosity. Eaten by sailors and pigs until they were gone. We could see just a peek of feathers, fluffed up and nestling into long sedge grasses. A guide speaking to a group of tourists in Mandarin pointing towards the little ball of feathers.

Emmy held my hand, quiet with anticipation, through the double doors locking off the tropical air from the temperate bio-dome. Obediently stepping through a sticky antibacterial gel to prevent cross-contamination. Wild viruses. Isak carried Jake, dipped his little sneakers in the sticky tray.

The second soaring, white dome was cooler than the humidity of Singapore outside and filled with large American trees, a small hillock covered in waving grass. A breeze moved slowly through and a flock of passenger pigeons circled overhead. Photos of Martha, the last of the passenger pigeons in 1914, demonstrated clearly that within two generations the program had successfully renewed the species. The pigeon DNA was just over a hundred years old.

Hidden in the grass, the heath hens pecked at scattered seed. The wonder of it seemed lost on the children, who dragged us through the crowd, keen to get to the next dome and discover it. But I loosened Emmy's grip on my hand and lingered, reading the boards and watching the renewed birds. Here now as though they'd never left.

Isak waited for me, smiling at my passion for the ancient world. 'You might get to dig up some fossils someday.' I'd barely started my studies. Just a few weeks into second semester on a dig in the Wicklow mountains and I was already in love with him. We were unstoppable.

Separated from the birds, but in the same temperate dome, three thylacines lay with their backs turned to us. Isak was telling the children the story of their extinction, the horror of colonial thinking—something dark and alien. Photographs of 'Benjamin', the last thylacine in Hobart Zoo and the sad old video of her pacing in her enclosure. 'Like a hyena,' he had said to the kids. Her mangy appearance, hanging head and incessant pacing. Nothing like a hyena in nature. The tale that her corpse was thrown out at the local rubbish tip. A preserved foetus in a jar. And something about the need for apex predators in the Tasmanian landscape. Their three stripy backs turned to us, refusing our curiosity.

The tundra bio-dome shocked our systems, controlled to keep the ground cold from beneath and the air cold from above. The children complained loudly and tourists dashed through, rushing by the greatest wonder of de-extinction, past the signage and video dumbing down detailed processes for the unscientific public, justifying the project—these animals were helping us stave off climate change by stomping down the tundra and activating some processes that hold carbon in the permafrost. Always so much information when the wonder is in the creature standing on soft grass, scattered with snow. Isak and Jake first spotted the young mammoth as we rounded the corner. It was so huge. No tusks yet. Its rich amber wool, its deep dark eyes. So unexpectedly beautiful.

Isak took the children out to the gift shop and away from the cold but I stayed in the tundra. Shivering, I met its great eye with mine. Wide and wet and dark, I soared into the depth of it, disconnected from myself. There was something of my truth, something I knew of myself living in the beating heart of this great creature. Its grassy smell, the wisps of auburn hair surprisingly sparse on its skin yet it seemed so certain in that cold air. I was lost to its power and immensity. My heart pounded with the thrill of it and, behind in the frosted air, three artificial figures—a Neanderthal family, crouched and waiting to be resurrected. And on the board beside them some hints at the human trial and the name—Dr Jeffrey van Tink, whose children I had au-paired years before in the nice house with the nice garden.

I still wear the locket Isak bought for me that day. A coiled mammoth hair like a rusted spring, pressed under glass.

Now in the dim room, the technician measures the millimetres of growth and plots sections of the image on her screen. My uterus and its parts and details. Things I don't understand and can only see in fragments around her too-close head. The scan is quick.

'We're all done here, Stacey. Do you have any questions?' She glances at me.

There is only one question that can be asked. 'Is everything okay with the baby?' And I know she is not the person to give me the answer.

'I'm afraid we'll have to wait for the radiographer and his team to write a report.' She taps into the screen, holds up an image of the embryo, curled like the sprout of a fern. My heart jolts a little, unsure if I am seeing normal growth. She flips the screen back out of view. 'If you go on the website, they will post images of the scan and a copy of the report for you. Have you logged on to our site yet?' She wipes the gel from my stomach, flipping the loose clothing over me without touching my skin with her gloved hand. I nod, wriggling off the side of the bed.

'And I see you have an appointment with Dr van Tink coming up so you can discuss your concerns with him.' For a moment, I did hear the beat of life. Fast and definite, as my own.

In the car Isak sits stiff and avoids my eyes. My insides twist at the sight of his fine hands, hard against the shield of the steering wheel. He measures his words, carefully planned.

'I want to go and see my family for a while before we have the baby.'

I sink inside.

'The kids are both in school and they can stay here with you.' He glances at me for a moment, just quickly. 'I don't want to disrupt them. I'll tell them I need to help my mum on the farm.' He is pale, his lips stretched thin.

Sick, frantic. 'Will you come back? This isn't it, is it?' Will myself not to cry. 'I can have an abortion if you want me to.' Silence between us ripples with emotion. 'But—' Our eyes meet for a moment and he shakes his head, obviously annoyed.

'That's a very loaded way of putting it, Stacey. I just feel like I need to do it now because it will be more difficult when there's a baby involved.' He sighs, looks at me with teary eyes. 'I just need to come to terms with this and I don't quite know how.' His voice cracks.

'I need you here.'

He touches my hand but he is resolved.

'I know it's a bit weird but it's just another baby really,' I try to soothe him.

He starts the car, calmer now he has cast off his anxiety. I have picked it up, wrapped it around my shoulders like a prickly shawl. 'You know it isn't just another baby,' he says. 'But you'll need me more when it's born than you do now and I can't see a time ahead of us for a long while when I will be able to go.' He takes to the road more calmly. 'I just need a bit of time to think it all through. And you know I miss my family.'

I buzz with worry, turn to the window with my tears.

He softens his tone, 'You'll be okay for a few weeks, Stacey. The kids are pretty easy when they're in school.'

Life is so fragile—little curls of being, tiny bundles of cells, the human heart. The delicate things; the most precious.

'I'll do it on the cheap, get another credit card. We'll have money enough soon.' His need to go settles in. Traffic is slow and we trace the coast back home, air-conditioner audible in the dense space between us. Even though cold air pumps out at me, oxygen feels lacking in the car. I sip from my water bottle, setting my eyes in the middle ground where rooftops fill the horizon in shades of red, brown and grey.

'I always think of us as rock solid.' My face is tight, breath shallow. Near tears.

'We are.' He grabs my hand and the car churns onwards, nearing our exit.

'You didn't even ask me about the scan.' Normally he would be in there with me, asking the right questions. Hearing the news firsthand. Perfect father.

'Stop picking at it, Stacey. We are rock solid, I promise. Just give me some space.' I brush aside tears, loose and silent, and we pull up at the kids' school a little early. A bronze-winged pigeon skitters quickly from the path of the car. I sigh deeply and we make eye contact, strong and resolute. Neither willing to disrupt the joyful days of our children. He squeezes my hand but I carry that first image alone. He still hasn't asked about the baby.

8 WEEKS

Isak is gone. Only yesterday, but the pit he leaves in my heart feels dark and heavy. I pull into the car park of the LifeBLOOD® offices fifteen minutes early. Sit in silence, sip water. The hum of traffic. Used tissues, burger boxes, a felt pen chewed to pieces, the skin of a banana. Out of control. I gather it together into a paper takeaway bag. Resolve not to feed the kids junk food while their father is away and leave the stuffed bag on the passenger seat. Have a mint, try to relax. They are sure to check my blood pressure so I need to calm down. Emmy drew a little person with a speech bubble saying 'calm' for our toilet wall. It has a caption—'think of a happy memory'. Breathe in through your nose and out through your mouth while saying *calm*. I breathe. Calm. He is in my happy memories. A Silver Princess eucalyptus droops over the car park. Long grey-green leaves hanging vertical. Rampant pink blossoms brighten the fading season. I parked in its meagre shadow.

The offices are in an old house, converted into consulting rooms and decorated in a classic style with hardwood floors and soft, creamy colours. It exudes order and cleanliness. Calm. Nothing like the public hospital clinic where my other babies were measured and dated. Waiting for hours in a mismatched row of vinyl chairs. And the last time, those blunt words—'Looks like baby has died.' They struck so hard; so unexpected. Delivered so carelessly, as though it were an everyday thing. I curled up like a dead embryo too. Dried into that shape.

The timber counter here provides mints for patients and convenient payment options. Neat, mature office staff wear blue and white uniforms and have sensible names—efficient Lauren and kind-hearted Sophie. They want me to feel I am in safe hands. I know Jeff is giving us the best care. There will be no blunt words this time.

'Welcome, Stacey. Dr van Tink won't be long. Please take a seat.' Sophie smiles at me. Neat and blonde.

On a large screen, a video plays promoting the work of LifeBLOOD® with smiling staff and neat-haired parents. A Petri dish and pipette allude to their laboratory work, a content-looking young woman in a white lab coat. Lots of happy women working in a clinical setting. Lots of happy women with pregnant bellies smiling back at them. Flowers in bloom. A family playing at the beach. A spotted ball thrown in the air against a blue sky. There is a rack of magazines. I stare out the window at the drooping eucalyptus. The screen replays the same footage, the sound low.

He will have landed in Johannesburg by now. I could message him but he will be driving. I know where he will hire a car, usually a Volkswagen, and he will complain to himself about how powerless it is compared to his car here, even if it is getting old. He'll be glad to swap it for the faithful LandCruiser when he gets to the farm. He will drive south and west away from the bustle and chaos of the city. It's a long drive so he will stop for some Coke and biltong at a service station. He'll be tired but he will drive as fast as the car can go to the dry town and the sparse vegetation. He will drive tired for hours, across towards the border with Botswana to Upington. He might see gemsbok, springbok, jackals, and take photos for the kids, a blurry selfie.

His mother will be pleased to see him and disappointed not to see the children. She will cook him breakfast—pap porridge then bacon and boerewors and eggs—he will try to eat it all and feel quite bloated. She will be positive about me when he complains to her that I don't cook like she does, but underneath her words she will prefer that he doesn't resolve whatever thing caused him to travel to see her in the first place. She wants him to stay. Bring the children back to their oma and their family, teach them Afrikaans. He will feel a little suffocated but liberated of his responsibilities at home.

He will drink a lot of Castle beer and complain about Australia, work and me, probably, to his cousins and his uncle. They will camp out in swags around a fire under a camel thorn tree and shoot a springbok, or better still an eland, which they will butcher on the spot and eat, charred and sandy off a pocketknife or in a white bread roll. They will drink together, bond over the killing, tell stories and walk out in the night to shoot jackals, full of Klipdrift brandy and Coke. He will realise he has changed, that he has outgrown them. That he doesn't really fit anymore and he will miss Emmy and Jake and me. His mother will tell him how people struggle to have a good life there and of all the people who have emigrated and are doing so well in Australia or England.

In a couple of weeks he will call and tell me he has booked a ticket home. His mother will have offered to pay for it but his pride will refuse and he will use the credit card to take her out somewhere for dinner and tell her that he's going to pay her back her savings in a few months. She will feel better about her future and so will he and then he will remember that his promises depend on me having this baby. And I depend on him.

A young woman with large glasses calls my name and I follow her down the hallway to a small room. She guides me to a chair.

'I'm going to take some blood, check your pressure and get you started. The doctor will see you after that.' She wraps my arm, pumps air into the sphygmomanometer. I can hear her breathing. Pressure on my arm. Release. She pricks my finger. Squeezes and gathers my blood on two white cards. Hands me a small plastic jar with a yellow lid. 'I need a little urine to test please. The door just behind you.' Warm jar in my hand. She dips, checks the colours. No comment. She smells of sugary deodorant. I sit back silent in the chair while she types into the computer record. 'Okay, we're done, Stacey. If you'd like to wait here, the doctor will call you through in a moment.' The language of bossing adults around is so benign but it leaves no choices. If you'd like to wait.

Jeff is a nice doctor. Smiling too, but without the makeup and perfect teeth of his staff. He has some grey in his hair and sharp blue eyes, crystalline and intelligent. When he opens the door and calls me through I can't help but smile. He is familiar, good at getting me to let my guard down. Isak reckons Dr van Tink would be in trouble if they knew I worked as his au pair once. That he might be accused of having groomed me; he definitely uses his charm on me. Isak is suspicious that I have a crush, I think.

Jeff's office has degrees on the wall, plastic anatomy. A uterus on his desk beside the computer with a discreet gash in the labia. Lots of branded stationery from companies—growth hormones, regeneration clinics, gene therapy. Clean advertising. A couple of fat books on human anatomy. Photographs of his adult children, who look vaguely like they did over a decade ago when I used to take them to school. Two beagles asleep on each other.

'So how are you faring, Stacey? All your tests look perfect. Nice strong heartbeat but how are you in yourself?' The counsellor would have written something to him, I'm sure. 'Any concerns?'

'Hopeful. I was relieved when I heard the heartbeat.'

He nods, seems to understand what it means to me.

'The tiredness is better.'

He had lots of volunteers but he picked me out for this because of my passion for his work in Singapore and because I lost my last baby. This time, he said, the baby will be very strong. Resilient. It will prove something about the need for this research and I will be doing something extraordinary. Me—making history.

This time, we will watch the cells divide, heartbeat like a hasty metronome.

He turns the image on his computer for me to see and points at it with his pen. 'Nice head formed here. Spine.' His pen follows the frond-curve.

'How does it compare to my other children?'

He smiles at that, mischief eyes.

'So far there's no real discernible difference. We'll expect a slightly longer cranium to start showing in the measurements next time. Looks good. You've done well.' I am the perfect patient. He turns the screen back towards him, taps on the keys. 'Now—' He reaches for a small plastic package behind him and holds it in both hands, thumbs pushing together a small lump in the plastic. 'This is a little device. A micro-ultrasound designed to monitor the embryo as it develops. It's still in its prototype stage and we are participating in the human trials.' He smiles with his eyes. Meets mine with his sureness. Hands me the packet. It's tiny, coated in a thick soft shell. Silica perhaps. With a plastic tail.

'It's intra-vaginal. Perfectly safe for the embryo and we just place it near the opening of the cervix.' I turn it in my fingers like a soft earring. 'It emits regular high-frequency soundwaves, just like an ultrasound, and the image is sent back to the server. You will be given access to the images. It records movement and change so we can head off any problems and keep you both in good health.'

PregCam™ is branded across the top of the package. 'How does it send images back?'

'It links into your wireless network. Totally fine.'

I question his confidence with this new device. Always, every day something new to amaze the world. I wonder at the risk to my tiny, curled creation, beating gently.

'Have you used these in many women?'

He is ready for my questions, seems to forecast my thoughts. 'Like I said, we are part of the human trials. They've shown great success in pigs. Here, take a look at the footage.' He turns his screen back to me again. 'I wouldn't risk this embryo, Stacey. It's safe.' Several spines, tails and limbs flash past in time lapse, grainy images. I am a sow. Isak would say something but I bury the pip of anger. 'I think this was the first prototype so the images aren't good quality. This one has a more refined processor in it so we should get some better footage.' Generous with his smiles.

'Can I think about it?' I'd rather discuss it with Isak. I explain that he's gone to visit his family in South Africa before the pregnancy gets too advanced. He might think it's already too advanced but I leave that out of my story.

He pauses a moment and I hand him back the PregCam™ packet. 'Timing is everything with this you see.' He leaves it on the desk between us. 'So we can't wait, sorry, Stacey. We only have a small window to install it without risk to the baby.'

A little shiver runs through my skin and I feel my resistance radiating into the distance.

He wheels his chair closer, 'So anyway. I wanted to get this done today.'

I mount a second wave of objection, but it is weak and I know he has won me over. I wish Isak was here. 'Am I obliged to do this?' I hear myself whine, like Emmy's refusal to brush her hair.

His sharp eyes drag my gaze to his. 'Well technically no, but under the communications clauses in our agreement we do need to keep you under regular care so we'll have to book you in for a lot more ultrasounds if you don't. And they're expensive.' He fidgets, knows he has hit the tipping point appealing to our budget. 'We cover the cost of the ones we have scheduled. If there are more required you will have to pay for them. It's up to you.' He returns to his notes.

PregCam™ seems innocuous enough. Pink and soft and quite tiny, about the size of a kidney bean. 'How does it stay in place?' Tail like a sperm.

'Just like a little IUD. That technology has been used for many years now. Won't be a problem.' Keeps at his notes. 'What is it that worries you about it?' He glances over, seems to convey there is no reason to resist.

I wonder myself for a moment. We really can't afford big medical bills but that isn't why I hesitate. The womb is such a silent, private place and having a camera—an audience—pointed at this baby so it can't even grow into being without scrutiny seems like the ultimate invasion. But I have already ceded control of my body to this pregnancy and I get the feeling he will have his way. With or without my consent. 'So nothing really. I suppose it's fine.'

'Great.' He looks up, smiles wide, eyes shimmer. He stands, leads me behind a curtain to a high gurney. 'I'll leave you to get ready. It's just like having a vaginal examination or pap smear. Just hop up on the bed when you're ready.'

My breath is short, quick. My knickers, a small dark pool on the floor. I push them inside my boot. Something so forlorn about my shed clothes on his hardwood timber floor. A lump rises in my throat but I lay on the narrow bed and drape a blue woven blanket over my bottom half. As if he's been watching, he appears as soon as I'm ready.

Places his hands on my knees over the blanket. 'Now, you need to relax. This is not painful and it will be very quick. Bend your knees up.' He lowers himself level with the bed and moves towards my feet. I hear metal clink. Gel. 'A bit cold now, sorry. Just a little pinch.' Something cold and metal, wider than I expected, pushing through the muscles. 'Now just relax, I'm going to open up the speculum.' I hear his breath hold. 'Good girl.' I feel like a farm animal. Sow. Close my eyes. Calm. The speech bubble. Breathe in through your nose and out through your mouth. Scraping feeling inside. He fiddles about. The metal releases, clicks and he draws it out. 'Right. All good in there, now pop your clothes back on and we'll link it up to the system.' My abdomen pulses.

I dress and wash my hands in his sink. I don't know why. It's not like I was involved in this procedure but somehow I am coated in bodily fluids. His soap is yellow and liquid, antibacterial. No smell to mask the vaginal fug in the air. I want to spray myself with perfume.

In his chair, he has his mobile phone in his hand, tapping away at the oversized screen. Pinching an image in and out. 'We have contact, Houston.' He smiles as if that joke has not been heard a million times. Turns his screen to me and there on his phone is my inside. A clear image of several vertebrae surrounded by lighter areas. Masses of tissue and organs I don't recognise or understand.

'It's very close up. I can't really make things out very well.' Swallow a lump in my throat.

'The technicians will though. They'll get all the images sent direct to them and be able to monitor the growth and development of the embryo each step of the way.' He is excited, staring at the images. 'Well done, Stacey, and thank you for agreeing to be part of this.'

I don't remember agreeing. It was more like not disagreeing. I want to clench the muscles around the baby. Keep it hidden. But it seems I am too late for that.

'Next ultrasound is booked and you have a follow-up appointment with me a week after. Contact my offices immediately if you need anything, Stacey. Anything at all. Okay?'

'Okay.' Not really. Not really that okay at all.

He nods. 'The ultrasound images will be on the website.' He puts the phone on his desk, folds his hands politely in his lap. Bedside manner.

Finally a question comes to me—'Can the whole world see it?'

'No, definitely not,' he says, serious and shaking his head. 'We have a very secure intranet. Firewalls and security codes all over the place. Don't worry.'

Everything is on the website. I nod and smile.

'We'll be in touch then.' He stands from his chair and herds me towards the door. 'Just let the girls at the desk know that we're done and they'll get you to sign off on the insurance claim.'

His hand on my shoulder as I walk out the door is hotter than I expected.

I stand at the counter. Touch the rosy wood and wait. Efficient Lauren beckons me to her end of the desk. 'I have another appointment booked for you, Stacey.' She sorts out the account and I stand silent, my cervix connected through the air, through the walls, to Jeff's phone. 'We will send you confirmation the day before.' Each pulse. 'The doctor said your account should be covered. Can I have your health provider cards please?'

I walk out the door leaving something of my spirit behind in the plastic packaging torn in two in his bin.

Pink blossoms from the drooping eucalyptus have fallen on my car. I take a chunky gumnut filled with rosy stamens for Emmy. My calm one. In the car I check my messages—nothing. He must be there now, driving through a different landscape.

In the silent evening, while the children sleep, I log on to LifeBLOOD® Bringing Life Out of Darkness and tap through the welcome page to 'Parenting Stage 1'. Then to the PregCam™ images. The pictures are not coloured. They are tinted in a chromatic blue scale. In the time lapse the movements appear jerky. The figure shifts. Turning around the screen. Spine again. Ribs and the top of a limb, arm probably. The darks and lights bouncing blue, pounding like a heart. Profile of the face. My heart shifts in my chest, shades of blue. Light and dark. It is nothing but everything to fall in love with your own baby. The bulge of an eye which will open and peer deep into my own. Wanting what I can give. Only I can give. The spine again and a shifting, like a sigh before sleep. What will be shown has been shown. Yet it is a magnet and I can't turn away.

I make a cup of tea and return to the screen. Gone. 'We apologise but images for this site are currently unavailable. Please try again soon.'

I tap through the pages—*What to Expect*—seems unlikely anybody can answer this challenge so I read on. *It is most important at this stage of any pregnancy to relax. The embryo is still in a fragile state and mothers must provide a peaceful and healthy environment in which their child can grow. Stress is a major risk factor so practise regular meditation or yoga . . . Why not join our yoga teacher online and be part of our mothers' fitness program? Click here to join today.*

I skip past the image of a woman in tight pants standing in tree pose. A pregnant bulge in her orange tank top. I can do asana in my sleep, thanks to my mother, but can't stand the thought of her false calm. 'Namaste,' she would say while Alex and I played endless rounds of Uno in a caravan in some stranger's back garden. Bored, we peeled strips of ply from the walls while she instructed strangers on goddess pose, warrior number one, mountain pose. She tossed the ply and the Uno cards in the fire pit, cursing us as 'little shits'. Despite this, sometimes I long for her. I write to her— 'I'm pregnant again. Congratulations granny. Due'—but I can't say when it's due; I delete the message without sending it.

I sip the tea and browse the rest of the site. *Our* mothers—not just me. Lots of advice about healthy food and no alcohol. The usual list for normal pregnancy, but this is not a normal pregnancy. Avoid all stimulants including coffee. *We recommend a wholefood diet, rich in protein and fresh organic fruit and vegetables.* Takeaway boxes have again filled the footwells of the car. *It is important to avoid alternative medicines for nausea as they are not subject to thorough medical trials and may impact the development of the embryo.* My mother would have a lot to say about that and I soon abandon the site—there is no comfort to be found in information. Message Isak—'went to an appointment today'—but there is no response. I send another—'Jeff says everything looks normal'—and I now have a camera inside me. I don't know how I will tell him this. 'I miss you.'

A great wind roars across the rooftops of the suburb. Something rattles on the front of the house and I walk barefoot on the cool tiles in the semi-dark. The floor sparkles with glitter. Emmy is asleep on her back, her arms above her head in careless abandon. I never thought of her when I made this decision. She wants a sister, like most girls, and she might get her wish, but it won't be a human sister. I sit on the floor by her bed, take her dropped teddy and hold it close, stifling sobs in its musty fur.

9 WEEKS

This time she doesn't use the diffuser and welcomes me with a smile and a handshake. She quizzes me about Isak's trip and how I'm coping without him and I manage some kind of clarity and good sense. She seems to relax, like she's got me hooked now.

'Tell me, how did you meet Isak?' she leans forward in her chair, as if she's eager to hear my story.

'We met in Ireland. He was travelling with a couple of friends.' They drank a lot. He was in a pub in Temple Bar, arms around a group of people, all singing. When I saw him I knew, my chest filled like it would explode. I remember that first eye contact like something blood-borne. 'I was studying.' Between the dark buildings of Dublin I found a room at the top of some narrow stairs. A residential college full of school leavers from rural Ireland and countries all over Europe, speaking different languages and smoking. Playing drinking games until late. A dark crevice in a cold, tall pillar. Always cold; noisy. Not conducive to study.

I am silent a while and she nods, clears her throat. 'Studying what, Stacey?'

'Archaeology.' It was the fieldwork that kept me enrolled. The chance of finding something like the bronze bowl and the finger bones Marco kept in his study. His history, he said, from Italy and he told me the stories of his family while I held the bones in my own hands, stroking the convex line between the knuckles. He smelled of basil and tomato, of summer and a real home. 'I failed the theory units but I loved the practical work.'

Then my mother would leave again and take us to a gritty shack in a caravan park somewhere on a winter beach. Enrol Alex and me in a strange school again. 'I had a lecturer who read us "Bog Queen". Have you ever read it?' She shakes her head.

Her ancient hair, untangling the precious beauty of it in the mild sunshine. For me, field weeks spent combing the earth in bare trenches, the chance of discovery, sherds and bone reconstructing lost lives—they were why I pushed myself back to school. Why I worked and saved. And I abandoned all that for the pull of my heart and then the ache for motherhood. To belong and connect. Isak made it all seem so pointless. I stopped caring about the past and lived in the present moments, with him.

'Do you feel any resentment towards Isak for taking you from your studies? Would you go back if you could?' She nods. A little smile. Perhaps she feels she is making some inroads.

'In some ways I am doing fieldwork.' I firm up my barricades, know she will want to talk about the pregnancy. 'And no, I don't resent Isak. He is a good father and my best friend.' She'll love that bit.

She shifts in her seat, looks at the time. 'Have you contacted your mother since we met?' She smiles warmly, I think she knows she's taking a risk.

'I wrote her a message.' And deleted it. 'She often goes on retreats this time of year and is out of contact.' I did not lie.

She tips her head on one side. 'Where do you think she is on retreat?'

'Somewhere in New South Wales usually. She moves around from the coast and into the mountains with my stepfather, Marco, sometimes.' I'm doing well.

'I sense that you get on well with him.'

The wise woman ruse with all the sensing and feeling, just like my mother.

'Yes. He was very supportive of me when I was young and I needed him.' Sent me money, no judgement. But I have not given him much back. I am no daughter for him.

'Wasn't your mother supportive?' Finally she digs deep but I expected it.

'She was, in her own way. But she was busy too, working as a healer.' Healer is a stretch. She was the agent of chaos so often. Plying her wisdom and esoteric methods to the clueless and vulnerable. 'She always means well.' And I know this is true.

'What will she think about you having this pregnancy?' she asks it with a strange emphasis.

'She will say it is my destiny because if it weren't then it wouldn't happen.' She would say just that.

'But you did choose this, Stacey. You need to be clear that this is your decision, your choice.' Feels like something she has been told to reinforce with me.

'Yes, it is. And destiny led me to that choice.'

She smiles at me as if I am silly. I was right to react to her, but I have kept it in check today. We part after making another appointment in a month.

12 WEEKS

I wish I hadn't worn a dress. I feel so exposed here, an audience of six around me with clothes hauled up to my armpits. Jeff is there, standing behind my head. The same officious radiographer tucks the paper blanket into my knickers, pulling them down a smidgen, dark hairs coursing out to remind them where they all came from. She squirts a clear gel onto my hard stomach and moves the scanning device. The screen is turned so I only see a slice of the action. Clearly I am not the main audience.

When I took this on I really didn't think about being treated as a science experiment myself. It was all about the baby. This is harder without Isak. He has always been there holding my hand through all our pregnancies and without him I feel hard and isolated. He has seen the scans online, he said. 'Looks just like a regular baby.' We can do this, he says. He's excited, but the words come from far away and I can't feel it today, in here.

Everyone tells us we are great parents and we should have more. Our kids are beautiful, sporty and Emmy is very intelligent.

It's easily said, of course, but I'm tired. I close my eyes. I don't know what to look for, anyway. Surely they have seen it through the PregCam™. Still, the air is thick with audience.

'She's moving her fingers,' says the radiographer. There are drawn breaths and I hear news I did not think would make such a difference.

'It's a girl?' I whisper, not sure if they will hear me.

'Definitely a girl,' says Jeff. Bold and smiling.

Emmy's longed-for sister—here she is. Just not quite the sister she has been waiting for. In the glimpse of screen I see a baby. Fingers and spine and baby-shaped head looking as normal as my other children, from this vantage point at least. Maybe they won't notice she is different from them, for a while.

'Looks good,' Dr Anderson, head of radiography, pats me on the shoulder. 'Well done, dear.'

I want to cry. They all clap as if I'm in a circus. Maybe I am. Maybe she will be one day.

There's nothing quite as hollow as that little death we saw on the ultrasound screen. That human shape refusing to beat or flutter. It seemed so real, yet fragile as dew; it was gone before it really began. What did it do to us to see that sad little thing? The image forever printed in my memory from the secret room of life. Then months of emptiness. Lifeless—as though I were strewn with salt. I thought I would never feel another burst of life in me but this child is reinforced.

This time the cells—well, some of them are mine and Isak's, but others were snipped and sliced and fused into our baby. There is not just us in there. Her whole genome was recovered and reissued: a new work using old materials. Somewhere in prehistory she has another set of parents. She is the child deposited in a tooth found under layers of sediment in a deep cave. Only accessible via a narrow tunnel, amid a ring of stalagmites, an ancient campfire. The fossilised remains of a woolly rhinoceros, butchered mammoths and red deer. She is older than the Bog Queen. Maybe she was buried with ceremony thirty-eight thousand years ago. Surrounded by flowers. A stone axe. From there she has come back. Back to us. I have excavated her.

At the kids' swimming lessons I imagined her one day, seven years old in a blue bikini, plunging into the pool, rolling over, skating through the water, shiny and laughing. Chlorinated water dripping from her hair. How much will she have of normal? To learn and talk with other children, not like her. I have watched the mothers with unusual children and I know I will be among them and I wonder how they feel with their little different one out there swimming with the four-limbed bright-eyed kids. I've had all that normal and now I will have something more; I'll have what they have. It doesn't take much to alter the development of a child. To turn its life and the parents' lives into something entirely other. For those parents, the child is the pivot around which everything turns.

Surely she won't learn to swim like other kids.

The team point to the screen and discuss the growth of my baby, 'their work'. It is quite in keeping with human embryonic development, apparently.

'What about the forehead?' They all turn, surprised I am still awake, I imagine.

'Did you say something, Stacey?' asks Jeff. Naturally he has the best bedside manner.

'The forehead?'

'Can't tell yet, I'm afraid, dear.'

'We expect some different cranial development to show next ultrasound, in a few weeks,' says Dr Dimitra, evolutionary paediatrician. I met her briefly in the IVF clinic. Her postdoctoral sidekick stands close, nods seriously at me. He wears a sticky label that says 'Eugene'.

'Remember, Stacey, the baby is also genetically yours. She will be something in between; we expect she may have a slightly pronounced supraorbital ridge. She will look a little different but not too different,' says Dr Dimitra.

'Like I said at our appointment, Stacey, don't worry. There will be some surprises but I think they will all be good surprises.' Jeff presses his hand on my shoulder.

'I think we're almost done, Doctor.' The radiographer speaks to the group, probably all doctors.

A museum piece for the next generation. A living museum piece. Possible titles for *National Geographic* articles they will write about her one day. Ultrasound images stored on the LifeBLOOD® server will be sold to exclusive media outlets. We've already signed the non-disclosure contract to protect our identity and the children. But not this child. They'll know her inside out.

Some of the doctors seem to be in a rush so Jeff flurries around the small room, shaking hands while the radiographer cleans up the gel.

'Everything okay, Stacey?' Jeff finally smiles at me. I nod, gathering my adrift dress back over my body.

'Well, I have one question—are there other mothers?' He seems surprised at my forthright question in front of his lofty colleagues.

Dr Dimitra answers me, her scent of spice and cosmetics close to my face. 'I'm afraid we can't discuss the details of other pregnancies,' she says, in a low voice.

'But—are there? Will she be alone?'

'One day there will be other people like her,' she says, cryptic and aloof.

A more senior man, one I have not met, seems to outrank the rest of them. He leans in to speak. Cold-eyed and pale. 'Our girl here will be loved by your family and then—well, we'll see how things track but all kids go their own way when they grow up.' He smirks, fat white fingers hovering over my belly. 'You'd better start thinking of names—maybe avoid Lucy?' He lets out a little laugh.

The screen goes still, then blackens. Our little secret is safe inside.

Outside in the car I search 'Lucy' and eventually find an image of *Australopithecus afarensis*, a crouched and hair-covered beast of a creature. Nowhere near human and much older by thousands of years than this baby's amended DNA. Hers might be Spanish or from the Steppes, or Croatia. All kinds of life has emerged from the melted glaciers and permafrost. Her ancestors dressed in animal skin, crafted jewellery, buried their dead. They were human, not like us but not an ape. She will not be an ape.

13 WEEKS

In the car park at the clinic I park under the same tree. This time I have cleaned out the car. It only takes the kids a couple of days to drop enough socks and food scraps to make it feel filthy again. For a moment, the serenity of order is good. This morning we started the day well but the Paleo breakfast has given me heartburn. My mother would say that means I'm having a hairy baby but that doesn't really bear thinking about. I have avoided the intranet but check my messages before my appointment in case I've missed anything important.

Dear Stacey,

Researchers in our actuary dept have been analysing the data on primate gestation across several species and have calculated an approximate gestation based on the size of the embryo at your 12-week ultrasound. Considering also the ratios and comparison to modern human gestation they estimate a 32–34 week pregnancy. I am hesitant to give you a specific EDD but, even in human babies, they

are only an estimate. We should get a clearer idea at your next scan.
See you at my rooms for your next appointment.

Kind regards
Dr Jeffrey van Tink
LifeBLOOD® Professor of Obstetrics and Paleogenetics

Human babies. Primates. It is difficult to think my child is not human. Her face, her hands on the screen from the PregCam™ all look the same as my other children. Five fingers, clenching and opening her hand. The curve of her spine. Her delicate foot. The bouncing image of her heart. She is, every part of her, mine. Inside me, growing day by day. Feeding off my scrambled eggs. I don't really care what they say, she's human enough to me.

The appointment proceeds as the last one. The same sensible names, the large glasses testing my blood pressure, squeezing the crimson juice from my finger. The waiting, looking at the plastic uterus. All is well, according to Dr Jeff, who tracks his warm fingers across my abdomen, silent and focused. His competent presence is reassuring, despite his obvious charisma. His ability to make me comply. He stands back quietly, hand resting on my abdomen.

'Stacey, when will Isak be back?' Gently, he waits for my response. I swallow hard.

'Um, next week he's due back. His mum is making the most of him being there.' I avoid his eyes, pull at the rumple of clothing under my back. Jeff waits for more. 'He might not go back to South Africa for a while after the baby is born so he will have a lot of visiting to do.' I've said this before too. Rehearsed a valid statement in response to a valid question. He holds my hand and helps me sit up from the narrow bed.

'We are concerned that you don't have enough support.' Silence for a moment. 'Is everything okay between the two of you?' There is no one to support me with this pregnancy, no one who can share all the truths of it. Only Isak. Just the thought of his name scrapes a raw graze in my chest. Jeff returns to his chair, wheeling backwards slowly as I reassemble myself.

'I have missed him, Jeff.' A lump in my throat, the sprig of tears. I stop myself. 'I've been busy but I can manage.'

'We can bring in a nanny, some cleaners for you if you like and take the pressure off you cooking. Get some help with the driving for you. If you're tired all the time it isn't good for the baby.' The house is sprayed with glue and paper, food scraps and glitter. I have no energy to clean or discipline the children. Their scooters fade in the sun of the back garden, dead oat grass casting seeds for the next season. Washed towels bleach into rigid forms over the clothesline.

Isak wouldn't like the invasion of our privacy, no matter how filthy and chaotic our house. But our diet—my mother would cringe at the things I feed myself and the kids. I resolve to accept some help. Sometimes it would be good not to have to cook and LifeBLOOD® seem to have endless money.

He taps away on his keyboard, practical and immediate. 'Right. Are you on the Paleo diet?'

'Yes.' The acid rises to the back of my throat. I swallow it down hard. 'But I grew up vegan and I think it's a bit much for me, all that meat.'

'Not so good, huh? Of course we aren't sure it's necessary so you can vary it if you need to. You've read the material on diet on our website?'

'It gives me heartburn. I've read books about it before. I thought it was debunked as being the best diet for us.' I was a bit surprised that I was meant to eat like that and we can scarcely afford all the meat. Isak loves it. 'Someone to cook, even just for the kids would be good.'

'We can get a home delivery system. I'll book it for you. The order forms are on our website. You order and they deliver. The cost is covered by us.' He is tapping into his computer. Prints out and hands over a prescribed packet. 'For the heartburn.'

Sun pours through the window, the shadow of venetian blinds across his desk and the plastic uterus. Silent. I hear his breathing whistle. I am waiting. I stare at his degrees from a German university. Medicine at Princeton. Some institute for genetic research in Barcelona. He is waiting and I'm not sure why. 'Have I missed a question?'

His magnetic eyes stare at mine. Anchor me to the seat. 'Yes— Isak. What's the situation, Stacey? Do we need to book him some counselling? One-on-one. He's definitely home next week, is he? You were both selected for this program. To provide a healthy family unit for this baby.'

I squirm inside. Grasp around for a response. 'I'll ask him. He just wanted to spend some time with his mother.' And get away from this. He knew it would be strange and had to have some space to come to terms with it. 'Before the baby comes.'

'If he doesn't come back, Stacey—' He looks at me sternly. Shakes his head.

'What? He will come back.' I know he will. He will never abandon me, or the kids.

He begins to rise from his chair. 'There's a clause about this.' His tone shifts. 'We will need to plan for it soon if he isn't coming back. She'll go to adoptive parents.'

I stand but I hold the desk. Shaking, the blood seems to drain out of me. I am thick and sticky on the red floor. I shrivel to nothing. Face numb. Jeff leaves the room and the woman with large glasses comes in with a jug of water.

'Vomit,' I manage and the bile rises out of me into a silver dish. She is quick. Holds out a warm, damp flannel and some water.

'Sit down.'

My hands shake but I push away from her. 'No, I've got to go.' And I bustle from the room out into my serene car. My heart racing. Close my eyes and cry silently. They might be watching me so I key the engine and drive through the traffic, tears dropping from my chin into the clean car. Through the traffic and the suburbs and winding streets to my own silent house.

I make a cup of ginger tea. Our back patio looks over the small yard with its hopeful vegetable gardens, filled with grass and lettuce gone to seed. A spindly lemon tree and a trampoline. Swing set and cubby house, balls, tennis racquets, doll's pram with a basketball in it, the scooters on their sides. It's tight but it's all there. I have a comfortable chair they bought for my birthday two years ago but I rarely get to sit in it. It was to read in, apparently. Today I sit in it. Sip tea. I call him but there is no answer.

Sometime later, clouds have darkened the sky and I wake up cold to the school pick-up alarm. I have missed a call back from him so I try again. Sip the cold tea to calm my nerves. Not sure what to say.

'At last,' he answers. Relief.

'My God, I miss you,' and I sob uncontrollably. I hear him breathing, repeating my name. A dog barks in the background.

'Sweetheart. Calm down a minute.'

I breathe. Think myself calm.

'Stace, I've booked a ticket home next week.' He waits silently on the phone while I cry again. 'You need to pick up the kids.'

14 WEEKS

The maternity clothes I had are old and faded. LifeBLOOD®
have given me gift cards to get some new ones but I spent most
of it on winter clothes for the kids. I managed to find one dress.
Not suitable to wear to ultrasounds. Beyond my chest it falls
loose and long, flowing like the gardens of Babylon, and more
cheerful than I have been for weeks. I am an ancient wonder
after all. The dress and I work together, unifying our mood and
approach to Isak's arrival.

The arrivals hall at Perth airport is packed with a large contin-
gent of robust and fair-haired expats from South Africa waiting
for the flight. They are quick to adopt the local winter wardrobe
and many wear sheepskin boots and jeans with shapeless jumpers.
Emmy has done her own hair into a haphazard bun, bits falling
around her face, and put on her new best dress, so she is too cold.
Jake is in his pyjamas and dressing-gown, playing a game on his
screen. He seems disinterested but Emmy watches the arrivals
doors intently with a firm grip on the welcome home card she

54

made. The blue glitter came off all over the back seat of the car, which I had hoped would be clean for a change.

'He'll be a while yet,' I tell the back of her crushed hair. She points at the arrivals board. His flight shows *Landed*. 'Even though the flight has arrived,' I tell her, 'he has to go through customs.'

'What's that?' She turns, little frown lines in her forehead. Glimpses of him in her sharp eyes.

'Don't you remember? They have to check that you aren't carrying any plants or animals or food into Australia so they don't bring new diseases here to *our* special plants and animals.' She nods, staring back at the gate.

I adjust the bow on the back of her dress and she ignores me as if my touch is part of her. 'I remember the long line of people and the man in the uniform who threw away my scissors,' she grumps.

'You have a good memory for a girl who was only five.'

I watch too, just as anxious as she is to see Isak. In my heart I knew he would come home, but part of me doubted, still doubts, that he will actually walk through those doors. The crowd is a band stretched tight, getting louder until figures begin to appear from behind the wall. Tension releases as each appears, pushing trolleys of suitcases, boxes, backpacks and packages of duty-free alcohol and electronics.

'Dad!' Emmy runs out of the row of seats and jumps at him. They are both smiling—unified, unbreakable. Relief fills my eyes with tears and I draw Jake from his game, pulling his hand out to his father. He is warm, smells of diesel fumes, holds me tight against his bulky chest.

'You've grown.' He smiles at me.

'You have too.'

He laughs.

'Yes, Oma's cooking and too much Coke, of course.' I can see the fresh energy in his face. Eased tension.

'Did you bring us presents? I made this for you,' Emmy interrupts to thrust her sparkly card at him, keen to put in place a principle of fair exchange, knowing her brother and I are not bearing gifts.

'Absolutely, for all of you from Oma and from me. They're in my case so we'll open them later.' He picks up Jake and props him on top of the trolley, wheeling quickly out of the airport into the night air.

The parking is costly and he swears about the discrepancy between the economics of life in Australia and South Africa. He drives out onto the freeway, in a hurry to get home. A speed camera flashes at us. He curses, 'Used to the roads at home. I got fined there yesterday, going sixteen kay over the speed limit and the fine was only five hundred rand—it will be a lot more here.'

Everything seems normal. Jake falls asleep in the car.

Eleven years ago in Dublin I could never have imagined the reality of our lives now. He was mischievous then, standing out from the crowd with curly hair and a wardrobe of European football shirts. We caught trains, held hands constantly and slept together in single beds at backpacker hostels. We went to concerts and bars and ate in the park, falling asleep on St Stephen's Green, in Hyde Park, the Luxembourg Gardens and Trsteno on the stone benches among the marble and greenery. There were other people around us, friends and other travellers sharing moments in sublime landscapes. The wonders of the world. But for Isak and for me there was only us. My gaze fixed upon him and his upon me. The wonders all around and within us. It seems so magnified to me, that time. Those months we walked like giants. Time stretched.

Along the quiet highway, concrete warehouses barricade acres and acres of horizon from our vision. We pass through it like a curse thinking only of the warm interior of our little house in the suburbs at the outer edge of the city. Spangled with souvenirs of those journeys we once had.

Isak carries Jake over his shoulder like a sack of grain, tucks him in. I wake Emmy and escort her, glittery, to her overstuffed room. Tuck her in with her menagerie of stuffed toys.

Finally, he holds me tight in his arms, kisses the top of my head. Tears rise in me but I force them down. 'Chamomile tea?' I ask him.

He nods. 'I need to wind down a bit from the flight. I brought you some little things.'

I make the tea and he lugs his bags into the house. Locks us in. On the table a little package wrapped in raw paper and a pile of colourful fabric. A print scarf, with zebras. Earrings and a matching necklace.

'They're made from bottle tops. Unbelievable, isn't it?' I turn the little treasures over in my palm. He pulls out another parcel, wrapped in gift paper. 'My mum sent this for the baby.'

'You told her?' A lovely knitted cardigan, bright green. A couple of T-shirts in tiny sizes with a rhino, a map of Africa. I unwrap them slowly and tenderly.

'Of course. She was very happy.' He laughs but does not hold my eyes for long.

'But you didn't tell her the truth, did you?' We are bound not to but over there he might ignore the rules of our agreement.

'No, I just kept things normal. I'm hoping we can keep things as normal as possible, Stacey. That's what the doctor told us to do and if we can just go with that, then I can deal with it.' He tries to smile. He is calm, at peace with it. For now at least.

His hand rests on mine.

'They told me it's a girl.'

His fingers wrap around mine, squeeze them tight.

'Emmy will be happy.' He smiles at the thought. Sighs and leans closer to me. 'I'm so sorry for leaving you like that, Stacey. I just . . .' He looks at me, teary.

'I know. I understand.' *I understand more than you know.* Sometimes I wish I could run away from myself for a few weeks. 'I'm all right. In that middle stage now, having a burst of energy. I had some ultrasounds and you saw them online, not that you can see much really.'

'They put all the ultrasounds online? Some were very close, blurry ones that looked like time lapse or something.'

I have the urge to stare deep into my tea or pick up today's schoolbag chaos erupting on the floor.

He kicks at a lunchbox by his shoe.

'It's not public, just for us and the medical staff.' I bend to pick up the empty container, bread crusts fallen on the rug. 'They installed a tiny ultrasound device.'

He picks up the crust and tosses it in the box in my hands, 'Installed? You mean put it in with the baby?' His mouth draws tight, pale.

'Yes.' I don't want to tell him. It's just so invasive. 'I didn't want to really but they said if I didn't we'd have to pay for additional scans and tests all the time.'

He shakes his head, takes the lunchbox from me and stands up. 'They bribed you?'

'Yes, I guess they did.' *Please don't be angry with me, it's not my fault.* I brace myself for his rage—too soon.

'Fuck!' He seems explosive. 'So did they inject it or what?'

It seems obvious to me how it got there but I tell him anyway. 'They said it wasn't risky to the baby or me. I saw it, it's tiny.'

'So they can see what's going on up there? All the time?'

She is under surveillance all the time. I try to forget it's there; talking about it makes it so real. Even in our most private places, anyone—everyone—might be watching the two of us.

'Just the baby. It's so close to her you can't really make sense of the picture. I guess they can.' I know what he's thinking. But I can't answer his unasked question, don't know what to say.

'Are we celibate then?' He looks tired, lines across his forehead etching back.

'No, I don't know. Maybe. I'm sorry, Isak—I felt like there was no choice.' I feel a panic rising, want to push the thing out of me.

'There wasn't. It's not your fault. It's those pricks at LifeBLOOD®, dodgy bastards. I'm sorry I wasn't here for you.' He tosses the lunchbox on the kitchen bench. Pours his cold tea into the sink and leans against the bench, staring back at me on the couch.

'Does she look okay to them?' He reaches into the fridge and finds a block of chocolate, snaps it loudly and returns to the couch. He cracks off a row for me and reaches for my hand. I touch a bruise on his nail.

'Boy's own adventures. Uncle Henrik and his kids out on the farm. You don't want to know.'

I laugh at him. He knows I'll hate the story, the slaughtered wildlife, the drinking. 'She's fine, just like a normal baby. So far there is nothing strange, nothing we didn't see on the ultrasounds for the kids. They say she'll be little and the pregnancy will not go forty weeks.'

'Do they know when?' The lines quickly deepening.

'Just best guess. We're about halfway.'

And we are not halfway ready, especially me.

16 WEEKS

Every time I come in here and wait in this room I'm faced with the same posters: the amputee man 'Nothing sweet about diabetes' and the hollow-eyed girl 'Pregnant and injecting?' Normally I am pragmatic and I can see the point, but they are like sand in my eyes. I am tired of trying to be calm for them. I didn't want to come back here alone but Isak is back at work, has already borrowed days off he hasn't earned. What I did to my baby is worse than drugs or too much lemonade. I volunteered her to be broken and made into something not human. I want to run and hide with her. I don't want to bring this child into being with all eyes turned to her. I tell Isak she is normal but she is a freak already and she always will be. I play scenarios in my mind where I pack them all up and go hide in a little town somewhere dry and inhospitable where nobody will know us.

They did a psychological profile before they started—so much for that! I came up stable but I feel myself unstitching. Taking my kids to school I hide behind normal, but each day it's getting harder.

'Stacey?' The same radiographer leads me down the dimly lit hall. 'Have you drunk all the water this morning?'

'Yes,' I snap at her, knowing it's not her fault.

She opens the door. 'Been to the toilet since last night?' Her head tips to one side, she fake-smiles.

I shake my head.

'Well, let's get in here and get started.'

I bet you say that to everyone, I want to snarl at her.

No dress this time, a skirt and a rounder belly too so altogether I feel a little more dignified, on the outside at least. I swallow down my irritation, try to hide it a little.

'Just a little cold gel and we'll tuck you up a bit here.' I breathe deep as she pulls gently at my clothes.

'Where are all the doctors?' I try to make some conversation.

'They won't be in here today unless something isn't right. They are just with another patient but they said to take the measurements. We'll record all the images so they don't miss anything.' She taps into the keyboard and starts the movements over my abdomen.

'Is someone else having a baby like mine?' They must be thinking the same things as I am. I wonder if their husbands are ambiguous, if their minds have turned tidal—surging and sucking back, dumping detritus on their shores.

'Every patient is important, Stacey. There are lots of unusual pregnancies and the doctor and his team try to make sure everyone is looked after.'

Treating me like a child. Deep breath. Lots of unusual pregnancies, they must have a whole army of 'research' on the way.

It's all right that they aren't here, really. Maybe I will find out more from her.

'There she is. That's a hand . . .' She clicks and measures, narrating the body parts but I don't really listen. I'm just looking, as if that is the only way to know something.

'She looks like a normal baby.' There's a tear in my voice.

'She is a normal baby.' Her sweet cheeriness makes it seem okay.

But she won't be normal when she's born. She might be hairy. She might have a jutting jaw, lumpy forehead. She might not be able to speak, ever. She might walk like a gorilla.

'She's not human, you know?' Maybe I shouldn't have said that, maybe she doesn't know the truth of this.

'Yes, she is human. She is your baby.'

It strikes so deep, that little sentence, like a charge quavering in my chest. She is. But she isn't.

'Just think, some people adopt babies and they still call them "my baby". Yours is your baby, even if she is not genetically all yours and your husband's.' Maybe Miss Radiographer is only half human. 'We have lots of pregnancies in here that have had gene therapy and they get born into normal babies.'

'Really?' Her pale eyes block any signs of understanding and I feel a sudden spike in anger. 'I won't even be able to take her to the shop without people staring at her and wondering what the hell is wrong with her.'

She doesn't say a word. Looks stunned.

'She won't be able to go to school. In fact she might not be able to talk or learn to talk. She might not learn to play with my other kids or learn to swim or ride a bike. None of us will ever have a normal day again.'

Not a word. It surges through me. Comes out with force.

'The whole world is going to change once this baby is born. Nobody will think of life the same way. And what do you think she is going to do when she grows up, if she actually does?'

I haven't let myself go there. I haven't really thought about the possibilities before, but slowly things come to me. The reality that not only is she different from our other children, she's also not ours in the same way they are either.

'She's going to be doing whatever they want her to do.' She's their property—to use for making babies, or testing drugs or whatever else they plan for her. I'm not even really sure. Jeff said something about developing new gene therapies to treat a whole range of things. She'll be strong. Strong organs. A big, strong heart. 'But she herself—she is of no real importance to anyone except me. Because I am her mother.'

And that last word is too much and I shake and quiver and cry until the radiographer stands to leave. She pulls her card out of the computer and points towards the toilets. Obviously upset.

A few minutes later I wipe the gel from my stomach and find the keys to my car. There really is nothing to do about it now. I am on the journey and there is no way out. What the journey means, well that is only just starting to become clear.

17 WEEKS

In the car park at the clinic Isak parks under the same tree. The car is littered with takeaway packages, disposable coffee cups and school socks. In a couple of weeks the attrition of my resolve is complete. We are always in such a rush, caught in the winding traffic to school, away from school. Hours spent in this tight little cocoon, Emmy reading aloud, doing her homework. Jake gaming quietly in her shadow. This pattern, firm as a binding cloth. Each day. Isak is enjoying the Paleo breakfasts as an excuse for a fry-up every morning and eats more of it than I do, marching out the door with a bacon sandwich for smoko. My heartburn persists, she grows on my stores. And tea.

I check my messages in the car park again as Isak finishes the last of his lunch, keen to multitask on his break.

Dear Stacey
All signs from your ultrasound are normal and the baby looks to be
growing as expected.

I understand you are having some emotional stress about the child so I have referred you to our resident psychiatrist as well as Fee, your usual counsellor. Please notify the staff at my offices when you are next there and they will make an appointment for you at a suitable time.

Kind regards
Dr Jeffrey van Tink
LifeBLOOD® Professor of Obstetrics and Paleogenetics

'Everything okay?' He brushes the crusts from his shirt onto the floor of the car.

I return the phone to my handbag. 'Yes, ultrasound is normal.' His gaze follows mine to the floor. We look at each other—complicit in ignoring the mess.

'Normal?' He laughs. 'Maybe their experiment has failed?'

We book in with Lauren and wait for a few moments for the woman with oversized glasses. Isak sits quietly to one side while she tests my blood pressure, stabs my finger, dips a card into my wee. He raises his eyebrows as if to say she's a bit odd. Her silent and efficient delivery of her service a sign that incompetence won't be tolerated. There is something comforting about things going wrong though. A reminder of our fallibility is a great unifier. More forgivable than perfection or absolutes. She leaves the small clinic room and Isak laughs and whispers.

'Bit tense aren't we?'

'I've had her every time. And she still doesn't talk to me.'

Dr Jeff opens his door, smiles widely at Isak. His eyes drop to my belly, growing rounder now.

'Welcome home. We're all very glad you've come back to support Stacey. Well done.' I feel Isak shrink to child size. 'Sit down. Now, how are you, Stacey?' His blue eyes are less intent on mine today. They dart between us, sharing his energy and enthusiasm.

'Still got the heartburn with this Paleo diet but I'm okay otherwise. Getting bigger.' From the base of my stomach, the hard swelling of pregnancy has risen. Almost imperceptibly, day after day. Forming and assembling, stretching me into its own shape. It takes control, there is nothing clever or noteworthy about my own efforts. Every regeneration of life shares this process but every time it is a miracle. None more so than this. My hand rests naturally on the expanding shape of myself.

'No more cramps or pains?'

'None. They stopped a few weeks ago.' I have waited for the signs that this has not gone to plan. That constant ache, ever sharpening, whittling into a howl. Clots of blood and spine. The bulge of blank eye.

'Well I don't like to get too ahead of myself but I do think we are past the danger stage. You could start telling your family about the baby. What do you think, Isak? Do your other children know there will be a new child in the house?' It's an unnatural way of putting it—I wonder if he tried to avoid saying 'sister'.

'Yep, they worked it out.' He's already told his mother but he doesn't say that. 'Now, maybe you can fill me in, Doctor, on what we should be expecting over the next few weeks and with the birth?'

'Our website has some detailed information there if you'd like to take a look. But I can summarise for you if you'd like.'

'I'm not keen on websites myself. I'd rather have it from the source.'

I know his belligerent face, his demanding.

'Well we're expecting a shorter pregnancy and the birth should be normal. We are keen for a vaginal birth to give the baby the best microbial start. We've found it helps with immunity. She should be just like a normal baby, perhaps a little smaller. And we expect her to look normal too. Fair skin, red hair. Her facial features will be slightly different but we can explain that away. She has your genes too so she will resemble your other children a little, we expect.'

'How will we explain how different she looks? That she's retarded?' Isak is provoking him. The set of his jaw looks ready to receive a blow, slightly raised.

'No. We don't like that term. We have a rationale for you that explains exactly what to say to people. In short, if anyone questions, you will say she has a rare genetic condition similar to Down's syndrome so you aren't sure how her intellect or speech will develop and she may look a little outside the norm.'

Seems sensible and possible to me.

'Fee was going to talk to you both about it. Talk it through.'

Isak sniffs, his colour rises a little. 'Won't our families worry that they carry the same genetic condition?'

My family won't care or ask. There's no baby coming from my brother.

'The details are all online on a website built for the purpose of explaining the condition. There is enough detail to confuse most people. It will be specific to the child's likely characteristics and the statistics will show it is so rare it is almost impossible.' Jeff taps into his keyboard, sends the link to Isak in a message.

'I see. All bases are covered. She's going to be a bit slow by the sound of it?' Isak almost taunts him but Jeff is calm, well-practised.

'We don't know, Isak. That's part of this. And you two are the best placed to teach her and support her to reach her potential. She might be just as bright as your other children. The fact is, this is a clinical trial and we are breaking new ground. Some questions just can't be answered yet. You will find the answers. In many ways, you will also be finding the questions.'

'Will she learn to talk then?'

'Signs are that she will. There's archaeological evidence and genetic markers of speech mechanisms the same as we have. You will be her teachers, so you will need to keep track of this and stay in touch. From our interviews, we know your other children were well within the normal range with developmental milestones and Emilia is quite advanced.'

Isak flinches at our daughter's name. 'You know as much as I do by the sounds of it.'

'Like I said, Isak, what we know and assume is all available for you on our website. Have a good read through it and next time we can discuss more specific questions.' He sutures the conversation and turns straight to me. 'Now, Stacey, I had a message from our young radiologist that you were "stressed", she said, at your last appointment. Are you going to seek some help from our psych department?'

I submit, nod fervently and try to move us out of here. I will not show up. I know that already.

'And you can both keep seeing Fee too. She says you are doing well.'

Jeff rests his hand on my shoulder as we leave. 'The two of you are doing a wonderful thing for this child. Relax and enjoy. It will be a great adventure and you are both very strong people. In three months or so you will have a beautiful baby. And she'll be very lucky to be with you all.'

It's almost as if he gave us this gift, but she is a gift we gave to him.

.

Reheated cannelloni for dinner and the kids pick out the pasta, leaving the skinless centres behind in a pool of sticky sauce. After school we mucked out the car so I reward them with a bubble bath, teasing Jake with sprays of bubbles, building him a giant bubble beard. Now the bathroom is trailed with wet towels and toys but I feel like a better mother. Tuck them both in.

I read to Jake for a while but Emmy rejects my offer and digs herself into a heap of pillows, propping her book up on the tail of a pink swan called Diana. I sit beside her, belly obvious now and she rubs her hand over it. 'I can't wait, Mum.' She pulls up my top and looks closely at my skin. 'Hello in there,' she says. I mime hello back to her with my fingers, waving from under my shirt. She closes her book and cuddles the swan, kissing the top of its head. I kiss hers. I can't help but feel I'm deceiving her somehow.

Isak has a glass of red wine and looks up the PregCam™ site. Time lapse images of her foot. The form of toes—five of them set wide. Splayed as frogs. The pulse of the heart. Movement of a knee and the foot. Walking the earth again but also for the first time. I sit beside him on the couch, both transfixed by the staccato image moving.

'Is this real time?' He moves the party invitations Emmy has scattered on the table. Places the wine bottle in front of me. Smell of muted berries.

'I didn't ask.' Puts his hand on my belly as if to transmit through my skin to our girl and back to the screen. She rises, the flutter of her trampling near my liver. 'I think it is. She's dancing for you.'

We sit together, three of us mediated by the screen. The glow of it upon us like a holy family. The moment is broken by a pop-up window asking for my password again and an error message.

'Unbelievable. Fuckin security.' We watch the blue circle swirl around and around, captured like prey. Isak leaves for the kitchen.

The page loads and a new screen appears—'LifeBLOOD® children Phase Two' and asks for my password again. 'What's phase one then, if we are phase two?' He has his hand on my shoulder looking at the screen. I sink inside at the unknowns I can't even imagine. He puts a wineglass in front of me and half fills it. 'Won't hurt,' he says. Coloured confetti sticks to the base of the glass.

He takes the screen, seeking answers we are meant to discover ourselves. I lay down beside him and leave him to his reading. Sip the wine and escape into sleep.

19 WEEKS

I've never really been good with cleaning but today I've really tried—for Emmy. Beaming and swirling, she gathers her forces for her birthday party. Here. Isak lured Jake to tidy the yard on promises of taking him to a movie while the partygoers squeal and run around the house, and they straightened up the trampoline, twisted paper streamers around the safety cage and filled it with balloons. Jake had to jump in there and pop a few but it still looks very party-worthy.

My gluten-free birthday cake has no nuts or sugar and is vegan for all her friends. The rich smell of the cocoa nibs seemed to trigger the baby, who fluttered and turned while it cooked. There are jugs of optional syrup and cream and I adorned the cake with a china fairy.

Oma's parcel is early and my mother's is late as usual, but when my phone rings, I hand it straight to Emmy, who shouts 'Nine' into the phone. Something coven-like comes out between my mother and Emmy when they speak and she retreats from me. They are collaborators.

I pull helium balloons back from the door and tie a few to a pitcher of water which Emmy has set up as a centrepiece for the table and thrown in a few coloured stones and a plastic unicorn. She has called it moon-water because the stones and the unicorn were outside on the trampoline. I love her imagination but it connects her so close to my mother. Despite me, they are alike.

Emmy comes out of her room with the phone. I can talk to Mum about the food—she'll be pleased it's all vegan. 'Here she is—I love you too.' I open with the cake story and she praises me. A charade we both know.

'So . . .' Someone else's cat parades silently across the precipice of the back fence. She has issued an invitation with a long pause. I am meant to tell her all.

'How are you, Mum?' That will distract her for a while. She tells me she's worried about Marco, who looks a bit grey, and she's been to Tasmania to visit some old friend I should remember and of course she's fine because she looks after herself holistically and she hopes I am doing the same. That's her lead back to me because she has heard from Emmy that I am having a baby, and I didn't tell her. The accusation. I am not a good daughter, no matter how much she tried.

'She said you've been to the doctors a lot.' She trails off, leading my responses. I know her style so well. I could pre-warn her, tell her things are not quite right. She'll understand that, the innuendo. That all care should be taken when speaking about the baby. But I let her talk about doctors and interference and the dangers of the medical profession and watch the cat walk back across the fence and drop into our yard.

Even though I wasn't really listening I tell her 'I understand all that.' And sigh.

'But how are you, darl? I sense your anxiety.' She leads me to confession. I resist. Tell her Isak went away for a few weeks, to cover the traces of truth. She is forensic and can easily find my hidden cache. I haven't practised this game in a while and I feel the risk. She rounds back to the doctors' appointments.

'They are being extra careful because of the last one.' She will know it's more than that.

'I'll do a reading on it, see what comes up.'

I groan audibly into the phone.

'Don't worry, you won't have to know about it. I'll only share if you ask.' Snippy now. 'When's it due?'

I don't know of course so I tell her how many weeks I am instead. 'Capricorn,' almost immediately—she could never help me with the home-school maths work but she can work out astrology so quick. 'Nice with your Leo girl. Are you letting her in for the birth?'

'Mum! Of course not. She's only nine.'

She laughs. 'I was stirring you. You have no sense of adventure left. Is that Isak too serious these days? I doubt it.'

If only she knew how adventurous we really are. It's a good time to stop. The mood is light so I say goodbye and she tells me she loves me. So much. Despite my resistance, it is a comfort to know she is there.

'I love you too, Mum.' And tears prick my eyes. A strange silence when the phone cuts. The connection still feels live and I try to imagine what she is doing across the other side of the country. Like me, maybe she waits for the link to break. I step outside into the weak winter sunshine. The cat is leaning against the wall of our house, eyes closed in the warmth. I startle it, and it saunters towards me, looks up a moment. Rubs against my legs. I scratch behind its ears even though I say I hate cats because they eat the wild birds.

Someone has come to the front door and the party madness begins. I've never really spoken much to the mothers of Emmy's friends. They are working mothers, or athletic types and I never know what to make conversation about. Some like to complain about the teachers, but I don't feel comfortable with it. Emmy always does so well academically I feel embarrassed to say anything negative. They all say 'Hii-ii' stretching it out a long time to seem like old friends, 'How've you be-eeen?' The fathers are more relaxed and smile at me, tell me they'll be back at the appointed time.

I've always felt a bit of an outsider. School was so inconsistent for me I never had friends like this. Emmy holds their hands, drags a posse of them to her room. Presents and paper and the smell of new art supplies. They seem to know her well and she is squawking about how she loves this and that. It's beautiful and the joy of it lightens me.

They bounce outside and I warm some arancini in the oven. Balloons pop and there is squealing and laughter. The cat is gone.

Inside they play music and jump around with the helium balloons. One is lost out the door. Gone into the immensity to wreak disaster on wildlife somewhere. I resisted this disposable lifestyle but the force of it is too much. We told Jeff we would like to move from the city and live down south somewhere, closer to nature. I am hoping the support they give us will drag us out of this suburb. I had feet in the earth for my childhood and Emmy is almost too old to enjoy it already. She wants to play netball, go ice-skating.

The door wrenches open, 'Pass the parcel time!' We used up all the scraps of Christmas paper and old school art and she has a bundle like a large misshapen watermelon. Scattered inside are special notes of love she has written to her friends, magical stones and some handcrafted coloured pencils made from sticks, which my mother sent last year. They hurt her hands so Emmy is giving them away. She hands me my phone with a song queued and instructs me to stop and start randomly. Her friends sit in a circle, serious and focused while the music is on, laughing and talking in between. The melon shrinks to a pip and soon the game is done. Piles of paper strewn everywhere. They eat, sing happy-birthday-to-you and soon parents come to the door again. They all had a wonderful time, thank you thank you they all say, prompted by the parents.

Gone. Emmy deflates and we lie on the couch together. She curls around me, squeezes tight but she can't get as close because of the baby. The effort has drained my energy to the last but she is happy and I feel good about myself as a mother. For the moment.

21 WEEKS

He has taken a longer break today to come to my appointment with me. In a colourful street close to the clinic we park outside a restaurant and order big bowls of laksa. Smells of garlic and ginger seem trapped in this satin room, trimmed with elephants. I know it will give me heartburn but the spicy liquid and noodles, saturated flora of broccoli and Asian greens is overwhelmingly delicious. We connect in silent food bliss. Isak leans back, hand on his belly.

'So good. I'll be glad when the kids are old enough to enjoy a bit of spicy food. If I never eat mashed potato again I'll be a happy man.'

'Or a chip. If I never eat another chip I'll be happy too.' We laugh and connect.

'Do you remember when we used to come here and share one of these? It never seems enough now. I'm so deprived of spice I could eat mine and yours too.'

'You're such a pig.' I laugh at him, reach for his hand. 'It's worth it though, Isak.' I sip water to quell the chilli burn, watch the staff shuffle around in narrow skirts.

'I know.' His gaze drops towards my stomach, tucked under the table. 'Their website has so much advice on what to feed her—raw, Paleo, high protein. That'll be your job, I think. Better make the most of this before we have to worry about her diet as well.'

'I won't be in a hurry to continue the Paleo diet.' The list of dislikes, don't-likes and this-makes-me-sick from Emmy and Jake grows every week.

'Laksa maybe—start her early.' He checks the time and we head off to our appointment.

.

Jeff's beagles are on his screen saver, one caught mid-yawn and the other looking up with baleful eyes. We sit in the familiar seats, constantly rehearsing the same scene. I always forget my lines. They come back in the night, when the chill of realisations wakes me and triggers the nerves in my spine, my neck, making me rigid and anxious. Fee is not much comfort as a counsellor but I have kept the appointments, mostly. Isak has brought notes.

'How are you feeling, Stacey?' Jeff knows my pulse, my blood, breath and urine. Has seen the inner sanctum of my uterus on a daily basis, thumbing through the images of my fallopian tubes. The inscrutable density of the placenta and the erotic pulse which waves across the screen.

I don't know what to say because he must know. He has seen in me. 'Good,' inadequate as it is. As she grows, I feel myself recede from everyone. It is hard to focus; to concentrate. Even though I am here I feel transported beyond the path of other people. It is as if I am partly outside my body, like the real me is living in my shadow. 'A bit of heartburn.'

'Do you still have the prescription for that?'

I nod.

'Mind if I feel your tummy today?'

'That's fine.' Tummy, a children's word meant to sound casual and friendly. They all use it. Awful. They don't realise how patronising it is.

'Hop up on the bed for me, Stacey. You're welcome to come and watch,' he addresses Isak. I see him flinch, know his thoughts.

Through my dress he presses around, feeling her outline in me. He traverses the boundary and works down, careful and firm, approaching my pubic bone. Lifts my dress and gently places the cold ring of a stethoscope under my navel. Smiles.

'Strong heartbeat there. Want to hear it, Isak?' He pops the dark buttons from his ears and places them around Isak's head, mindless of the strange intimacy. Hunched down under my dress they listen, eyes fixed on a middle space somewhere lost in the beat, beat, beat. The rhythm of her life in creation. It is as if I have gone. The burn of laksa rises in my throat.

'It's quick.' Isak's voice is light.

'No quicker than your other children's will have been in utero.'

'You really think she's going to fit in with the other kids?'

'It's up to you two to make that happen, Isak.' He folds down my dress, pats my knee. 'We don't expect her appearance to be so outside the norm that she won't be accepted by others as part of your family. We want her to be brought up by you just as if she was one of your own.'

'She is one of our own,' says Isak and I know that he is committed. I know because he will defend her as his own.

Jeff smiles wryly. 'She's also our research, Isak. This is a joint project, we are partners in this.'

Isak stiffens and looks at me, holds my gaze. We read about this—the study of her growing up. When she grows up, if all goes well. She will have a good life and any medical trials done on her will not put her life at risk.

'She is precious to all of us,' Jeff says.

I am still on the examination table. There is a long silence and Jeff is the one to break away.

He dips his head. 'It's not too late if you want to terminate.'

The statement sucks my breath out.

'You need to be certain of this, that you can raise her with your family.'

'You don't normally terminate this late,' says Isak.

'Well she might survive as a prem baby.' Jeff cleans his hands with antibacterial gel. 'Someone else might raise her.' The smell is acrid and I want to get out of here. 'Stacey, what are your thoughts? It's a courageous thing you are doing. You are bearing this—not alone, mind you—but it's your body we are discussing.'

But it's not. I am ours: I am hers, theirs, Isak's. 'It's done, Jeff. She is real now and we are already doing this.'

He smiles, his shimmery eyes locked on mine in awe, satisfied as a glutton. I liked him once, but this child has changed what I see.

24 WEEKS

Pressure is tight in my abdomen from my full bladder and the ever-growing mound of the baby. I went shopping with Emmy, bought maternity jeans and a buoyant, blousing top that she picked for me. Too colourful. Excited to be shopping for new clothes instead of second-hand ones, she wanted to buy baby clothes but settled on a bunny-rug and some bibs. She is victorious over Jake—a sister will be all hers. She bursts with it onto the world of schoolteachers and friends who coo and fuss over me. I am a voodoo doll, constructed of blood and falsehood. Bound tight with scraps of flesh, grown in a Petri dish. Button eyes. I smile and thank them for their well wishes, lie to them about getting to swimming lessons in a hurry. Lie to them more. They offer help with kids. Stick me with pins.

Jason, the new radiographer, calls me in and begins once again the ritual. The laying out, the bearing of flesh, the squelching of gel and the cold. He presses hard into my belly, round and round. Clears his throat to break the silence.

'She's getting bigger.'

I can't think of words to respond with so I smile weakly at him.

'I'm just measuring the placenta.' He clicks and taps on the keyboard.

It is dark and terrestrial. A great, temporary organ which grows again and again with each child. A thing of magic, rubbed on the face of witches. I saw Emmy's in a kidney dish but I had no urge to feast on its nutrients.

'Do you think it's the same?'

'The placenta?'

'Yes, do you think it's human?'

'I don't know. That's something to ask the doctor next week.'

'Interesting thought though, isn't it? That thing there might not be human. That massive organ there like a parasite or something.'

His eyes shift sideways, wary of transgression, breaking a taboo.

Sometimes, the cells of the foetus cross the barrier into the mother. Parts of the baby transfer through the placenta, leaching out into the mother's body, creating anew parts of her tissue, installing the code of her unborn baby into her heart and her brain. She is no longer herself as she once was. She is a chimera, parts of her forever altered with the DNA of her children, human or not. I am not me any longer. I can feel her writing herself into my bloodstream. Ancient codes uttered in the pulse of our being. *Homo neanderthalensis* tracing back into the world through our cells.

25 WEEKS

My unity with her engulfs me. Isak and I walk on the beach in silence before our appointment. The blast of late winter storms has driven mounds of dark, ribbony seaweed onto the beach and our steps sink into the stinking heaps of it. It is tangled with white, elliptical cuttlefish cores and wrangles of kelp. Sandy pieces of sea sponge and tubular forms wrenched from the sea floor. Amid this mass glisten cans from Asian grocery stores, packages with Chinese script. A worn length of wood, crafted once by hand, bears the holes of many years in the churn of the ocean. Detritus of fishing expeditions. The hard corpse of a broad fish patterned like honeycomb. Isak bends to pick something from amid the mass.

'Batman.' He holds a small plastic bat wing. 'All this stuff will rot away but Batman survives.' He laughs. He would like to live closer to the coast.

'There must be something symbolic about that.' Though I have no idea what. Wind blows at his hair.

'We need to be superheroes, Stacey. That's a lesson for us from this. All the stuff around us seems like a big tangled mess but we'll survive it. It's all going to fade away into the past and Batman, here, he'll still be sitting on the sand watching the clouds roll by.'

'I love it when you're philosophical.'

'I'm a high-vis poet but you don't give me any credit.'

It's true. I have lost my generosity, especially with him. I hold so much inside.

'This baby—'

'You're very self-absorbed when you're pregnant.'

Strange that he chooses that word.

'I feel like I've been absorbed.'

He checks the time. Doesn't respond to my disappearance.

'Come on, Batman, it's that time.'

.

The usual tests of blood and wee with the large-glasses woman seem even more distant and in a few moments we are in Jeff's office. The plastic uterus is in pieces on his desk, veined plastic and ovaries, the false sinew of the vagina muscles heaped beside his keyboard. No leaching placenta cells visible on the pile.

He is a little formal in his greeting and I feel the hangover of our last appointment.

'I am worried about the birth,' Isak surprises me with this. Why didn't he share this with me?

'How about you, Stacey, how do you feel about it?' He clears his throat, defrosts a little.

I pause. 'The others were okay. I try not to think about it.'

He clicks through his ultrasound images.

'Don't they have bigger heads?' Isak asks.

I feel the force of it, pressing into my pelvis. Her head.

'You mean *she* has a bigger head.' I see my wings spread. I am her shelter.

Jeff smiles at my response. 'Well if you look here.' He points to the measurements on the screen. 'Her cranium is much like the shape your other children's will have been. Their heads grew into a round shape, like a soccer ball, in their first year and hers won't. Her head will stay that shape, we think. Like an egg, or a football.' He flicks to another screen, turns to Isak. 'We aren't completely sure, but I can assure you that the brain of a newborn baby and our girl here are both four hundred cubic centimetres. Her face, though, has more robust bones than your other children so we'll have to monitor the birth closely and intervene if we need to.'

I never want to focus on the horrors of birth. It just happens, plots its own course. No amount of anticipation will prepare me.

'What does that mean exactly? Can I still be there?' He is anxious, a shrillness in his voice.

'Yes, of course. And I will be right there, don't worry. There is no way I will let anything happen to either of them. If she's in the right position, her chin will be tucked into her chest and the shape of her face won't impact on the birth.' Jeff smiles over at me, nods reassuringly.

'Have you done this before? Has someone given birth? I see on your website there was a phase one of this,' Isak pursues.

'Phase one was a different kind of clinical trial. There were no live births.' He stands from his chair. 'Now don't worry. Everything will be fine. Take her somewhere nice for dinner while you have some time without a baby.'

'Yeah, thanks for the advice.' Isak takes my hand and draws me away from the doctor and his plastic uterus.

In the car, the warmth makes me sleepy.

'I'm sorry, Stace. You have every reason to be self-absorbed.' He holds my knee as he drives.

'It's okay. Don't worry. Thanks for asking about the birth.' I have been afraid to ask the questions.

'Not sure you want to know too much though, love. Don't think it will help on the day.' He has been there each time, each moment of labour for the other children. Unique in their own ways.

'Birth is about surrender, Isak. You can't know what will happen—not for any birth.' Deep inside, though, I know this is different. There is reason to worry; reason to ask. I try not to think of the mechanics of it. The visceral tear of memory.

28 WEEKS

Isak is missing my appointment today, keeping a little time in credit at work in case he needs it later. I walked the kids into school this morning, stopped to watch the honeyeaters sucking the pollen out of grevillea flowers. Spattered with rain. The moment so sweet. Jake's teacher wanted to ask about the due date but I rushed away, eager to see Emmy's artworks up in the school hall. She has held back on the glitter, fashioned a colourful elephant patterned with Hindi swirls. My bladder is hard and we sit in the classroom for a moment while she shows me her maths book. The tenderness of her efforts with fractions, not quite right. So close. I wonder how many more of these days will be so simple and so sweet. I have had a little cramping, but kept it quiet. They will find out why soon enough. It can't be a problem or the PregCam™ would know.

I am back in the imaging centre with Jason in a blue shirt. Another scan.

'Yes I do have a full bladder, yes I do need to go but I haven't.'

'Well hello to you too.' He laughs. 'Come on, let's go check on this bub then maybe you should take yourself out for a nice lunch. You sound like it's getting to you.'

'That's an understatement.' My gait has changed, the heavy front of me causing me to lean back and counterbalance it. Some days my lower back is very sore.

He gives me a bedside-manner smile. I sigh and follow him to the same room. He sets me up on the bed, gels my belly and looks me in the eye.

'You know, I realise that this must be a very difficult experience. It is absolutely not normal to be having a Neanderthal child, no matter how much they tell us to pretend like it is.' He looks in my eyes and touches my hand. I am surprised, pull my hand back.

'Sorry, Stacey, I'm speaking out of turn. They record these sessions but I haven't switched the webcam on yet.' He slows down a little, turning the lights around on their long stems.

'They record this too, not just the scan?'

He nods, eyes wide.

'I like you. I just want you to know we are under surveillance in here. You should know this stuff.'

I am shocked, but pleased. 'We'd better get started or they'll start to wonder.'

'Jason.' His finger hovers over the keyboard, waiting to start. He looks over to me. Warm eyes piercing into mine.

'Before you start. Will they record the birth?'

He flicks on the webcam.

'Absolutely, no doubt about it. Now, here we go. Oh, look, there she is! She's turned over.' He runs the cursor over the shape of the nose—just like the other kids. He measures her. She is small. Complete. Big, dark eyes, I imagine. A little well rises up. Baby. My baby.

'Looks like she's moving down towards the birth position, Stacey. They have an EDD down here of thirty-two weeks but it looks like she's getting herself ready. Might be a bit early.'

A little charge inside—a thrill. Fear.

He looks at me. 'You'll be fine and she will be too. Don't worry. Look at her, she's gorgeous. Preemie babies at this age are . . .' His phone rings. 'Normal' he might have said, or 'usually fine'. I know he has broken protocol and wonder if he's in trouble.

'Yes, yes. Yes, I'll ask her.' He nods at the phone. 'They want to know if you've had any of the normal signs of labour.' Serious.

'Um . . . cramps a bit, but only mild ones the last couple of days. I thought they were just expanding pains or Braxton Hicks.' My face is hot, anxious.

'Just as a precaution, they want you to go down to the hospital and book in. They are sending a taxi.' They're panicking and now I am too.

'But I need to go home, get my things. I have to pick up the kids from school. It might be the last time I can do it for a while. They'll be expecting me.'

'Calm down, Stacey, calm down.' He holds his hand over the phone as if they can be blocked out. 'Don't stress, love, it's only a precaution.' He gets up from his seat and moves away a step or two.

'Please, can I call Isak?' I want to cry. 'Is it really this fucking urgent?' Jason listens to the phone, looking away from me. Quietly hangs up.

'Okay, now just take it easy, Stacey. We can slow things down a bit. No panic. They've asked me to go with you to your place, pack a few things and take you to the hospital. It's not urgent but they want to monitor you. You might be there for the rest of your pregnancy, so we can take some time to get you organised and comfortable.'

I shake inside, my throat filled and hard.

'They don't want you to lose her. You understand that, don't you, Stacey?'

'Yes, I don't want to lose her either.' Sniff, close my eyes.

'Now, I'm going to get someone to organise my appointments. Take a moment and give Isak a call.'

.

In the dim light, the frozen image of her knee on the screen glows across my face. I tap Isak's name and the phone rings.

'Everything okay?' Tight panic in his voice. I tell him the story knowing he is already rearranging our children and his work hours in his thoughts.

In the silence after the call I feel her fluttering, reminding me of my full bladder. We share this urgency. Pressure bearing down like rock. Amid the tangle of my intestines and organs her purpose prevails. She will walk this earth, I know it.

The door opens and Jason appears with a wheelchair.

29 WEEKS

I didn't even know this was a hospital. Low and leafy on the banks of the river, it is tucked behind houses and a car park. It is a transplant clinic, not a hospital, according to the signage. Birds call, various trills and squawks rising above the hum of healthcare and gadgetry. The décor is soft, earth toned. Inspiring verses embossed into the cement walls. *Our body is a machine for living. It is organised for that, it is its nature. Let life go on in it unhindered and let it defend itself, it will do more than if you paralyse it by encumbering it with remedies—Leo Tolstoy.* It wraps around the corner. I have read it over and over, annoyed by the break between 'go' and 'on'. Puzzled by its endorsement of no remedy. Secular words meant as the wisdom of ages, which seem comforting but aren't. Comfort, perhaps, when a transplant doesn't work.

I am instructed to stay in bed, avoid long walks around the hallways. Each day they take me in the wheelchair out into a garden overlooking the river and each day I sit and stare at the moored boats and large houses stacked like cubes ascending up the banks. I stare and feel her there. Insects in the breeze, a flutter of wings. The sun of spring is gentle for a short season and I have time to watch it pass. Its days burst and wane, blossom and pollination. I am having a baby and yet I am paralysed and encumbered with the waiting. Each day measured by pulses. Each day scanned and tested.

In the afternoons Isak comes with the children, brings flowers or chocolate, fruit, things to read or wear. I wait for them but when they come I am tired suddenly and they have complaints and homework and are hungry. The room is close, despite its size. Emmy likes the private bathroom, the hospital-grade soap and wears the latex gloves down to the cafeteria. Isak pushes the wheelchair and we sit overlooking the river. Glass intervening between us and the insects. There are tall mounds of ice-cream bathed in luminous sauces. Creamy coffee for Isak. He apologises for his indulgence. I tell him I don't care. I feel like I'm watching them through a screen, smile at their stories, voices masked by a whisper in my ears. Constant, it takes me into the womb, where I am held, transfixed.

I am not sure what they tell me, not sure what they say, have no memory of our conversations. They laugh and talk between them as if I am present. Perhaps it seems as though I am. I feel the warm press of their faces against mine. Their blessed smell of coconut shampoo and coloured pencils. They wheel me back to my room, park me up in the band of sunshine from the window. I cry when they leave. Finally notice the pictures they have drawn for me. The effort of crayon and glitter. Jake's script embossed hard into the paper. Backwards letters. The gush of love.

He returns one evening alone, looking tired. I know he has driven almost an hour home through traffic, left the children with someone and come back here. He has brought two takeaway containers of laksa. I smile for him because I know he deserves me to, try to rise from the pulse of the machine.

'Can we go and sit outside somewhere?'

I nod and he leaves to find a wheelchair. Through the winding hallways we leave a scent trail of spice all the way to the river, outside to the garden.

'You seem really out of it, Stace. Have they drugged you up?' He opens the soup. Places one carefully on my lap, bolstered by a wad of serviettes.

'I don't think so. It's just . . .' How do I tell him of the way she has slurped my mind through the placenta, that I am no longer myself? That she has bled into me and I into her. 'I don't feel like myself.'

'I'm worried they've done it to you.'

I close my eyes. The cold air off the river brings the insects of night. They rush against the lit windows, gentle collisions.

'I spoke to the doctor.'

'The baby is fine,' not sure if I am asking or telling him.

'Yes, Stacey. I have been watching her at night through the PregCam™ after the kids go to bed. It's kind of mesmerising and it makes me feel close to you. I know that sounds weird. Pretty fucked up really.' He laughs, sadly.

'I hate being in here. I feel like an object, a machine or something.' The image of a pink lamb immersed in clear liquid. Eyes closed, tubes and valves fused to an artificial uterus.

A plastic bag, blood pumping into and out of the lamb, pulsing and beeping. 'I just want to scream.' Tears.

He removes the soup and holds me.

'What happened to the lamb?'

'What lamb?' He is gentle but he looks at me like I'm half mad.

'The lamb that was made in the artificial uterus.' Years ago, when we were kids. 'It was all over social media. Years ago.'

'Dunno. You want me to find out? It's probably hopping around in a paddock somewhere.' He is wide eyed, afraid of me and what I might be. I know his look of worry and fear. They are entwined.

'Why did they choose a lamb?'

He shakes his head, rubs his temples.

'A lamb, Isak. Lamb of God, Isak. I feel like a human sacrifice. Do you understand?'

I know he doesn't.

'You wanted to do this.'

He's just a regular guy—simple hearted.

'I know. They could have used a plastic uterus like they did with the lamb. They didn't need me. They had proof that it works without people.' All day I have thought of this.

'They did need you. A child can't be born without parents.'

They can, in theory. They proved it years ago.

'The lamb was.' I almost yell at him, voice high. I pull back. Calm. Try to still myself.

'She's not a lamb. She's your baby. A person in there who will love you just because you are her mother, doesn't matter what you do.'

A mosquito lands on my arm. Its delicate probe immersed in my flesh.

Isak slaps it definitively. Sits back in his chair. 'I just want this to be as normal as possible, Stace.' Normal is so elastic. His voice is husky and low, I know he has tears.

'She will love us, not just me.'

He smiles a little and I know I must assure him. Not send him away with that tangled-up look. 'I hate being observed, Isak. I didn't realise it would be like this. They have their camera up inside me and they hook me up to machinery, monitors and scanners. They beep and nurses take notes. They don't even need to speak to me. I could be that plastic sack of amniotic fluid. I could be those tubes of blood.'

'When we take her home, I will take some time off work and we can pack the kids in the car and go somewhere down south. Augusta maybe, or Windy Harbour. Somewhere peaceful where the kids can swim and nobody will scan you or take blood tests. We won't take a camera, it'll be private. No phones either.'

I love him so much—his practical solution to this.

'Promise?'

He holds my hands between his. 'I promise. Now I have to go.' He stands. 'But it won't be long and we'll be collecting shells on the beach with the kids and our new baby. Okay?' He wheels me away from the cold night. I can still smell the laksa and I sleep quickly, dream my mother is stroking my hair.

30 WEEKS

Early in the morning, I step onto the cold floor. Liquid rushes out, trails down my legs like a current. Around the arch of my foot. I stand still, holding the metal bed with my left hand. It feels like a torrent but when I look at the pool on the floor it might be a mouthful. A tear duct. When they know, there will be urgency, phone calls and calm words. I step into the bathroom, stand before the mirror. My face rosy, hair ragged. The round belly is low and I feel her pressing down. She is ready, but I am not.

In the shower, I wash my hair. Anoint myself with soap. My hand rolls around and around my belly, the feeling comforting. Soon the nerves will swell and pain will be all that I am so I gather myself and stretch these minutes under the warm drizzle. Swirl of soap and hair and amniotic fluids gushing around on the tiles. I wrap myself, dry each part. We will not be the same again. The machinery of birth alters me, alters our family and the world. But she will be. Through me she will travel, through the muscles of my body, through my labour, my arteries and cells. Stretching me into the shape of her, taking my flesh to its limits. My abdomen tightens, another trickle of warmth down my thigh and something drops on the tiles. The soft bean of the PregCam™. I leave it there amid the soap and wrap myself in a fresh white towel. Soon they will know.

In my towel, I ring Isak before they tell him for me. He is primed, ready with a plan. A man with purpose. I dress in my gardens-of-Babylon dress, do my hair. Breakfast arrives, then Dr Jeff. I prop myself gingerly onto the pile of pillows and slowly turn the scrambled eggs.

'You'll need all the energy you can get, Stacey. Eat up, don't mind me.' He flips through the clipboard of observations on the end of my bed, looking over at me as if to verify what he has read is true. There's a gleam in his eye and he's cheerier than usual, his shoulders straight and jaunty. I know he is excited to see 'his creation'.

'So your waters have broken, say an hour ago?' He stares into my eyes, more hypnotic than usual. I nod and he notes the time.

'Are you going to wait and see if I go into labour?'

'Yes, we'll give you twenty-four hours and see if things happen naturally. Was there any colour in the fluid?' His pen poised.

I shake my head.

'The birth plan is to keep it as natural as possible so let's just wait.'

'You have a birth plan? Don't you think I should know what's in your birth plan for me?'

'Relax, Stacey. Your birth plan is just based on what we know about you. We didn't get time to discuss it in depth. You've sprung this on me a little you know?'

'Well, what does it say?' No cutting me under any circumstances.

'It's in your document file—' He opens his mouth to speak but I shout.

'Fuck your website, why not talk to me about it?'

Jeff raises his eyebrows and steps back.

'It's okay, Stacey. I'll get the nurses to bring you a tablet with the document up on it.'

I try to breathe, not give way to fury at this moment when I need him to be at his kindest.

'Can I make changes?'

'Yes, but it's very simple so there probably isn't anything in there you don't ascribe to yourself. We based it on your previous births and our own intentions to keep it as natural as possible. We want her to have the best head start we can give her.'

'No drugs?'

'No. An epidural late in the birth if you really need it. It's important to keep any variables out of the process. If anything goes wrong, we want to know what it is. So any drugs will interfere with our knowledge of that.'

'You're excited.'

'Of course. We're doing an amazing thing here, you and I.'

'Isak too.'

'You are great parents. She's very lucky.'

I want to slap the sparkle from his eyes, but I lower my gaze and sip some chamomile tea instead.

'I'll send a nurse in to update your obs. They'll call me when you go into labour.'

He hangs the clipboard back in its pouch and pats my hand. 'I'll ask one of the nurses to come and read through the plan with you.' He flicks back the curtain to the hallway. 'You need to relax, get a bit of sleep and eat what you can, Stacey.'

I text Isak—'might be a while, no rush'. I finish all I can of the eggs. He returns—'okay. Organising kids. There soon.'

From the window a flush of yellow wattle surrounds the low foliage and a honeyeater busies itself, shifting the blossoms, which shake in a strong wind. Cloud cover mutes the morning light, growing dark with storm. I try to breathe deeply and not imagine the next few hours. The ordeal of giving life is always a journey of fire. Some stories might be shorter or involve less horror but there is suffering in even the mildest of experiences. I watch the bird and try not to step back but in my memory is the sensation of soft flesh slipping out of me, that terrible feeling of trying to hold on to a baby that is already lost. Trying to hold the muscles tight to stop it leaving. The force of expulsion tearing through without mercy. Agony compounded by the pain of death. And the aftermath of bleeding and tears and dark, dark days.

·

When I wake, Isak is sitting in the chair by my bedside reading something on his phone. I smell coffee. He smiles and puts his phone aside, grabs my hand.

'Any pain yet?' He is wearing the green Ireland T-shirt he wore for Emmy's and Jake's births.

'Lucky shirt again, huh?' I adjust myself on the pillows and a dragging pain, deep in my belly, tightens across my abdomen. A sharp response in my lower back. I breathe deep into it, drawing my focus inwards. It goes on. Eases but remains as an echo.

When I open my eyes, he is standing over me, stroking my hair. Brow drawn together.

'Want me to call them?' His breath is short and coffee scented.

'They'll come soon enough.' I try to relax in the interval. 'Have you timed it?'

He raises his phone.

I see nothing on the screen, my focus holds only myself, Isak, a small perimeter around us both. It is as if the world has shrunken, yet it is as full as it can be. I sip water, wait. As expected, the tight, sharp cramp returns. It spreads, dragging me into it until my whole consciousness is immersed in my abdomen, kicking and scratching at the gateway to life. Grinding against my lower back. I curl in on myself, roll on my side and am swallowed whole. Released. A nurse at the foot of the bed. She lifts the sheet, my dress, presses her hand around on my belly. Her touch is molten iron. I bat her hand away. She speaks to Isak.

'Stacey, they're going to take us to the birthing rooms. They asked if you'd like to go in the bath for a while. It'll ease the pain.'

I nod and it returns. Absorbs me into its force, gorging itself, taking me further into its throat. Tightens.

They move me into a wheelchair. I see the floor of the elevator, chrome plate distorting our reflections. Later my bare feet, the garden dress thrown over the back of a blue chair. Warm water around me, dim lights. I try to talk to Isak between the contractions.

'It's really bad in my back. Not like the other kids, as far as I remember.'

'Want me to tell them?'

I nod. Grab his hand so he can't leave me.

Tightening again, it holds me rigid in the water, pitched at the highest point for long moments. The water runs warm against my feet. A nurse comes in, her hand in the water on my skin. Words spoken around me as if I have gone. Far away. It does not stop. Takes hold of me again and again, determined to consume me. Determined to squeeze me into its hot gullet.

In the hiatus, they lift me from the water. I pull myself down against their grip, but someone is behind me, lifting me up.

'Come on, Stacey, you have to get out of here, you've lost some blood. We need to check how far you've dilated.'

'Is it time?'

I am back in a room, in a cotton gown, no pants. There are people around me. Jeff. He bends over my raised knees. I feel pressure inside. The flick of latex gloves.

'Yep, time to start pushing.' Isak is behind my head, holding both hands. His face is pale, tired, eyes wide. I wonder what horror he is witnessing.

Then it grabs me, tears me down, down. I cry out. Throat sore. My knees are bent up on the bed, some hands on my feet. It sears, burns—my flesh stretching. Tearing. I push against it, push further into the pain, into the tear. Can almost hear it rip. My voice rasping like a beast. Let me die. Please let me die.

I breathe, push again, further into the pain until I feel the bulk of her head emerging. Held breaths.

The surface tension finally breaks with the swell of another motion, rising and tearing forward. I surge, rise up from myself into the night sky. See the spire of the church. A lamb. My voice like bees held in the air.

Isak meets my eyes. 'She's nearly here.'

'Yep, one more push and her head will be out.' Jeff's face shines with sweat and thrill.

Like gathering cloud it rushes in, swirls into my whole self.

On a dreary night in November I push her into the world, a trail of my spine grating into fragments. And finally, in the slipstream, all of her is given. The air utters something like wonder.

They speak, lift her. Isak jerks out of the way. She is on my body. Bluish grey. My accomplishment.

A loud beep and flashing light. They take her. To my left I see them suctioning inside her mouth, cover her. I cannot breathe. I watch it all. Waiting.

Waiting.

Until finally, she cries.

POST-PARTUM

Tiny and fair-skinned. Doctors and nurses huddle around her. Counting, measuring. Gasps and exclamations—amazing. Someone says 'well done' to someone over there.

The contraction continues, now almost painless, expelling the placenta and various bloody clots and liquids. Finally the pull of stitches and an icy pad to reduce the swelling. All is numb. I see the nurse carefully collect it all in a silver dish.

Isak looks exhausted, kisses my forehead and holds my hand. A silent sentinel, he looks over at the stainless-steel trolley where she is under scrutiny. Looks at my eyes. The knot of serious faces around the trolley holds my gaze a moment and he looks again.

'Everything okay over there?'

Jeff turns to us, smile like a new father. 'Oh, yes. Just a minute and you can have her back.' Through the group, a young woman with a camera is focused closely on her. Tracing every inch of her. Each moment the sinew between us stretches. Aches. They lift me, replace the sheets and finally cover me with a thin blanket. My head still turned to the trolley.

A nurse wraps her in a cotton rug and hands her to Jeff, who looks down into her face, smiling. 'Isak, come and take this beautiful child.'

He does not hesitate and I know he has bonded with her too.

Jeff hands her to him. 'Do you have a name for her yet?'

Isak looks at me.

'Asta,' I whisper. And he brings her to me at last.

I know she is mine. Like a gush, the force of motherhood flows from me painting her in my blood again. She is twisted into every cell of me, bound like a helix to my core. Her little face like a pixie, broad cheeks, a wide, flat nose. Perfect rosy lips. A generous spray of russet hair. I touch her cheek and she opens her huge eyes. Like nothing I have seen, the irises dark blue and wider than normal. The whites reduced to a narrow rim. It is this that sets her apart more than the shape of her face; sets her apart from my other children. Yet she is mine, perhaps more mine. And I more hers.

Isak gasps at the sight of her eyes. A wonder. And perhaps that quaver at the end, the edge of horror.

I begin to unwrap her, unaware that the audience has turned to me. Jeff circles the bed. 'We are going to have to put her under some heat for a few hours, Stacey. Just to monitor her and make sure she is okay. Don't let her get cold, okay.'

I wrap the rug back around her, stroke her cheek. A nurse pushes a mobile plastic crib into the room, lifts the lid and plugs it into the wall.

'Now, let's get her stable and then you can have her back.' Jeff reaches down to take her but I hold her a moment more. Printing myself in her gaze. Those eyes, human eyes but not human.

'You'll get your time, Stacey. Let them make sure she's okay.' Isak takes my hand. 'Asta.' He says it as if to himself. 'I like it.' But he looks a little puzzled.

'I thought she needed something unique. Asta Mary, I thought.'

He smiles and shakes his head. 'Why Mary?'

'After Mary Shelley.' I don't think he gets the connection. 'The author.' There were a few classics in my mother's suitcase library. I don't mention what she wrote.

A blonde nurse comes to my bedside. 'Stacey, let's get you to a shower and back in your own room.' And she lifts the blanket. The new sheet already bloody.

Back in the room, they have cleaned and arranged flowers by the window. Prop me up on rustling pillows. I am sore now, the numbness has gone and cramps continue in the aftermath. The frozen pad renewed to take down the swelling. I feel war-torn, my body a soft jumble of shock and organs trying to re-establish order.

Isak is gone—home to sleep and to speak to the children. There are strict instructions, he said. The website is very specific about who can come to the clinic and visit. Only the parents and their children. No other relatives can know where the clinic is, or visit. Strictly no unauthorised visitors. They gave an address for flowers and gifts, to be delivered offsite. This is not a hospital, it said, but a clinic designed for limited public access. Part of our non-disclosure clause apparently.

I don't know what time of day it is but I am energised, can't sleep. Waiting for them to bring her back to me. I stare at the flowers. Not the same ones Isak brought me before. The orange lilies are gone. Instead there are gerberas, white chrysanthemums.

Pink rosebuds. From the dewdrop on the roses I can tell they aren't real. A card with 'love Mum' printed in someone else's handwriting.

A woman in uniform with outrageous lipstick brings in a tray and sets it up. 'Would you like a hot drink? Tea?'

I nod, and open the lid on hot porridge. Banana bread with fresh berries. I am suddenly hungry. This is not like hospital food so I make the most of the special treatment.

Afterwards, in between the rattle and chatter of the hallway are submarine moments. I wait, breathless. Trying to see through walls. To check that she is real.

When I wake, she is there. Sleeping like a stone, incongruous in the plastic crib. Red digits track her heart and breath. A white cap on her head. Tucked in. I wonder how many people in this clinic know what she really is. If the nurses are blind witnesses, stepping outside into the world with no knowledge of the wonders they have been privy to. I lay on my side, she lays on her side. Knees curled up. My eyes are fastened to her. As if it is the only way to know her. The prickle of lactation radiates around my nipples. She stirs, opens her wide eyes. Hungry for each other's flesh, milk flows.

I call for the nurse. She opens the crib like Tupperware and disconnects Asta from the digits, which hold still at that point. My breath is short and I take my baby to me. Need her. Tearing at the hospital gown. The nurse opens the back of it, bearing both breasts, swelling by the moment. Veins visible. My milk has never come in so fast with my other kids. Asta's wide mouth fastens immediately, her suction definite and satisfying. Relieving the pressure on my left. I sigh deeply, entirely drawn into the act, into being the feast.

Eventually, she leans back and we gaze into each other. As the light enters her eyes it seems to fill the facets within, illuminating her irises with sharp blues and reflections. Many moods of sky, centuries deep. Sinking into her I feel her soul and know her. A person unlike anyone else. Though we are all unique, she is more spectacularly unique than any living thing. A film of thin milk rises from her lips and I wipe it away with the corner of the rug. She is worth every moment of the torture of birth. Every tear and stitch. I will heal and she will always have been born. She will always be a wonder.

I hold her up to release any held wind, rub her back. Turn her to the right and she latches on with a ferocious suck. I am drawn in once again, mesmerised in the movement of her cheeks. That shape of her jaw. She has adapted me to her. I see the shift in me. But it is not a shift into a primal state, it is an elevation.

How strange I am to myself. Once I would have draped and covered myself, controlled the baby's mouth, but here she controls me, my desire for privacy overridden by her will. She slows now, drifts into satisfied sleep. I sit there with her for a long time. Holding her close.

A nurse comes to check on us, places her in the plastic crib and reconnects the monitor to her finger. Takes my blood pressure and inquires about my wellbeing. I can hear Emmy in the hallway. My heart leaps.

'Mumma! I made you a card and Dad has brought you some chocolates.'

'It was meant to be a surprise.' He is still weary, but has been home and changed. Emmy is by the crib, transfixed by the sleeping baby.

'Oh, Mumma. She's so beautiful.' She is hushed. 'I don't have red hair like her though. It's so pretty.' Jake climbs up on the bed, curls onto my lap.

'No, she's very unique.' Isak smiles at me. Hands me some chocolates and a little package, which I open. 'For the baby. Father's job to give her her first toy.' He has found a little stuffed mammoth. I laugh.

'Oh, you must have hunted the whole city for this.'

'Surprisingly, no. She was in the toy shop in Morley. Couldn't believe my luck.'

Jake looks up at me. 'Dad should've gotten you one, Mum. You love mammoths.'

'I do. But Asta will love her mammoth too.'

'Can we open the plastic lid and put it in with her?'

I nod and Isak opens it. A sucking noise. She stirs but does not wake and they place it under the blanket, facing her.

'I miss you, Mumma.' Jake tucks close into me and I flinch at the pressure on my swollen breast. Asta stirs a little.

'Careful, sweetheart. I'm a bit sore.'

He sighs. 'When will you come home? Dad tried to make nachos and they were all dry and hard.'

Isak feigns disapproval. 'Oh, come on, mate, you've had some good pizzas too. And plenty of international cuisines—Chinese, Thai, Vietnamese.'

'I see a theme.' I wag my finger at him. 'Plenty of leafy greens when I get home. I have saved up all my best salad recipes. No more Paleo diet.'

'Damn—I liked that Paleo diet.' Isak smiles, enjoying the normal conversation. The security of it amid all the strangeness of the past couple of weeks is a relief.

Asta slept through their visit. Masking her beautiful eyes under those massive eyelids. To the kids, at least, she is normal enough to not warrant a remark. With her eyes closed, anyway. The ordinariness of their lives suspends them in a net, a reality so solid they do not realise that their feet have never touched the ground. It is secure enough for now. How long it will hold, I am not sure. How she will alter their lives is something we can't know.

.

The light through the window is fading to evening now. The clanking of dinner trays and the smell of food. I eat a little, the post-birth numbness wearing off. More frozen pads. A hot water bottle for the cramps. She wakes and the nurse comes, I am guessing the monitors are connected to their desks or something.

'Time for a bath for this little one,' she says. 'Doctors say you are to bath her and one of the doctors is on her way to see you so I'll get it set up and when she gets here you can start.'

I'm barely fit to walk to the bathroom so I'm glad to hear there will be someone to help with the bathing. I can't trust myself just yet, both of us too fragile. Too precious. She is awake and silent, watchful. Looks around, staring at the light on the ceiling. Firelight and sunshine would have been all the light her people knew. A dark-haired woman peers around the door. Smiles as if she knows me.

'Can I come in?' She steps inside before I respond. 'I'm Dimitra. We've met before but I'm going to be working closely with you now that the baby is born. Asta, is it?'

I nod. Dimitra is pretty, in a remote way. Long silky hair, dark and heavy. Light eyes, intense but detached.

'Now, let's get her bathed before the water goes cold.' She opens the crib, picks up my baby without asking. 'Are you okay to get out of bed? Or do I need to call a nurse?'

I rally, not willing to let her take Asta to bathe without me. Pull myself up, still wearing the gaping hospital gown. The swelling makes it awkward to walk but I find my dressing-gown and follow her to the bath. She places Asta on a change mat and waits for me to catch up.

'We thought it would be good to have someone with you when you bathe her for the first time. Just to discuss some of your reactions to her.'

I don't know what to say. 'So, am I under study too?'

'No, but we want to make sure that you are comfortable looking after her. Just to explain, I am a paediatrician and I have specialised in evolution so I've studied Paleolithic infants and children. My role is to observe Asta and also to support your family by caring for her health and development.' I finally reach the change table and Dimitra takes her hands from the baby.

'How do you get to study Paleolithic infants?' I begin to unwrap the rug from around Asta, who lays still, looking up at me.

'Archaeological samples. It is amazing what we can find out just from those and the situations where they are found. We know more than you can imagine about growth, diet and childhood. From things such as fossilised dental plaque and the microbiome, ancient bacteria.' She's obviously passionate about her subject and good at it too.

Asta's tiny hands are more stout than long. I remember Emmy and Jake had long fingers as newborn babies, like miniature versions of adult hands, which fattened up into baby hands in the first weeks. I examine Asta's hands, hold them between my own fingers.

'She's very little.'

'Well we didn't know what constituted full-term but her size is consistent with what we know of their newborns. Signs are that she will grow fast. Has she started feeding?'

I continue to unwrap her tiny form, light down covers her back.

'We think that will go. Some human babies have body hair when they're born.'

I flinch. 'She is as human as I am.'

'Yes, she is a different type of human. We just aren't used to it yet, Stacey. You are right to correct me.' Her eyes lower but she smiles.

'You think it's funny?'

'No, of course not. I've got a lot invested in her too and I'm pleased that you defend her.' She pauses, stares at Asta. 'It's just amazing that there are two breeds of human again. It's going to take the world a while to come to grips with it. There are theories that we should breed some of their genes back into ourselves for the strength of our species.' She picks Asta up and lowers her into the bath, eyes roaming over her wide body. 'Would you like to wash her?'

I immerse my hands beside Dimitra's, the sleeves of my dressing-gown dropping into the bath. Asta watches our faces and I wipe her tiny body with what seems an enormous flannel. Dimitra steps back a little and watches us.

'What do you notice, Stacey, that makes her different from your other children?'

'Besides the eyes, obviously.'

She nods. 'Well, she will have some traits from you and Isak.'

I wipe the flannel across her chest. 'She is broad. Her shoulders and chest. So she seems stronger.' Such tiny feet. 'Her legs are denser, less frail-looking than my other kids' legs.'

'She'll be a strong girl. You'll be feeding her often, I think. I'd like you to start recording it for me. How often and how long she feeds. I've got an app for you to put on your phone to record your daily obs.'

'The water's a bit cold, let's get her out.'

She laughs. 'No, let's not yet.'

The water is making my skin bump.

'She's cold adapted. I want to observe her response to cold and heat. That's part of my research.'

Already cruel.

It's noticeably cold but Asta does not react to it. No goose bumps. She continues to look at us with the same steady gaze. Dimitra dips a finger in the water and finally brings a towel.

'We can do more of this later.' She wraps and holds Asta, takes her to the change table. 'Would you like to dress her?'

I am faint with tiredness but I push myself, don't want to give her up.

The tiny disposable nappy seems oddly shaped on her but it's not quite clear why. I stick it together but while it fits around the waist it seems to be tight around her legs. 'We might need another size.'

Dimitra looks at the awkward-fitting nappy. 'I'll see what we can do. Leave it for now.'

I top it with a singlet and wrap her in a flannel rug with little ducks. Tired now. Dimitra takes her to the crib and I fall deeply into the bed, lights are dimmed. I lie watching her sleep, tracing the line of her profile into my memory.

The link to the LifeBLOOD® BubBot is on the website. I hit 'install'. It needs access to all my information, as usual, and I accept the terms and conditions without reading them.

We have not taken any photos of Asta. It seems strange but I have not even thought of it. I know there was a camera in the birth room but I have not seen the pictures or the video that was taken. I add a temporary photo of a pelican on the lake near our house.

The app has a list of reports to create for each week with blanks for diet, behaviour, growth, milestones, questions, photos and video.

All information shared in this app is only available to author-ised parties and affiliates of LifeBLOOD®.

I tap 'Create Report Week 1' and boxes appear for each. In Photos & Video I click on the icon to capture photo. Asta is out of the plastic crib, sleeping peacefully in the open cot beside my bed. As I near, her cheeks move as though to suck.

I save the draft of the report and pick her up to feed her.

The doctors are keen to get us out of the clinic. I'm assuming it's for privacy and the need to keep her birth discreet. I have the same nurses every day and Asta and I have not left the room since she was born. Dimitra is pleased with her feeding and her weight gain, even though she is small. We have appointments and the BubBot. Fee checks in and hands me some brochures on post-natal depression. We speak at length about how to respond to questions about Asta's 'condition'. I am blurry and don't write it down. Some final examinations. There is little to pack for Asta except the mammoth and some custom-made re-usable cloth nappies in a variety of colours with little animal pictures. A few things for me and the sagging maternity dress, freshly laundered, to wear home.

Dimitra visits to discharge us and provide a lengthy set of instructions. Keep visitors minimal, avoid people showing signs of sickness, no flower pollen in the house, try to keep her away from public places for a while until she is bigger. Take her for a walk every day. She needs to go outside for her immune system to develop. Feed on demand and report anything, anything at all. Under no circumstances put her or her real identity at risk. There is a media embargo and no publicity coming from LifeBLOOD® until we are advised otherwise. Dimitra's remote persona shows signs of cracking. Small beads of perspiration on her upper lip. Her mash-up accent noticeable. She is frightened. I am not. I look at Asta and everything about her seems right and normal. Our unity is a shield against the eye of the world.

In Isak's arms, she looks particularly tiny and he holds her
high against his chest. Her newborn face changes every day and
today her skin is becoming fairer, almost translucent with a bluish
tinge like the fairest of them all. A nurse escorts us from the
clinic to our car, newly cleaned and equipped with a robust baby
seat facing backwards. Heavy-grade sun filters are fitted to the
windows around the seat. LifeBLOOD® had given us a credit
card and instructions to buy all new baby equipment so one night
Isak came to visit after dinner with an online catalogue and we
picked out a new pram, bassinet, cot, change table, baby bag, an
ergonomic baby carrier and a lot of linen and bibs. With our other
kids I had a second-hand cot and re-used what I could. I would
have given anything for a new pram. I battled to fold and unfold
it in searing-hot car parks; immovable sand and food particles
were lodged in the stitches of the seat and it was awkward to fit
into our small car. It's still in the shed.

So we got what we could get from them. Within a couple of
days it was all delivered to our house and Isak had assembled
the flatpacks. Never had we spent so much money at once.
Each new piece of furniture in our house has been purchased
after a tax return or paid off during the interest-free periods,
each instalment impacting our ability to buy clothes and pay
for swimming lessons. If only I had been able to do this for the
other kids. I wonder how they will perceive all this new stuff,
when their own lives have been lived on such a sparse budget.
At least, perhaps, they will benefit from some of the financial
liberation we will have.

In the car it seems miraculous to be free and Isak doesn't hesitate. Drives with purpose from the clinic out onto the highway. Sighs and smiles at me. Checks the rear-view mirror and adjusts it for a view of Asta, even though she is facing the other way.

'Fuck, I'm glad to be rid of that place, Stace. The cafe is like the Cantina Creepy. Poor bastards.' He searches in the console for his sunglasses, which I find in the glove box and clean for him on the edge of my dress.

'Did you see any babies? I never saw any babies or pregnant mothers except me.' I hand him the glasses.

'No. Couple of teenagers though, obviously having some limb regeneration or transplants or something. Too sad for our kids to witness that.'

'We're so lucky.' We gaze at the long line of traffic onto the freeway, appreciating our escape from suffering. 'The car's nice and clean.'

'Yes, they had it detailed for us. Imagine that job, huh?' He laughs. We both know the layers of food and filth that were caught in the back seat. 'So, they've made good on their promise and we have a new LandCruiser on order.'

'You chose it already?' I know this is something he's dreamed about.

'Yeah. I got a green one for you and got the camper pack so we can take the kids out in the bush.' He is boring with the detail. Excited. 'Plus an annex for shade.'

'Well, you picked it so you can clean it,' I joke but there's a little bit of truth in that.

He laughs and jokes about 'getting all the best jobs'.

'At least the old one's clean now—we can keep it.' The slow crawl of traffic past the river gives pause to our day. Spring is so volatile. The storm of last week is long past and the heat is already making drivers impatient. Seagulls drift on the slow bounce of the tide and the city seems to crack open as its moisture evaporates. West-facing windows of posh houses, so desperate for river frontage that they border the freeway, are shuttered and blinded. Soon summer will bleach everything. He deserves the car, I know. I have navigated us to this place and he has been my passenger.

'Come on, people,' he speaks to the traffic. 'Is she okay back there?'

I unclip my seatbelt and kneel on the seat, my hand by her head. 'Still asleep but a bit sweaty.' I crank up the air-conditioner.

'She doesn't look that different from the other kids. I reckon we can take her in to school to pick them up. They'd love it.'

'I was going to wait in the car with her.' They want us to be discreet. 'Or go through the kiss-and-drive.'

He turns onto the exit, still crammed with close traffic, and soon we are in the slow crawl of the school car park. The siren calls three o'clock and a wave of frantic mothers mount the kerbs in their SUVs, haphazard and angular wherever there is space. Crushing native grasses planted each winter holidays. Someone reverses out of a space ahead and Isak darts into it, a little crookedly. I can feel the victory boosting his mood and he almost skips to the back door and unclips Asta.

I am still tentative so he carries her up the bush-lined path past various parents and children, laden with schoolbags. Nobody looks at her. No stares. At Jake's classroom, Isak leans through the door with the baby, ready to show her off. Kids push past him, eager to get home. Jake drags his teacher by her hand over to see the baby.

'Oh, sweet,' she coos. 'Did you look like that when you were a baby, Jake? I bet you were that cute too.' She touches Asta's cheek, and I retract inside. Jake laughs, grabs his bag.

'Come on, Isak, we have to go and get Emmy.' And I take his elbow, pull him from the doorway. 'I'm exhausted. This is a bit much for me yet.' I overstate things, want to get away. No questions. Please, no questions.

Emmy is the last child left in her class, up on her knees on the mat, bag on her back. When she sees both of us with the baby her face reverses from steaming impatience to glowing joy. I feel mine do the same. I remember that desire for a sister of my own. She is lucky her wish was fulfilled. Emmy dashes from the door, her teacher several steps behind.

'She's been so excited, talked of nothing else all week. I've heard all about her beautiful red hair.' Miss Healey smiles down at the baby and I shrink inside, frightened of revelations.

Emmy pulls off the cap, 'See, Miss Healey. Like sunshine and rust.'

'Watch the baby's head.' Isak pulls the cap over her long head. I want to explain, lots of babies are born with distorted heads. The fontanelles grow and it will be round like everyone else's.

It's just for a few months. But I am silent and the conversation moves on. She seems to not notice.

'She was a bit early,' Isak is explaining. 'But she's fine, just smaller than usual for a newborn.'

Then she opens her eyes and the teacher baulks, takes in a sudden breath I dread.

'Wow, she's got big eyes.' Polite. She looks deeper, I surrender. 'I don't think I've ever seen anyone with eyes like hers before.' She pauses, staring. 'They're so beautiful, and very unusual.'

I step in, very close to Isak, and she retreats back to find personal space. I look at her seriously in the eyes. 'We need to be a bit discreet, Maddie.' A knowing look. Just enough.

'Oh, things are not—oh, I see.' She swallows hard. 'Oh, I'm sorry to hear that, Stacey.'

'We don't know how much of an issue it is just yet,' says Isak. 'Let's not get too ahead of ourselves.'

'It's okay, I understand. My sister has a boy and you just have to keep things as normal as possible.' She reels back her enthusiasm like untouched bait. Emmy detects the shift in mood and goes quiet. On the way to the car she looks up at me, and reaches for my hand.

'Is Asta okay, Mumma?'

Among the blooming grevillea, small birds dart about. I don't want to quell her.

'Yes. She's fine. But you know she's been born a bit early so we need to be extra careful with her.'

Isak straps Asta into the car and Emmy slides across into the middle, staring down into the baby. 'She's a bit delicate. Don't worry, sweetie.'

'It's okay, Asta. I'll help look after you.'

Isak passes a pump bottle of hand sanitiser between the seats and the kids dutifully kill their bacteria. Its sharp scent fills the car and we rejoin the streaming traffic of the freeway, curving off onto an arterial road that funnels into various housing estates. Ours has a tired entry statement of bas relief pelicans in flight, eroding from rammed earth. A nod to the remnant wetland at the heart of the estate, now devoid of mosquitos. Frogs silent. The streets meander like small intestines, diverting into terminated streets. I call ours the gall bladder but it could just as easily be an appendix. Not a dream house but at least it is ours.

There's a caterer's disposable tray of lasagne in the fridge and cleaners have been through and sanitised everything. Not a speck of glitter is left in the carpet and dirty fingerprints have been wiped from around each light switch. Daddy-long-legs are gone. My ease has not returned. The spare room has been transformed. Painted and filled with the new baby furniture. A bucket for dirty nappies and a pile of clean ones.

Isak looks over my shoulder into the room. 'They ordered a nappy service for us.' I want to cry. Not sure why.

'She doesn't have any clothes.'

He leads me to a white cupboard, hanging with soft coloured onesies. A few tiny dresses. Little jackets. No labels, all handmade. 'Custom-made. Must have cost a packet.'

'It's kind of weird.' He laughs, places Asta into the bassinet and wheels it out into the dining room.

'And you expected something not weird?' He flicks on the kettle. Kids retreat to television.

Night and day bleed together. Salty and fresh clouding one to the other, become brackish. Bubbles emerge from the earth. Slow rising to the surface. Breaking in the air. Languid movements beneath the skin.

Slithering creatures live within me. Leak out, spurt and spray. They dry and become wet again, leave a firm crust all around.

I am submarine, subterranean.

Sublime.

I am consumed, in the belly of the beast.

Utterly gone.

I breathe enough only to stay alive. Enough to feed her. Rising to the surface, breaking through only to fill my lungs. Just enough. I am necessary. Not the purpose.

Milk and blood, blood and milk. Whorl together. My blood is her blood, her milk is my blood. She burrows into my flesh, sucking me in with a force beyond refusal. A force I can't deny. I ache for her, nipples sparking and tingling for the pain of her mouth. The sweet agony of it. My foot taps against the coffee table, neck stretched up, mouth open. I roar silently at the ceiling as she latches on. Breasts weighty and red, she needs and needs and needs and I leach out, leak endlessly. Marinated in my own juice.

Her wide mouth is a gateway to ease, a portal into agony. I rock back and forth amid damp cushions. A bottle of water at my side only to replenish what she takes. Nothing left for me but I want nothing more. We are locked together in eternal love. Her tiny nails clawing at my armpit, drawing down more milk. My body obeys and refills. Endlessly abundant.

A fly buzzes at the window. Television burns quietly in the corner. And the world goes on.

She grows. And each day her appetite increases, so I yield. Make more, give her more. She stretches back with satisfaction. Her arms and fists reaching.

Sometimes we roll together in a tangle of sheets and fitful sleep. I turn on my side, the swollen breasts stifling my movements. She fixes herself to them as they pass her mouth. Latching on without thought or need. Pure instinct. The drive to have me.

The nights and the days. I have forgotten my name and the chapters that have gone. I have no knowledge of what will come or how I have moved from place to place. How they have all lived around me. Their coming and going in a world above the surface, where the wind blows and the sun shines. Down here, inside this thing we slip into the gullet. So slick with saliva that little force is required to swallow it down. So many things here that I cannot name. Through the miasma all I see is her eyes, her cheeks drawing in, the rim of milk at her lips.

·

Isak's eyes, lids low and concerned. He bends to me, touches my hair. The phone rings and he speaks for us. The doorbell rings and he speaks for us. Brings me water. In the wood on the cupboard I see patterns swirling, ancient symbols. Twisted faces caught in a yell.

The dark-haired doctor comes. Her accent a merge of British and European. She smiles and takes the baby. Weighs and measures. Twists her legs and feels her stomach. Turns her over on the floor. I don't remember what she says. Isak is there and she speaks to him. Then she sits beside me on the couch, looking down at my bare breasts. Piles of tissues and bibs all around. Her hands feel like razors, pointed at the ends. Her touch slashes at my nipples, tearing open the red crescents. I rear back. Can't move away. Silent. Mouth wide open.

She speaks to Isak and they are nodding. Worry.

When she is gone he comes with a tube of cream. Soft as butter. His touch eases the raw flesh. But before it can seal, they fill and swell. Hot and bursting. Asta's suckle tears the wound wide. Skewering through my chest, pinning me to the couch. Stitching back and forth, binding us together in relief and suffering.

·

I have become the mother she needs. Who I am and who I might have been have gone completely.

·

The bones of a bird are hollow, which is why it can fly. I have been hollowed, my marrow drawn out through my nipples. And so I have risen, arms outstretched. Higher and higher, buffeted now on air pressure and currents. They have driven me south with scarcely a bump in the road. The children have finished school for the year and we are all packed in the enormous car. Baby sleeping, landscape and ecosystems transforming as we tear past on our way to a caravan park on the coast, far from home.

Isak relives his love of Ed Sheeran and plays the songs over and over until the kids are singing along to 'Galway Girl'. He has dressed in his shamrock T-shirt because it always brings him good luck. I know he must have a need for sanity, clarity. Some words from me that will bring us back into the same orbit. Ireland is our touchstone. He is trying to be joyful and make contact. I lift my arms and rise to him. Willing myself back. Emmy is in the middle, wearing a wide sunhat, bright birds on her shirt and bare legs. There is a giant bottle of sunscreen in the console, insect repellent and a bag of lollies I never would have bought. While I was feeding they have changed positions, abandoning me by the roadside while they set a course of their own. I am trying to catch up. We are attempting unity and hoping the glue will dry.

Jake sings along, tapping on his tablet at some strange game. Immersed in two diversions, eyes darting. Isak smiles at me, turns the volume down.

'Enjoying the ride?' Handsome today in his new car.

I nod. 'I love holidays with you.'

He grins wide. 'I thought we'd lost you for a while there.' Squeezes my hand.

I thought I was lost. A group of black cockatoos flash white tails at the car, dipping dangerously low. Their slow wings taking them just out of reach. 'Where are we staying?'

'Hamelin Bay. There's a nice caravan park there and it's on the beach. Shady and close to Augusta but out of town. Nice and quiet.'

I've been there as a child but I don't want to talk about that. I take a lolly and settle into the journey. The further we travel, the more it is like a return to a faint childhood imprint. The coast, small towns and shifting character of bush with unique trees—tuart, marri, jarrah, karri—words like lullaby.

We left here when I was very young, my mother fleeing my father and taking us to Byron Bay so she could live more alternative. It never lived up to her hopes so on we went—Warrnambool, Launceston, Port Fairy, Leura, Armidale, Katoomba and back and forth so I couldn't keep track. Eventually I was old enough to leave. The rubble of that still stands between us, as surely as the kilometres of coastline from here to there. She rang, sent a card and some hand-felted boots for Asta, no doubt made by one of her many old friends.

'Did you speak to Mum?' I know he did. He would have thought it only fair after he'd called his own mother.

He nods. 'She was in Katoomba, back with Marco. Poor bugger is sick and can't run away from her.' His weatherboard house in the mountains was always cold. My last stand with her happened there just as I finished school. 'She thought Asta was beautiful but Mary is an awful name, no surprises there.'

'She probably thought I did it to annoy her.' I take another sherbet. She will have thought of Bible Mary.

'She did speak to me for a while though.' He looks furtive, a little wary of my reaction. 'I sent her a few photos of the kids holding the baby.' He hands me his phone. He's taken over the BubBot app for me, uploading images of Asta asleep and in the arms of Emmy. I see how she has grown, quickly, and I hadn't noticed. Fully soaked in breastmilk. It breaks my synapses and undermines my memory. 'She is helping treat his cancer with diet. She said it seems to be working.' Isak rolls his eyes, no patience with non-medical treatment.

I am not quite so critical. She has had a lot of experience, but I just don't forgive her for my messed-up childhood. The other side of the country is only just far enough away. My brother has never come back from London, like I have, so I think I've done well to get this close and stay in touch with her. I scroll through his reports, dutifully recording my feeding and her sleep.

'Alex sent you some flowers from London.' Last time I saw him, we walked across Blackheath to the station on my way to South Africa to meet Isak's mother. I was already pregnant with Emmy and I knew the holiday years were over. He told me I'd make a great mother because I knew what it was to have one that was shit.

'Did you speak to him?'

Isak shakes his head.

'The flowers were lovely but I had to put them on the back verandah. Too perfumed for her.' He looks in the rear-view mirror. 'How's she going back there, Em?'

'Still asleep. I wiped a bit of spew off her chin. I think she's dreaming.'

'You're a good big sister.'

We turn south on Caves Road, which twists past forest and tourist destinations we have never been to. A stand of tall, pale trees marks another shift in the landscape at Boranup forest. The cathedral of karris, so pale and tall, render us all silent. We turn west to Hamelin Bay, descending into a hollow filled with peppermint trees.

Isak checks us in and drives to a small cabin in the middle of the park. There are sparse tents, hanging with beach towels and bathers. Evidence of barbecues. Worn shoes askew by the zipped tents. Once the door is unlocked the kids push past us, running into the small cabin and claiming bunk beds. Both at the top, of course. Isak transports our luggage and modest food supplies and I carry Asta, who wakes at my scent, turning her open mouth back towards my chest. Calling her low grizzle. Milk leaks through my shirt and drips onto my stomach and we settle into the pastel couch. Almost as soon as they arrive the children want to go to the beach. I don't make them wait. This feeding might go on for most of the afternoon. They close the door. Voices fading in the distance.

The cabin creaks in the breeze, branches scratching against its metal cladding. Inside is pastel and grey, blinds slightly open. It smells of shed skin and disinfectant. Seabirds outside. Her cheeks draw in and out, her brow furrowed with intensity, desperation. The hours of driving have left her ravenous and she draws deep on my flesh, reopening the wounds that have started to heal. My nipples have turned leathery and dark, protruding like a finger, but she has the power to force them to the limit of endurance. Skin stretching thin as a membrane. As the initial rush ceases she claws at my armpit, coaxing my body to make more. I dehydrate quickly, finishing off the last warm water from the bottle I had in the car.

I poke my finger between my nipple and her lip to break the suction and peel her off, laying her on the couch so I can fill the bottle. Open the blind to let in some fresh air. My heart races as I stand face-to-face with a stranger on the porch of the cabin next door. He doesn't look away, but stares at me through the window. I screech and close the blind. Asta startles, cries and rolls onto the floor. My heart is racing. I check her over and she latches on again. I am still shaken when Isak returns with the kids. He rushes to make them sandwiches. Once the kids have the network password, they are silent and absorbed in games and we lay on the bed into the late afternoon. I tell him about the stranger.

'Do you think it's them, that they are watching us all the time?'

He strokes my cheek. 'I hope not.' He smirks and we laugh a little. 'They know where we are, in case anything happens.' He reaches for my hand, 'I think it'd be better if you did the BubBot, Stace. I only notice some things but you're right up close with her. Have you read what I've sent?' I skimmed, not patient enough to sit and read through his notes on our feeding, her nappies, the responses of Emmy and Jake.

Surely some things, my thoughts, have to be private. 'You've done a great job and I don't think I'd do any different. Anyway, I don't want them to know it all.'

'But that's what you're doing, Stacey. It's a medical trial.'

Asta is snuggled in the pram beside our bed, fast asleep.

A medical trial. 'She looks like a baby to me. Is that really what you think of her?'

He raises his eyebrows, a mix of surprise and horror. 'Of course not. Look at her. She's so sweet.'

I know he's trying to treat her like a normal baby. 'She's not like the other kids though.'

'No, but they are all different.'

'She's more different.' Trying to dig for what he really thinks.

'The feeding is different, that's for sure. I don't remember you being so intense with it before.' He runs his hands through his hair. 'I mean, she's always hungry and your tits are huge.' He looks at them, leaking again through my clothes.

'Nice way of putting it, Isak.' There's no escape from them and the smell.

'Sorry, but you know what I mean.'

'I do feel like it's all that I am. Right now anyway.' He takes my hand and tears come gulping.

'You're amazing, that's what you are. To do this, you are so brave. You didn't know what was going to happen to you. You might've ended up with anything. It took courage.' He kisses my fingers and I can't help but smile.

'Stupidity too, I think.'

He pulls me closer, runs his hand over my waist.

'Don't start things you can't finish.' Kids outside the door.

He laughs, looks over at the door, the baby. 'But I'd expect nothing less from a girl like you. Remember that time we did the Ring of Beara and you suggested—'

'I didn't suggest it. I just said I wondered what it would be like to sleep on the druid's grave.'

'That's not how I remember it. I remember waking up with a sore back though.'

'And freezing cold.' He's cheering me, bringing us closer.

'Maybe now that we might not be always so fucking broke we can seriously think about going back there.'

Evening cools down the cabin quickly and I get up to close the windows. Wind pushing around the long hanks of peppermint trees. I can hear the sea.

'We need to get them all passports. Did we get a birth certificate yet?' Not sure why he thinks I'm that organised.

I shake my head. 'Did you fill out any forms?'

Isak takes my phone and searches for birth registration on the government websites. 'They should've done it in the hospital. It says the forms are given to us by a midwife, nurse or doctor.'

He opens the BubBot. Uploads a photo of Asta sleeping in the pram. *Big sleep. Having a good holiday in Hamelin Bay. Very hungry after the big drive down from the city. Please send us the registration of birth form, we didn't get one at the clinic.*

'Want to go get fish and chips in Augusta for dinner?' he calls and immediately the door opens, Emmy runs to the bedside.

She's bouncing, hair ragged with salty water. 'Yes. Can we all go? Will Mum and the baby come too?'

'Okay.' I nod to her. And we pack them in the car to drive even further south.

.

Emmy holds the steaming paper parcels on her lap in the car then we set up our picnic beside the beach on a grassy foreshore. Seagulls rally around, in the air and on the grass, one with a missing leg and a couple of terns with red beaks and dark heads, less arrogant than the gulls. The kids throw them our scraps and they circle and squabble. Isak straps Asta into the baby carrier on his chest so we can walk on the beach and the kids run out on a timber jetty. Dead blowfish, scraped scales dry in the sun. I step around the gore of bait and entrails.

Dark brown river gives way to the sea here, creating a place between the two. It is only a short walk to Flinders Bay and the wind-battered lighthouse of Cape Leeuwin. I remember the force of the wind on the coast as a small child. The terror of being swept away into that endless wild sea. Whale-watching tour boats are moored for the evening and we walk along the pathway through a dense stand of stunted peppermint trees, crafted by the harsh winds into a twisted arc. Further on, we find steps to the beach. Wide and white, it squeaks under our bare feet. The kids run in the wind, straight towards the breaking surf. My heart leaps and Isak calls for them to stay out of the water. Jake drapes kelp over his head like a wig. Emmy chases him with a stray claw. Fine white sand is airborne, merging with the mist of ocean spray. There are dogs and people in the distance and the wind pulls at my hair, clears me.

Isak walks ahead, far up the beach with Asta and, though her absence draws at me, I let them go and hope it will be bonding. Sitting on the sand I look out to sea and am sure I see the spout of a whale in the distance.

.

In the car on the way back to the cabin I check my phone. There is a BubBot message. 'LifeBLOOD® births are not able to be registered.' I tap a response without thinking, 'Why???' Anger rises up.

'Fuck, Isak. I sometimes want to just shut out the technology.' He looks over. I've shattered his bliss. 'They said they can't register her birth.'

'Why?'

'Well I asked them that.' I check the phone again. Again. Night is deep in the forest and he drives slowly, watchful for the wildlife that hops and runs out onto the road. Check it again. Then it rings and I answer it right away.

'Hi Stacey, this is Jeff. I've just had a call from the office that you had some question about a birth certificate.'

'Yes, that's right. Isak and I wanted to know how we could get one.'

'Why?'

'Well one day we might go on a holiday and need passports. And, anyway, shouldn't we get one for when we need it. Whenever, I don't know.'

'We can't register with the government as a birth.'

'Why?'

'Technically, she's not a human birth.'

Silence. Trying to process this statement.

'Look, she's not alone. Lots of babies don't get registered for various reasons.'

The pulse in my ears belts loudly, face prickles.

He continues, 'You can't. Like I said, she's technically not a human birth. She'd be considered fauna.'

The phone shakes in my hand. Want to throw it out the window.

I try to speak but my voice cracks, 'You and I both know—she's human.'

'Yes we do, of course we do, Stacey. Just not the same kind of human as everyone else.'

Isak pulls the car into the park beside our cabin and takes the phone from me. I realise the kids have heard everything.

'Look, Doctor—Isak here—I think we need to sort this out.' He is silent. The chirp of Jeff's voice on the line. Can't make out the words. He is nodding. 'Right. Well I guess there's nothing we can do about that.' Nods some more, the chirping of Jeff goes on a while, softened now, 'Well thanks for calling us back.' He ends the call.

He looks at me and shakes his head.

'It means so much though.' School, bank accounts, passport. 'I even had to have it to register Emmy and Jake for basketball.' Passport. I don't say it—it will rise up, engulf me when he realises.

'I know,' he says flatly. The enormity of it suffocates our conversation and we stare into the narrow strip of glow from the headlights.

.

In the night long branches of peppermint trees sway and dip in the wind. A piece of thick rope hangs, its end broken into a ragged fray. It moves back and forth. I feed the baby in the dark on the couch while they sleep. Watching through the glass door. The silent tents. Waves break and hiss across the dunes. Trees creeping with invisible life.

.

Next day we drive to an ice-creamery popular with tourists and their children. Isak wears the baby carrier and tucks Asta in facing towards him, a soft hat pulled down low over her head. It is her eyes that are most remarkable now. Babies so often have long heads from birth that it's not so strange but her eyes are a sure sign that there is something unusual about her. I press into the layers of people and order ice-cream and eventually we find a shady place by the little creek and relax for a while, kids busy in the playground.

'I think she needs some sunglasses,' he says. 'Some dark ones that'll shield her from prying eyes.' I like that he is protective. It's a good sign.

'Ask them on the BubBot report.' I try to comfort him with my willingness.

He nods. 'I think they make them like goggles with a strap around them. For babies.' Isak dips his finger into the pistachio ice-cream and puts it in her mouth. Laughs when she responds with excited suckling.

I shake my head to scold him but have no heart to make an issue of it. Across the creek are several penned emus so we walk across a small bridge to see them while the kids enjoy their play. Two emus follow us along the fence, necks dipping. Their eyes always seem to suggest they have been deeply offended. I try talking to one but the offence seems to worsen and it thrusts its beak towards me through the wires. Asta is awake and watching, hands beating excitedly.

Isak pulls her from the carrier and faces her towards the bird. 'Look, Asta, Mummy is scaring the emu.' Her broad mouth stretches into a huge smile, toothless and astounding.

.

The proximity to the beach has filled our new car and our ears with sand. Even Asta has grains of it in her ears. She pulls at them occasionally and calls to me as we pack the car for the drive home. I carefully clear the sand with a wet tissue. And give her a final feed before we head off. Isak takes the kids for a last walk to the beach. By mid-morning we are on the road. The days are hot and we are glad of the air-conditioning and shades of the new car. Isak diverts to a side road and follows the signs to a chocolate factory. Emmy notices we are going a different way but he won't tell her where. There are squeals of delight when we pull into the crowded car park. My heart races with the thought of the people and heat inside.

'Isak, I don't want to disturb the baby. We'll wait in the car.'

'I'll bring you something.' He leaves the car running with the air-conditioner on.

I unclip the seatbelt and lean over to check her. She is a little sweaty and red-faced so I turn up the cold. Kids return with chocolate moulded into shapes and smothered over pretzels. The sweet density of it hangs in the air. We return to the road, meandering through new ways. Isak follows signs to small towns and we find ourselves eventually in Nannup. I am suspecting he has an unspoken plan.

'Where are you going?' I clip at him.

'Home—eventually. I thought we'd go through Balingup. Weren't you living there when you were little?' The road bends back and forth, tracking along the river.

'Yes, very little. You know that.' It feels familiar though, the uneasy stomach lurching as we curve left and right, left and right.

He looks at me, glassy-eyed, a little shattered I know. 'I've never been there. I thought we could check it out.' I have not been back since I was about five, even though Dad lived there, last time I spoke to him.

'Even if my dad's still there . . .' I don't want to see him.

'I know. I just thought it would be nice to see the place. Nice for the kids to make some connection with their history.'

'Why now, Isak? I'm not my best, emotionally. You know that. You know how it is with my mother.' But he likes her. Thinks she's a cool parent, not like his.

'Calm down, Stace. It's just a drive-through. We're in the neighbourhood anyway. We won't stop.'

I breathe. Try to go with it and not infect the family with my reaction.

'I'd really rather not.' The road and river twist in tighter curves, hills rising and falling on either side. Forest and farms. Places selling their own cheese and cherries. We are on our way so I settle back into the seat watching the landscape. Pine plantations and narrow bridges. The sharp descent to the tea-coloured river. There is some faint familiarity as we round a tight bend and descend towards the town. Weatherboard houses. The hot stillness of the air. I recognise the scent and the intersection onto South Western Highway. A small row of colourful shops. The mark of artistic locals. My mother scrawled her own signature on this place, bearing two kids in a fibro cottage in the hills somewhere up a gravel track. There was bush, farm animals that belonged to other people and a lot of long grass bleached pale in the sun and rustling with snakes. We played on a wooden verandah. It was hot or very cold and there were lots of mandarins and apricots. We turn left and quickly leave the edge of Balingup. I stare out the window at the rising hills, the dark patches of forest at their caps.

'Are you okay, Stace?' Isak pats my leg.

'You know, if it wasn't for Alex I think I would never have survived.' Tears sprout, trickle. 'My parents were only interested in themselves.'

'Sorry for surprising you. It's a nice little town. Very pretty.' He has no idea how it felt.

'Very pretty.' But we always did live in pretty places. My own children live amid houses and highways. Nothing pretty about it. 'But that didn't make it good, not for me anyway.'

We stop in Donnybrook at an enormous playground and set the children free from the car. I set up under a tree with Asta and feed her in the shade. Isak walks across the railway track to the bakery to get something for lunch. In the heat, her skin is rosy and damp. She feeds with desperation, ferocious at my nipple. I take off her hat to cool her and cover us with a cotton bunny-rug, lean back against the rough bark. She quickly exhausts the left and I change her to the right, sitting her up in between to burp. We are like one, choreographed and comfortable.

Isak returns and seeks out Emmy and Jake, who have drifted away into the twists and slides, climbing the pinnacles of rainbow. He hands them each a pie, telling them off for not staying within sight of me. I know his reprimand is also meant for me. Perhaps I learned something from my own mother after all.

'Emmy, love,' says Isak. 'Hold the baby for Mum while she has some lunch.' Emmy grows before my eyes, thrilled at the responsibility and I can't help my smile.

'She's not finished feeding yet.'

'She's never finished feeding. Haven't you noticed?' He laughs and reaches for her. I break the suction of her mouth and wrap her in the cotton rug. Hand her over to Emmy, who leans back beside me against the tree. I cover myself and take hold of my own pie. Emmy smug and smiling at the baby, whose wide eyes are fixed on her sister.

'When will her head go into the right shape, Mum?'

I look at Isak and he clears his throat.

'It won't', he says quickly. Eye contact with me. Waiting.

'Why? Is there something wrong with her?'

'No, what makes you think that?'

'I'm not a baby, Dad, I can hear what you talk about.'

My heart sinks. I let him speak, afraid of what I might say. How much truth I will tell.

'Yes, there is something different about her, Emmy. Not wrong with her, just different.'

'Is she gunna die?' She tightens her grip.

'No. She's healthy enough.'

'Well that's good. I don't want her to die. I love her so much.' Emmy's eyes fill with tears. So do mine. She holds her close.

'Don't worry, Em,' I say. 'She's going to be fine. She just might not be the same as you and Jake.' How not the same, I don't really know.

'You mean like a disability?' She creases her brow, eyes still teary.

'Not really,' says Isak. 'There's nothing wrong with her. She's just different. But everything works just fine.' He thinks for a moment, collecting our rubbish. 'It's a bit like we have this fantastic new car and everything works on it and it's perfect and amazing, and that's you. You're like our fancy new car. And Asta, she's like those old-fashioned cars you see at the show. Vintage cars. The ones that go slower and don't have air-conditioners. But they still work fine. It's still a car.'

I look at him, puzzled by his analogy, which doesn't make it any clearer. Emmy has lost interest in the explanation but he waits for her response. Nothing. She has the baby's fingers in her mouth. I take Asta from her and she runs back to the climbing ropes.

I can't help but laugh at him. 'That was a terrible explanation. You really need to work on something that makes better sense.' I punch his arm lightly.

'I know. It was the first thing that came into my head. We've got a bit of work to do.'

'Well you do, that's for sure.'

'I didn't hear you do any better.' Isak laughs.

·

We drive without stop for two hours. The landscape dries, paddocks become progressively lighter as if bleached by the sun. The grey talons of dead trees clawing at hot blue sky. Absence of reliable rain again has leached the life from the farmlands on the periphery of suburbia. It is as if they sense the impending doom of development, content to await the bulldozers and heaps of sand. Refusing life. The heat of the city is a membrane, almost visible. A haze of tight particles. We re-enter it, sealing ourselves into the security of its hold.

The kids go back to school for the new year and each day Isak takes them on his way to work and each day I pick them up.

Each day I sit on the couch and feed Asta, which seems to take more hours. I change nappies and upload a brief report to BubBot.

Each day I try to push her needs away from the small nest of time I might have for my own needs. Or the needs of the other children. But her needs surpass those efforts and often I don't shower. Don't help with the homework.

I smell of sour milk and a splash of milk or vomit lands on my shoes or clothes and leaves a patch.

Each day I say I will cook a nice dinner or something at least and don't.

Each day I hope I can walk into school with the baby and nobody will speak to me or want to look at her. I get there early so I can get a close parking space. Try to avoid the kids' new teachers and their new questions.

I try to keep her eyes and head covered in public.

I am gradually fading.

Mondays the kids have basketball training. Thursday nights Isak and I take them to their games. It is still light until quite late.

On these days the world is a jury and I am on trial. I cancelled swimming lessons and the cleaning service. Isak said he would cook so we can get back to normal. Try to claim our home back from LifeBLOOD®.

Each day I take her for a walk early in the morning before it gets too hot. Each day, that is the best and most normal thing that happens.

I push the pram around the twisting streets, concentric curves leading to a lake in the centre of our estate. It is a small lowland. Once, perhaps it was the heart of a larger wetland, but now it serves to collect winter rains from the streets and prevents any flooding. It is also a receptacle for any floating or mobile plastics, garlanded around the fringe of reeds and rushes that border the water. They spray for mosquito larvae every year. Despite this, swamp-hens stalk through the grasses like royalty and several wood ducks and black ducks sail slowly through the thick brown waters. Sometimes there are dragonflies hovering at the surface. Movement beneath the oily film. Ripples and rising bubbles. She-oak trees were planted around the concrete pathways several years ago and they have grown quite tall, dropping a mat of needles beneath that suppresses the grass. Under the trees are small flying insects, midges perhaps. When they are very thick we breathe them in and Asta coughs.

Few people walk this path in the mornings except a couple of lone seniors with dogs off the lead. They show no interest in the pram but nod to greet me, so I feel safe to roll back the insect screen, which serves also to hide her from view. She is active then, testing out her voice and calling to the wetland birds. They are impervious to the wonder of her presence and continue to forage, stalk or float. Sometimes I take her to the small hide at the end of the hot path to see if there are more intimate scenes of these birds but it smells of urine and is tainted with scrawled words and empty bottles. I have tried to overcome my aversion to it so we have that other view, but it's quite awful. We walk past the playground on our circuit of the lake. Empty in the early mornings. What will it be like when she breaks free of her pram and wants to swing or climb or slide like other kids? I wonder if it will be possible, in her dark glasses and hat. A secret agent among the innocents. But she, perhaps, the most innocent of all.

I have brought Emmy and Jake here many times, waiting on the park bench in the shade while they complete a circuit. Sometimes we have taken a picnic lunch and sat together on the crunching grass or amid the she-oak needles, munching on sandwiches made more flavourful in the open air. Speckled with midges. They have tested out their balance on scooters and bikes on these pathways. Lost balls in the long reeds and struggled to get kites airborne. Sometimes with friends. I wonder if those normal days are over.

I feel as if I am grieving for the life I once had even though it seems to still be intact. For who I was and what our family used to be. On the periphery, a gathering force rises each day. Assembling above our knees, our waists, blocking our view and rising upward to tower overhead. We are built on falsehood. One wrong move and it will crumble to the ground. An unstoppable force. It will surely crush us all and turn our world into aftermath. These are the secrets I walk around the lake. My fears; my guilt. The invisible passages I trace into the future.

·

On a hot day while the children are at school, Dimitra comes for a three-month check-up. She rings the doorbell promptly at nine while I am locked in baby-mouth, sipping the last well of cold tea from breakfast. Asta knows my finger will try to prise her from my nipple so she has learned to clamp tight and not allow me to break the suction. I stand with her attached and open the front door, dragging a sour-scented bunny-rug. Left breast bare. The air is searing outside but Dimitra smiles like a goddess beside the dead plants and skewed paving bricks on our porch. High heels and manicured nails, she carries a professional bag. Black. There is a stray clove of garlic on the tiles near the front door, a piece of Lego, coagulated dust and hair. I have never set foot in the world she must inhabit and it is anomalous to have her step across my threshold. Shame burns my cheeks a little. I smell of sour milk, have become slack with the record keeping on BubBot.

She greets me with a smile and seems to not notice the dust or the breast but welcomes herself, tells me it's nice and cool in my house and reaches for the baby. Asta frowns at being forced to let go and continues to suck at the air in the doctor's arms.

'Would you like a tea or coffee?' I cover my chest and lead her into the living room.

'Maybe later, Stacey.' Her English a little stiff. 'You are welcome to go and have a shower if you would like to. I will sit with Asta for a while. I have tests and things to do but they can wait until you are more comfortable.' Like an unfamiliar aunt, she makes herself at home. 'I've been looking forward to spending some time with her.' I am tired and the shower sounds like a relief. I rush it and dress, my breath a little shallow with anxiety. Not sure what she will think or say or do while she is with my baby. In my house.

When I emerge, she has cleared the coffee table, covered it with a white cloth and set up her computer, some equipment that looks like it's for pathology tests, an empty package, a change mat and a breast pump, a tape measure and scales. Asta is wrapped neatly and stares up at her.

'Stacey, I'd like to first interview you about how you are going and I'd like to record our interview with the webcam in my computer. Is that okay with you?' She turns the screen to face me and begins.

'Firstly, how are you feeling?' Rich lipstick smile.

'Okay. I mean, I'm tired but I've recovered from the birth.'

'Tired because of the feeding? We recommended a nutritional plan, it's on our website. And the company has offered to supply meals to your family but you have cancelled all the support you had.'

'Yes, I'm tired because of the feeding.'

'We need to run some blood tests on you, Stacey. Check you out. Please make an effort to eat well. We can help again. Just tell me what you need.' I am told off and I know I have neglected myself. Isak cooking and buying takeaway. 'How about sleep?'

'Asta is sleeping well. Six hours at night, feeding at about ten and then somewhere around four-thirty in the morning. Then we go for a walk.'

'Can you nap in the daytime?'

'Sometimes I drift off.' Often Asta detaches, spread wide on my lap, and sleeps. Saturated with my milk. I don't tell her that sometimes I stare at the television, blank and burning with exhaustion. Lose consciousness and return to her, mouth wide and seeking me out. Then the alarm sounds on my phone and we bundle ourselves into human shapes and collect the kids from school.

'How are you feeling about the baby?' She reads from her screen. Questions prepared beforehand.

I look at the bundle in her arms, now sleeping. Smile. 'I adore her.'

'Anything else?'

'No.' She is beautiful, fascinating. I can't believe that she's real. I'm terrified of her, what she might be doing to us. To me. I think she has power we can't imagine or understand. She is magnetic to me, absorbs me.

'Are you concerned about anything?'

'Yes. Other people mostly and not being able to keep her hidden enough. That people will notice she is who she is, and not one of us.'

'Which people?' Lips purse up a little.

'At school. The kids' teachers, other parents, people at the shops. Anyone who visits.'

'You've had people visit?'

'No. That's the point. How can we have anyone visit? Can't you at least let us get to know other people with children like Asta?'

'We can't do that, sorry. There are none nearby. I won't lie to you, Stacey, there are other children but they are all in quarantined locations, like you. We have scattered them around the country. We modelled it on a witness protection program that was very successful. LifeBLOOD® have decided to keep a media embargo on the birth of Asta. It's all about minimising the risk of harm and exposure. We want the best outcome for her and publicising her birth is not in her interests right now.' She seems proud of this but I would like to know how it is for someone else. She rocks Asta, whose cheeks suck. Always ready for more. 'Our scientific papers will come out eventually but you will all be de-identified. I thought you would be happy with that. What else concerns you?'

'She is so hungry. I wonder if she might need more than I can give her. I have thought about giving her solid food, even though you said to wean her at seven months.'

'I will do some tests on her but the more she feeds the more your body will respond and make more milk. This is the way breastfeeding works and your milk will change to meet her needs and her demand. You just need to let her lead the way. But we will test your milk too and see what she is getting. No solids, Stacey. You must check with me first.' She produces a hand-held breast pump and passes it to me. 'One hundred milli-litres when you are ready. The theory is that the Neanderthal babies transitioned from breastfeeding at seven months and were completely weaned at fourteen. We have this information from dental samples of Paleolithic infants.' She sighs. 'It's very reliable.'

She turns the webcam to face the change mat and puts Asta down, carefully unwrapping her from the light rug. I can see she has grown, broadened around the shoulders and chest. She is changing shape, becoming stronger. Dimitra tears open the cloth nappy and hands it to me. Pulls the singlet over Asta's head and films her naked.

'Could you please get me some clean clothes for her? We are going to remote monitor so I'm giving her an injection.' She begins measuring the length and circumference of each limb in several places and I dash to the small bedroom, not wanting to miss what she might do to my baby. When I return she is taking her blood. There is a large syringe on the table. Asta cries low and soft, her deep blood siphoning slowly into the small tube. Then another. And another.

'Isn't that enough?' I step towards her.

'Not yet,' clips Dimitra. 'Just sit.' She completes the third test tube and pulls out the needle.

Asta looks at me, pupils wide and dark. My nipples prickle and leak.

Dimitra marks up the tubes and places a latex glove on her hand, feels around in Asta's mouth. 'I can feel the little buds of her teeth. She will get her premolars first, you know that?'

Asta tries to grab at her fingers.

'No. Really?' Just want to pick her up.

'It's on our website, Stacey. Please try to read it and keep your-self informed. It's there to help you. She will cut her molars before her incisors. Your other children will have cut lower incisors first and we expect Asta's will be earlier all around. Any signs of teething yet?'

I can't remember all the things she tells me. She holds the baby flat with her latex glove.

I sit forward, tension rising in me. 'Not that I've noticed.'

'Well she's going to start growing them quickly in the next three months but please keep a record and check her mouth. I will leave you some sterile gloves. What about her hearing and sight?' She lights up the inside of Asta's ear with a tiny device, an image appears on her screen of her inner ear.

'Um, I think she hears fine. She responds to things.' Asta shrinks away and Dimitra removes the light. 'The children's voices. Birds and things. Her eyesight is very good for a little baby. I notice she watches things at the park a lot, focuses on things for a long time.'

'She should have more acute distance vision so we are keen to track that. We are not sure on hearing but it is likely she will hear a wider range of sounds. You must watch her for otitis media. Any pulling of the ear or hot ears and fevers, contact us immediately.' I assume she means ear infection. Dimitra turns the screen and types in some notes. Asta bats her hands together. 'Can I get that milk sample please, Stacey?'

I raise my top and fit the plastic funnel onto my breast, nipple poking into the end, then squeeze the handles together. Milk sprays out immediately, hitting the hollow bottle with a fine spray. It runs between pumps and fills the small bottle rapidly. I hand it over.

'You've got a good supply there.' She shakes it, a creamy haze coats the sides.

'It just never seems to be enough for her. She's on all the time.'

Dimitra nods. 'I'll see if there is anything we can help with. Please try to be more diligent when you record the times and duration of your feeds. It will help my research for future children.' She seals and labels the milk bottle. Packs up the table and, finally, dresses Asta in a fresh nappy and singlet, wrapping her and handing her to me. 'I'll get some clothes sent to you based on these measurements too. And I've prescribed you a multivitamin, which will be delivered. How about a cleaning service again?'

'I said no before.' She looks around, disdain finally showing. 'But I don't think I can do it.' She nods, taps into her phone.

'I do think seeing your counsellor again might be a good idea Stacey. You have a lot to adjust to here. It will help to have someone to talk to, who knows the situation.' She stands with her black bag and I nod because she is probably right.

When she is gone, her perfume lingers in the air. Asta and I settle into position. She groans and reaches for my chest. Latches on, brow furrowed and eyes focused on mine. I can see the ridges above her eyes now, her face changing as she grows. I run my finger back and forth across the hard bump. Each eyebrow protrudes slightly. When her teeth grow, it will be apparent that her face does not resemble the other faces around us. Fragments of Dimitra's conversation come back to me and I wonder about the red lump on her arm, which I hadn't noticed to ask her about, and especially about the other babies in quarantined locations. I enter the time and feed into the BubBot and 'are we in quarantine?'.

Half an hour later my phone pings 'not officially'.

His hair like yellow leaves sticks to the enamel of the bath. He is wrapped in a towel, blurred by bathroom mist. Shaving his face in a clear patch of mirror, which he has wiped with his hand.

'I wish you could take the day off.' I am on the closed lid of the toilet wrapped in my dressing-gown, cheesy with breastmilk.

'Have a shower, Stace. I'll make the kids' lunches and do breakfast.' I obey, peel off my pyjamas, turning so he can't see my ravaged body. He looks over at me, eyebrows arched.

'Sorry but I'm a wreck and I don't want you to see me this way.' I hold my hand over my loose belly.

He kisses my shoulder. 'We're both a bit wrecked, don't worry about it. We're in this together.' He laughs, drops his towel and pushes out his gut. 'Not exactly eye candy here either.' He leaves to get dressed.

'I'll take the kids to school if you're feeding them,' I call through to the bedroom.

Asta sits in her bouncer in the kitchen, watching Isak at the bench. Her legs kick when Emmy speaks to her and she grins widely. Emmy sits on the floor beside her and eats toast. He has made me tea and toast with honey. Lunches are done.

'Have you been walking them into class?'

'No,' Jake answers for him. 'Dad's been doing kiss and drive. Every day.'

'Yeah, every day,' says Emmy. 'And when you pick us up you say hurry up the baby is asleep in the car, or you come and get us early before the bell even goes.'

Isak makes eye contact with me and I nod gently.

I swallow down the anxiety. 'Emmy if you and Jake help and get ready nice and quick, I will walk you in.' Try to smile.

'With the baby?' She puts her face next to Asta, whose hand tangles a fist of Emmy's hair.

Fear rises up in me. 'Just go and get dressed,' I snap. And they scatter, the tone of coming fury something they are too familiar with. I have not revealed all this to Isak, this turmoil that comes on each day as I get in the car to pick them up, how I navigate around people. Coffee and toast in hand, he sits knowingly beside me.

'You just have to face them, Stacey. We can't live in a bubble and it's not fair on the kids if we try to.' I know this. 'At some point you—we—have to be confident to go out into the world with her and face the questions. They told us how to handle it.'

'I find it easier with you there.'

'I want you to do it. Soccer and netball start after Easter and they'll have training and games. You don't want to miss out on that.'

'Of course not.'

He's so involved in soccer, reliving his own heroic tackles.

'Just face them at school.' He drains the last of his coffee. 'They're just a few suburban parents and a couple of teachers. They might not take any notice of her at all. Most people are only really interested in their own children anyway.'

'Everyone wants to hold other people's babies, Isak.'

He pats my knee, so confident.

'Not if they think she is special needs. You watch. Mention that she has a rare genetic problem and they'll be less keen. Guaranteed.'

But he won't be there.

.

I wear my lucky mammoth hair locket and carry Asta on my hip, her tinted glasses on and a crocheted beanie rising in a point to camouflage her head. I pull it low to hide the rising ridges of her brows. As she grows, her facial features are becoming more distinct, especially her jawline with her wide mouth and receding chin. Her nose is wide and flat, not so unusual in a small baby but as she grows I imagine it will be more apparent. We walk the familiar path lined with grevilleas, darting with tiny birds after the spray of reticulation. The heat has eased a little, days shorter, and the gardens rebound slowly as autumn starts to drizzle.

Jake holds my free hand, backpack on. Drags me around to his class first. Emmy won't leave my side. I avoid eye contact with a couple of parents, helping kids organise their bags, and walk with Jake to his desk. Children's artworks are pegged to lines across the ceiling and Jake shows me the ones he's created. His teacher, a redhead in her twenties, is listening to children read. A queue of them at her desk. She doesn't even look up. Jake joins the other boys constructing something with blocks on the floor.

Emmy's new teacher this year is much older and clearly grooming the kids for high school in two years, setting homework and paring back the games and artwork in the room. There are few parents and the kids are learning to be independent, organising their own day. Emmy does not need me there but pulls me by the hand. As the only other adult in the classroom, Mrs Hughes comes to greet me. We have never met, though I have written several notes about early departures and being unable to fundraise or volunteer. Isak attended the parent information session. She is warm, extends her hand.

'Nice to meet you . . .' her pause asks for my first name so I tell her. 'So this is the famous Asta.' She smiles and extends a finger, which Asta seizes with her wide hand.

'Does Emmy talk about her a lot?' Nervous question.

'Endlessly. We've been doing a poetry module this term and studying odes so there are some wonderful odes to Asta in Emilia's writing book. "Ode to Asta's Rusty Hair" is quite memorable.'

'I'd like to read them sometime. Maybe you can bring them home?'

Emmy smiles, pleased at the long-awaited union of sister and teacher. 'See, Mrs Hughes, she does always wear baby sunglasses. She has very sensitive eyes.'

'Yes, I see.' Mrs Hughes looks at me, as if seeking information. I ignore her and look back to Emmy, who watches expectantly. Uncomfortable silence.

'Well, have a great day,' I turn to leave.

'Um, Stacey . . .'

'Yes.' My face heats and I know I am blushing, anxious.

'A quick word?' She turns to her desk. 'Emilia, go outside until the bell goes. The others are setting up for the assembly.' She beckons me to sit in the small school chairs. Heart racing.

'Sorry to nab you like this but I have been concerned about some of the things Emilia has been saying about the baby. I have a duty of care to make sure everything is all right so we can offer support to the children.'

My breath is shallow, Asta sits awkwardly on my lap and I adjust her. Delay. 'Um, what do you want to know?'

'Is Asta healthy? Is there something not right with her? Emilia is very anxious about her, and about you too.'

After Asta's birth, Fee coached me on how to respond to these kinds of situations. It seemed simple at the time and LifeBLOOD® are very clear about what to say but somehow I am blank, uncertain. Mrs Hughes' steady eyes fix on Asta, then me. Back and forth. She can see through the lenses of the sunglasses. The beanie drawn back, Asta's brows, wide face, broad mouth.

'She's an unusual-looking girl, were your other two anything like her?' Fake smile. I don't trust her.

'No,' quick and defensive. 'She's different. Just different that's all.'

163

'I don't mean to pry, Stacey. I'm just concerned about your daughter and if there's an issue with the baby we can help to support her. To deal with it. It's hard on siblings when there's a new baby, and even more so when that baby has special needs.'

'Special needs? You mean you think she has a disability?'

'I never said that. I'm just trying to work out if there's something we can do to help Emilia.' She waits. I have no words to add and my heart is racing. 'We're a community and we look out for each other.' Panic rising. I tighten my grip on Asta and get up from the low chair.

'Thanks for your concern, Mrs Hughes.' And I walk quickly from the classroom. The bell rings for the start of class and I rush to the car, drive quickly home.

Asta and I lock in on the couch and I text Isak in panic—'I think Emmy's teacher has guessed.' He doesn't respond.

An hour later, he walks through the front door.

'So I had a call from the school counsellor and she wants to speak to us. I said we'd be there this afternoon before we pick the kids up from school.'

I fill him in on my conversation with Mrs Hughes, realise it makes me look very inept at explaining things. 'It's my fault.'

'Well, no shit, Stacey.' He's annoyed. Short with me. I shrink inside, face tingly with anxiety. He heats leftovers in the microwave and eats them on the couch. Asta suckles, looks over and smiles around my nipple. He ruffles her hair. 'You just have to lie, Stacey. They told you what to say.'

'I don't like it though. She doesn't have a disability.' Just the word makes me want to cry.

'I know. They said to tell people it was a rare genetic condition not a disability.'

I don't know that it makes a lot of difference.

'And what do you think they'd conclude from that? Mrs Hughes said she was special needs.'

'Look, we'll go and reassure the counsellor and hopefully that will do it.'

At the back door, a butcherbird flings itself at its reflection in the glass, seeing a palm tree in the living room. It bashes itself softly, over and over.

.

The counsellor's office is in the school administration building. When we drive up, Jake's class is out on the sports oval playing baseball. His little figure on the pitch so familiar. A small version of his father. There are plenty of parking spaces. Isak opens the back door and takes off Asta's hat and glasses, unclips her.

'What are you doing?' My voice is shrill. Try to settle down.

'Not hiding, Stacey. They want to know so if we let them see then they might be off our case.'

He can't tell them the truth. I grab the hat and stuff it in my bag before he locks the car.

'We tell them what we've been told to say but at least if they see her they'll understand why you cover her up.'

I don't like it and I am panicky but we walk into the school administration offices. The counsellor is tall and blonde, striking blue eyes. We have never had a reason to meet her. She shakes Isak's hand, then mine. She glances at the back of Asta's head.

'I'm Anna. Come in.' Her office is uncluttered, with comfort-able chairs. There are several plants and a wide window onto the sports oval. Isak sits, cradling Asta. Her strange and beautiful face. I want to hide her, to keep her safe, but there she is, exposed to the eyes of the world. Isak chats nervously, commenting on the birds in the garden around the school and asks if she ever sees magpies swooping the children on the oval. Trying to charm her. She shifts in her chair, looks at me, avoids the baby.

'Stacey, Isak, you know why we're here.' She looks directly at Asta. Eyes fixed, then consciously shift back to me. She is distracted. They dart back to the baby.

'Yes, Mrs Hughes had a conversation with Stacey about it this morning.' Isak sits forward, 'There's a time and place for these conversations, Anna, and Mrs Hughes chose the wrong time and place to confront my wife.' I didn't think he would take this angle but he is firm and assertive. I rub my fingers across the locket, back and forth. Genie from the bottle.

'I apologise. No, that wasn't following the right procedure but I'm sure Mrs Hughes was just trying to engage in a casual conversation.' She glances at me—young and pretty.

'You can't engage in a casual conversation when you are talking about disability.' He said he wouldn't use that word. He avoids my eyes. Asta flails her arms in his lap and the counsellor is distracted by her. Isak holds her little hand still. 'It's serious and a parent is very sensitive about the wellbeing of their baby.'

'Yes, I understand that. But we do have a duty of care to your other children so if they are having difficulty coping we need to be able to support them. To help them understand and deal with the change to the family dynamic.'

Asta grabs his ear, looks up at him. Draws his attention, then, 'Da.' Loud and distinct. Joy inflates me inside and Isak's face glows. I see tears in his eyes and he swallows hard.

'See, she doesn't have a disability,' I say.

Anna smiles. 'How old is she again?'

'Five months,' he says. Not quite.

'She's very advanced then.' We all look at Asta, her wide mouth seeking out Isak's earlobe. Anna laughs nervously. 'Perhaps you can tell me why Emmy is so concerned.'

Isak is a little tremulous, 'You can see she looks a bit different. Well, genetically, she is different.' He's going to tell her the truth. I rise from the chair a little, look at him. His eyes dark and stern at me and I sit down, reprimanded silently. 'She has a genetic condition. It's very rare and that's why she looks this way.' Anna's eyes dash between us, assessing our relationship, the signs of cracking. I can see she is suspicious. Her light eyes see through us.

'I don't think she believes you, Isak.' He glares at me.

'It's an inherited condition,' he continues. 'Like Down's syndrome, it causes a variety of symptoms and abilities so we aren't sure what to expect from Asta and how she will develop.'

'Is it chromosomal?' She glances at me, tries to engage me in the conversation. What I might say could unravel everything. I am silent.

Isak pauses, 'Yes and no.'

She is puzzled now.

'Does it have a name? Then I can do some reading around it and better know how to help.'

'We don't want your help.' The words are acid and I spit them, raised bile. She squints.

'Stacey.' He stands up. The counsellor stands too. Both above me, looking down. He is white with anger. Asta's face still and staring.

'Okay, now everyone be calm,' her well-schooled voice. 'Let's just sit down and keep talking.' She sits slowly, and Isak follows. 'Now, I can see there are some stresses in your family life. Whatever they are, let's just focus on the children here. I can refer you to an external provider for relationship counselling too.'

I want to cry but suck it down. We are both silent.

'It's very difficult to have a child with special needs and we know, there are other families who face these challenges.'

She makes us another appointment for the end of the week and Isak mumbles about being sorry and getting time off work for it. She shakes his hand, avoids my eyes but I touch her damp fingers.

.

In the days that follow, he is remote from me and focuses on the children. Speaks to them, feeds them. Goes. I am a leaf in the sun, slowly drying out, curling in on myself. I could crack and crumble into tiny pieces, unnoticed under foot. I could dissipate into the earth in a moment. Fragments of dust and cellulose merging into landscape.

The night before the appointment he breaks through my husk.

'I'll go to this appointment tomorrow. I don't think you are up to it, Stacey.'

I feel my blood rise in anger. He thinks I can't deal with it, that I'm rash and stupid. I say nothing of this. Agree it is a good idea. 'What will you say?'

'I'll say what we are meant to say.'

'About me?'

He lowers his eyes. Reaches for my hand and sighs deeply. 'I'll say you have postnatal depression.' He pauses, waits and looks at me. Waits. 'I think you do, Stacey. I think you have postnatal depression.' He waits. 'Have you thought you might?'

I am altered. I feel her blood in my blood. 'Maybe.'

'You are not yourself.' This is more true than he could possibly imagine.

'I don't know if I will ever be the person that I was.'

He shifts, sits beside me with his hands on mine.

'You will be. Don't worry. It will pass. And she's growing up so fast. Before you know it, she'll be weaning and then you'll start to feel your energy come back.' His eyes are a little glassy with tears.

In some simple, practical way I know he is right but he can't see the invisible workings of her traces, circulating through my heart and brain. The way her difference has become normal to me, made us one in our alien-ness.

There are moments when I am home with Asta I feel such oneness with her that I think it must be what enlightenment feels like. Feeding her, changing her, bathing her, putting her in her bouncer, I am in orbit around her and completely fixed on her beauty. In awe and in love. Her little body grows robust and strong and she is more mobile each day, turning over, pulling herself up on her arms. Almost crawling. At five and a half months, she can sit and sometimes I prop her with cushions to make sure she is safe, but she isn't fragile like my other babies.

Each day and most of the night I nurse her. She feeds and feeds and feeds. And as she feeds, my own flesh withers and shrinks. I tell them, through the BubBot, that she needs food, but each week the message comes back to wait until the right time. I push my body further, giving it to her, every last piece, every last drop. I am her sustenance. And all of this while the television chatters in the background, a new bird-flu virus, people suffering, dying, blowing each other to pieces in another place, a monster storm season in the Caribbean again. Then the relief of watching people cook and renovate houses. It stays on the periphery of my consciousness. My attention is with her.

Today Dimitra is coming so I shower and dress before Isak leaves with the kids. The cleaners went through the house yesterday. I took Asta for a long walk while three women repaired a week's chaos in each room. They sent a message when they were done and we came home to the scent of disinfectant and a defamiliarised house. For a day or two everyone tries to keep it clean, a little afraid of the neatness. I leave Asta on the floor in the living room and clean up the breakfast things. When I return she has moved away and is half hidden behind the couch. The doorbell rings at exactly nine.

Dimitra is sculpted into a red dress today and greets me with a smile, trailing a carrier on wheels filled with her equipment. Perfume of sweet spice. In the living room, Asta has moved again, her legs and broad feet visible around the side of the couch. I pick her up, sit her on my lap while Dimitra sets up the table with her tests. Her laptop camera trained on the two of us.

'Stacey, I gather from what Isak put on the BubBot that you are not feeling well. Perhaps we can do some tests, if that's okay with you. I want to assess you.'

'For what? Postnatal depression?'

'Just some quick questions. We use the Edinburgh test so it's well tried and very reliable. I'll film our appointment if that's okay with you too.' I nod and she starts to read from her laptop in a formal tone. 'Have you been able to laugh and see the funny side of things? A, as much as I always could. B, not quite so much now. C, definitely not so much now. D, not at all.' She waits.

'A.' It is quite clear what the right answer is so I give it. I don't want her to prescribe me any medication. She looks up, eyebrows raised. Continues with question two. 'B,' I respond. If I mix it up and don't seem quite so perfect, perhaps she will think I am being honest. Ten questions later.

'I'll just submit your responses, and . . .' She waits, staring at the screen. 'If you answered the questions truthfully, then your score puts you in the low range.' She widens her eyes at me. Knows.

'I told everyone I was fine.' I know it's obvious that I'm not.

'You're doing well considering, in my opinion.' She shifts in her seat. 'It's not a foolproof test, it's very basic. If you are feeling sad or struggling, please talk to me or I can make you an appointment with Fee if you would prefer.' She reaches for Asta, changing the subject. 'She looks so well.' She raises the end of the sentence like a question and I know this implies a response is needed.

'She's growing, as you can see. Feeding a lot. I mean, really—lots. I would like to feed her something else. I know you've said to wait but it is pushing both of us to wait.'

'Six more weeks, Stacey. It's important for her microbiome and that is going to help her immune system so I'm sorry but you really must wait. Just remember that feeding her is the most important thing you are doing at the moment.' Dimitra lays her on the change mat, measures her limbs, head circumference.

Looks in her mouth and feels around with a gloved finger. 'Did you know she is cutting teeth?' I hadn't noticed. Dimitra adjusts the camera on her laptop and photographs Asta, zooming in with the touch screen. Asta squirms, coos at her. Weighs, notes. A sample of breastmilk and blood. It's all very officious and organised but when she is finished she does not leave. She stays beside me on the couch, while Asta settles in for a feed.

'We had a team meeting last week at LifeBLOOD® in Sydney and we were discussing your family situation and how we might do the best thing by all of you.' Her eyes cool and serious.

I jolt. 'If you were all discussing our family, don't you think one of us should have been there?' Isak should be here now.

She sniffs and nods, will not engage in me criticising their system. 'There is a common feeling that it would be good for all of you to have a bit more space.'

Not sure what she means. 'A bigger house?'

'Yes. Some distance from being in the spotlight and more space outside too. How would you feel, and how do you think Isak would feel, if we put you on some property, got you out of the city?'

We have never thought we could move, especially onto 'property'. The idea of it is a relief.

'Neither of you have any family connections in the city.' She waits for my response.

'No.' She would know my family connections. 'Where?'

'We had somewhere in mind, not that far from where you had your holiday. Just a couple of hours south. Between Bunboory and Mandoora.' She struggles to pronounce the towns. Probably only seen them marked on a map.

'On the coast?'

'Somewhere close to the beach, they said. There's a property available there now with some natural bush and a little pasture for animals.'

'Can we discuss it first?'

'Yes, yes, of course. But Isak's company have a refinery there and they have a position ready so we can't wait too long.'

'You've already contacted them?'

'It's a beautiful place, Stacey. If you and Isak are ready, we can send you down to take a look.'

'I'll talk to him.' But I know already there is no choice. That they have honed in on Isak's own desire, that they know he will say yes because it is what he wants. I want it too.

'It will mean less support from us though Stacey. We won't be able to continue with cleaning services or meals. But it is generally felt it will be better for you to have some space to bring up Asta.' She looks firmly in my eyes. 'Dr van Tink has a lot of confidence in your discretion.'

When she has left, I put Asta in the pram and we walk to the lake. I take a bag and collect the blown wrappers and dropped bottles as we walk under she-oaks and along the grassy bank. The prospect of wider landscapes to walk in lifts my spirit. I will never need to see Mrs Hughes or that counsellor again. Emmy will complain, miss her netball team and her school. Jake will be easily lured by a quad bike. Familiar swamp-hens wade in the low water amid reeds, seeking out modest prey. Small black coots float unremarkably on the surface. I am already saying goodbye to them. We will move and it is my choice too, this time. Maybe I do have some control.

.

We drive south in the winter. The long straight of the freeway, rooftops without end. Remnant farmland. Eventually the forest each side of the road. It burned in the summer, a wild uncontrolled blaze that threatened towns and made it to the news in the city. Tall dead trees stand dark amid the ragged regrowth, fringing around the bases. Light green in contrast to the char of the trunks.

The road transitions subtly, becoming less bright and massive. Forest thickens and closes in around the highway. An ear, soft and rounded on the road. Its edge trimmed with visible fur, surrounded by a mash of bone and flesh, tumbled pale organs. A thick tail still intact strikes out across the white line. It moves in the breeze of the car. I am queasy at the sight, almost feel it in my gut as it disappears beneath us. Dragging our lives into an unknown future.

Isak turns the music loud and sings with the children. The forest greens as we drive, broken only by occasional side roads, marking the turns in to small towns, all ending in 'up'. Rivers marked with bilingual signage—all ending in *bilya*.

At last we turn from the highway and follow a wide curve through sparse bushland, scattered with houses. The road opens out on the horizon and we all gasp. Stare. The car slows and layers of coast and water are stacked beyond in a wide panorama.

A warm, settling feeling glows in my stomach. Birds and shining winter sun and a broad stretch of tea-coloured water capped with slow-moving sprigs of foam. A single gull suspended in the air, wings unmoving, is held high by currents and we, suspended here for a moment, buffeted yet calm and sure.

Round a corner, we trace the bank of the estuary. Gentle curving road amid a natural trellis of old trees, peeling papery bark and up on the right, overlooking it, are houses, spaced apart amid tuart and peppermint trees. The GPS leads us to a banner of leaves in the wind, which marks our driveway up to a new house.

The air is briny and cold and the kids jump about in the back seat like a chemical reaction until they are released. Asta is quiet and watchful and I upload a photo of her to BubBot.

I can see why they chose this place for us. Primordial with its entwined paperbarks, gnarled as wizards. The brownish water, fringed with broad beds of reeds and tea-tree. Birds of all kind— black swans, pelicans and cormorants, gulls and ducks. Lizards no doubt and hidden possums. The water quivering with life. And across from us, a broad bank of sand dunes, protecting us from the coast beyond. The beach audible from here on a big day.

I know this is where I will stay.

ONE

Their first day in a new school and they rush from the car in rain-coats. Windscreen wipers beating madly and Asta tucked in the back seat in a low beanie. I want to walk with them in the sunshine to meet their new teachers but I am left here to wonder in the rain. To hope for them. I park outside the school for a few moments, not sure what to do with my day. Asta drifts to sleep in the warmth of the car and I drive into the town, up to the lookout on the beach.

Veined with sea foam, the waves curl and crash, spraying high into the wind. Mist hurls back, dampens my shaking car. Black coastal rocks bathed and tangled in a lacework of foam. An endless race of breaking water headed for the coast one after another. A great queue out there across the expanse.

The sea has risen with the storm, grown as if there is more of it. It triggers images of the future. Perhaps somewhere across the ocean there is a coast depleted when we are overwhelmed.

A band of sunlight falls on the green horizon, distant flecks and sprays of white-capped waves tell me this churning will go on for a few hours yet.

The car windows have misted over with our breath. The lovely child fills her baby seat with her broad body. She sleeps soundly, her wide lashes fanned against her pale cheeks. Mothers with blond children walk by, their little ones packed tight against the wind, and she is here, hidden from view in the still-cold air of the car.

Sunlight reaches us at last, despite it the sea is roaring and lumpy, crashing white across the black rocks. It is as if some great, multi-limbed beast is crawling across the sea floor raising up the surface, showing me what it can do—how the ocean knows, that the tide comes in to meet her and witness her return. Those same droplets and molecules that drifted along the European coasts of her people, that bathed their broad feet and gave them crustaceans and molluscs of inordinate size and plenty. Yet here, now, it is dark and wild. It tears at the living and delivers its dead to us, tumbled carcases, weed and retching stink, laying like aftermath all along the coast.

.

Leaving Perth, after living there for eight years, was almost unremarkable. There were removalists early in the morning and a last walk around our park. I stopped under the she-oaks, thankful that our new home would have nicer places to walk. The swamp-hens and coots went about their daily routine and Emmy and Jake said goodbye to their playground.

'Do you remember that day we had a picnic here and that kid Elijah rode off on Jake's scooter while we were playing?' She's been crying at school about leaving.

'Yeah, I see him at school sometimes,' said Jake. 'He's mean.'

'I remember,' I told them and wanted to cry, just for a moment. Emmy remembered the picnic menu for the day, even the sparkling apple juice I had taken with us. I have failed them as a mother this past year. Been so absent.

'I can't wait to take Asta for a picnic,' she said, and tickled her under the chin. She found some of Jake's old pram-toys when we were sorting out to pack and hung them around Asta's pram, which now jingles as we walk, and unearthed one of her old favourite hats, which just fit, despite the fact that Emmy had worn it at three and four. I moved a lot as a child, I told her, and never had old things because we always left them behind, so having your brother's and sister's things for your own is very special.

I know Emmy will miss her friends so I tried to offer her some extra encouragement to bond with Asta, shared my own experience of being a new kid at school, some highlights anyway. Isak and I had tried to keep it stable for them and we would have stayed there until they finished school, even though we never really liked the suburb, but that has changed now.

Isak is pleased to have the change and it was easy for him to move into the new job with the same company. He had imagined his life as endless days of the same thing in the same place with the same people, but at least this offered something new. They didn't ask us to sell our house so we are suddenly landlords, after years of living on a tight budget. The title for the farm, as we like to call it, is in our names already. That's all we can do for your family now, they had said, from this point we will help you with Asta's needs only. But that was more than we could have ever achieved before, so Isak was happy. A farm, small as it is, is a great symbol of masculinity and adulthood with his family and he is excited about having a few animals. We could plant some orange trees and cultivate our own garden without the burden of debt, he said, or relying on farming for income. We can buy a little boat and take the kids out fishing. There are crabs in the estuary and a good sea breeze in summer. For Isak, this truly is the best of all possible worlds and I have never felt so optimistic about a home in my life.

We took the kids out of school for a few weeks to move and settle into the house and they went back after the winter holidays. Jake's tablet was left uncharged for an unthinkable number of days while they trekked around our ten acres. Emmy carried a backpack stocked with survival snacks, her homemade first-aid kit, a wand and a jar filled with glittery water. Jake heavily armed, thanks to birthday packages from Isak's family. I took photos to send our mothers and to Isak at work and Alex. Thirty years ago, that would have been us, without the crossbow or rifle. 'Did you win the lottery and not share with me?' Alex messaged back. I didn't reply.

Hours later, hair flat with rain, they came running across the small paddock shouting 'Mum, Mum you should come and see what we found.' A couple of times I followed them into the stands of tuart and peppermints to see what it was—a magical hollow inside an enormous tree, perfect for a cubby; the rusted remains of half-buried farm machinery, which they spent hours excavating; a few twisted old citrus trees still bearing tiny fruit, which I peeled for them and they happily ate, even though they were just so sour. The shelters they had found from the rain— inside a fallen tree, ashy from an old fire; under a few stray sheets of corrugated iron that might once have been a small shed. When summer comes, I told them, this will be somewhere to watch out for snakes. They retracted like city kids at the mention of snakes so I softened it with learning how to avoid them and treat them when you find them. A lesson I learned many times over, spotting dugites here, tiger snakes and brown snakes elsewhere. In winter they're asleep, I told them and off they went again, more filth on their boots than they had ever seen. Faces shining.

Some days it rained heavily and they spread toys around their new rooms, leaving partly unpacked boxes and unwrapping familiar things like it was Christmas again.

One of the first big tests, though, is how they settle into school. We booked them straight into winter sports—soccer for Jake and netball for Emmy—to help them make friends. The burden, now, is on me to get them to training and school and do it with Asta. Trying not to overthink, to pre-empt the reactions of parents and teachers and children. Trying not to let myself wind up into a tight coil and hide us from their gaze.

·

By mid-afternoon, the rain has eased and I pull up a little early at the school, take the pram out of the car and strap Asta into the seat with a blanket and her beanie. My mother, quite unwittingly, sent this one as a gift and it fits perfectly, crocheted in shades of purple and trailing off in a tall point like a pixie. The perfect disguise for her head. We have upgraded her glasses to more therapeutic-looking ones, lightly shaded to protect her eyes, and I am prepared to respond, calm and factual.

The path into the school is lined with roses, recently pruned into tortured stumps and leafless from winter. Orange school buses queue like a rack of sliced loaves. I walk quickly in the cold and wait in an undercover area, scattered with picnic tables. It is quiet and several people arrive to collect their children, waiting outside classrooms. Despite my efforts, I notice my breaths are short and a little panic has crept in. A digital bell sing-songs and a ripple of movement surges through the classrooms. I can see Jake on his knees looking out for me, his teacher doing final goodbyes, dismissing small groups of them at a time to quell the grabby rush for schoolbags. Only three of them are left on the mat and she comes to the door with them, searching the parent group so I approach her with a smile.

'Hi, I'm Stacey, Jake's mum.' I offer her my hand and she shakes it quickly. She has the neat dress and styled hair of a good teacher.

'Nice to meet you, Stacey. I'm Isabelle Harper. I guess you're wondering how his first day was?' I nod, peer over my shoulder. 'I won't keep you because I know Jake's sister is here too, but he had a happy day and seems to have connected with the boys who play soccer.' She looks down at Asta, who is smiling and watching all the kids rushing around with purpose. I turn the pram away, face heating slightly.

'Well I'm glad to hear it, thanks for letting me know.' And I take Jake's hand, leading him away a little too quickly. 'Where's Emmy's class?' I breathe, trying to soften the panic.

'Over there, Mum.' He points up a narrow walkway and I push the pram against the flow of parents and children. Most are absorbed in their own lives and no one makes eye contact with me. I can stay a little anonymous. Emmy is the last one left in her class and is helping the teacher with a small row of aquariums at the back of the room. I park Asta on the verandah, facing out towards the garden and order Jake to look after her for a minute so I can meet the teacher. Emmy drops what she is doing and dashes over to me, grabs my hand.

'Mum, this is Miss B and she's got some mealworms and some eggs for silkworms and we're looking after them and waiting for them to change into something else and we're all guessing what they might be and what they might look like when they change. We're just checking them before we go home for the day.' Her exuberance and anxiety are yoked together, much like my own.

'Nice to meet you.' Miss B wipes her hands on a towel and squirts antibacterial gel on her hands. 'How was your first day, Emilia?'

'Good. Miss B is really nice, Mum, and my group is closest to the aquariums, just here.' She taps the lid of her desk.

'I gave her the job of worm carer to help her settle in. I thought it would give her a sense of belonging and she has to nominate a couple of helpers every day so she will get to know the kids.'

'Thanks, that sounds good.' I don't know what to say so I step back as if to leave and it gives the signal to Emmy, who collects her bag from the rack outside and takes hold of the pram, kicking off the brakes. Miss B follows me to the door.

'Looks like she's a great helper with the baby.'

And Emmy turns the pram to face Miss B. 'This is Asta, she's my little sister.'

My palms sweat, I battle an urge to react.

'Hello Asta,' and she steps towards the pram.

My breath is shallow and fast and I take the pram from Emmy, pushing it slightly away to signal our need to leave. I know I am rude. 'Sorry, I have to get home. See you again.' I smile awkwardly at her.

'See you tomorrow, Miss B,' Emmy calls and we stride off. In the undercover area I leave the kids with Asta for a moment, parking her again to face into the garden.

'Just don't let people mess with her, please,' I hiss at Emmy, jamming the pram brakes on hard. I breathe deeply, then go into the school office to organise more uniforms and get details for the bus and canteen. My eyes pivot to the children too much and I know I am not calm. Not dealing with it as I'd hoped and not ready for parents and questions. Less ready to offer an explanation for Asta.

·

For our seven months' meeting, Dimitra has set up a video chat so I put Asta into a jumper, fastened to a doorframe, and turn on the laptop after the kids have gone to school. As planned, at ten the call comes through. She appears, presentable as always, in a clinical office with rows of books over a sink in the background.

Everything tidy. A sure sign of someone who is completely demented, my mother always said, but Dimitra seems quite the opposite. Doing her best to hide it, says my mother, her long dress touching my leg.

I turn the webcam to focus on Asta, who is serious about kicking herself off the floor and flies in and out of view. Her stocky legs hold much more force than my other children's and I have bought her some size two leggings, cutting off half the length to fit her and pinching in the waist to hold them over her nappy. Dimitra watches with an indulgent smile, reaching out to touch her keyboard.

'I'm going to guide you through weaning her, Stacey,' she says, although she can't see me. I sip lukewarm tea, swallow the truth that I have already started. As soon as we left the city I felt like their view was not so close. I bought organic apples and cooked them up myself a couple of weeks ago, sieving them carefully for any seeds or skin. Added some oats one day. Ridiculous, Isak had agreed, you can see the girl needs more than breastmilk now.

'I've ordered you some pre-packed meals and they are being couriered over today. They should arrive in Perth tomorrow and be with you Thursday morning.'

'What's in them?' I wonder how different they are from what I have given her.

'They are high-protein, Paleolithic foods. We don't want to shock her system so we are keeping it consistent with what they would have eaten.'

'What protein is it—mammoth?' It is meant to be a joke, of sorts, to lighten things a little but it falls flat.

'High protein designed particularly for her age.'

I turn the webcam to face me. 'Dimitra, I don't want to feed her mammoth. Can you please tell me what's in them?'

'There are several varieties, designed by a dietitian in consultation with our team. They contain protein sources that were eaten by people at the time, at least the ones we have readily available, like rabbit and venison. I think they included moose, which we imported from Norway especially and there is some mushroom in them. You can also start to feed her a little egg, lightly scrambled without anything added, except perhaps a little breastmilk.'

I'm no mathematician, my mother used to say, but I know a tangent when I hear it, and she'd give me a knowing look. I have mentally ordered venison and rabbit from the butcher in town, buried the mammoth meat in a hole in the garden.

'We'd like you to get her some pets.' She changes the subject.

'Okay,' stay focused, 'what kind of pets?'

'Anything you and the family would enjoy really. We would hope she might have contact with small horses perhaps, rabbits and poultry. You could get her a dog but just a small one and non-shedding, in case they have some aversion to each other. A poodle or Bichon Frise perhaps. Avoid cats if you don't mind please.' She pronounces Bichon Frise with a French accent.

'Why?'

'Potential allergens.'

'Okay. I think we were going to get some chickens anyway. Isak is building a pen already.'

'Good. Birds are good for her. You want her to be able to touch them and, when she is on her feet, we want her to run around barefooted among the animals. It's important to build her immune system.' She taps at her keyboard. 'I've come to expect, Stacey,' she makes eye contact across the screen, 'that you never read the website content that we have put up to help you.' I am a child. 'But I suggest you do, especially regarding diet.'

I leave her screen, take Asta out of the jumper and put her on a play mat on the floor. Turn the camera on her. Dimitra speaks while I do this.

'How are the rest of the family settling into the new house and school?' I imagine she would call this 'duty of care'. How I hate that term.

'Fine. We love this house and the land around it.'

'And how about school. Are you taking them?'

'I have taken them,' once. 'But most days now they catch the bus. It stops down the road for them.' It sounds well adjusted. Tidy.

'Okay, well if you could please send me some data for our development records. I have listed the measurements I need in an email, and weigh her please. Take careful note over the first two weeks of her response to solid food. I would like you to put all this into the app. Will you do this please, Stacey?' Asta is on her hands and knees, rocking back and forth.

'I will.'

'Thank you. You are doing a great job, Stacey. She looks healthy and is developing really well. I will book another appointment in a month, unless you have any concerns.' I pick up Asta and wave her hand at Dimitra. The screen stills and her frozen image stays for a few minutes, until I exit out of it and take Asta to feed on the couch. On the television, a record-breaking fire tears through the Canadian wilderness and a coal-seam gas plant has exploded. Dead geese are heaped with a bulldozer. I change to the cooking channel.

•

On Saturdays we follow the fixtures for netball and soccer, regardless of the state of the weather. Jake has been absorbed into his under eight team like a hero returned, proudly wearing his black and blue strip for the whole day, despite the whiff of it. It is their first year using full-sized goals, girls and boys tearing about and giving it all they have. The cold gives me an excuse to rug Asta up and no questions are needed about why she hides there in her pram. I sit on a fold-out chair beside her, shoulders turned away from the other spectators, spurning chit-chat. Isak often runs the line, flag in hand, or stalks the edge of the pitch, cheering them on and shouting encouragement.

Asta dribbles with teething, front ones this time, at the bottom. I give her rusks but she bites them with her molars and smashes them up, so it is little comfort. Despite my aversion to them, I have given her a dummy and she loves it but often pierces the teat with her back teeth. I keep a three-pack in the back of the pram for Saturdays. Emmy runs off to play with girls from school who have siblings in the team. After the end-of-match talk by the coach, we drive across to the netball courts. Soccer shifts each week, different grassy ovals in various places, including some of the small rural towns nearby, but netball is always in the same place, cold and windy and too close to the beach for winter sport.

The girls were hesitant to include Emmy at first but she is such a good player she quickly became a contender for the regional junior team, so now they all adore her. Jake is always bored and hungry during the game, dragging Isak away with his demands for food and company. I watch every move, determined to give her the attention she needs. I see mothers on their phones during the game, missing goals shot and agile intercepts, mothers talking to each other on the sidelines. I stand apart a little, just enough to shun their conversation, frozen with cold and attentiveness. My mother never let me play netball and, even if she had, we never stayed anywhere long enough for me to feel part of a team. I want better for Emmy, for her to feel part of things, even if I am on the outside. More so now than ever before. Now I am on the outside of the outside.

.

When the courier delivers the baby food, I put it on the kitchen bench and, while Asta has her nap, walk out under the trees to dig a hole. Under the canopy, the wind roars loudly and my face is cold. I choose a place discreet enough for Isak not to notice. Ground breaks easily, rasping against the spade. It is dark sand, denuded of most undergrowth, probably by years of cattle grazing under the trees.

A few arum lilies have popped up in place of the native species—leschenaultia, zamia palms and grass trees. Long trampled, seeds unviable without a blaze. I dig deep through the wet soil, blackened layers. Make a wide hole to swallow whatever rare creatures have been processed into pink mush for Asta. I will not risk feeding her mammoth. I will plant something here to restore the native bush instead. I imagine a row of blue-blossomed leschenaultia enriched by those nutrients, growing longer with each delivery of pink food.

I take control of the BubBot app, diligently filling in all the details required. Organised and accurate, just as they want it. Isak makes jokes about my newfound approach, but I know he takes it as a sign of recovery. It is a sign of descent. I am controlling the ruses, covering my deceptions. I have tried to raise myself above my mother—to be stable and organised, which she would admit as her two biggest weaknesses. There are reasons for dishonesty though, I tell myself; rationalise that it is for Asta. I should be grateful that I have learned techniques for subterfuge from my mother. The worst of her weaknesses—I was never sure what was true.

Asta loves scrambled egg and cooked apple and oats. I bake field or Swiss mushrooms and process them in the blender. Isak roasts venison on his barbecue under the back patio on the weekends, grinning with his beer. I know he misses his family, wonders how we will ever be able to travel again, now we have an unregistered child. It means so much to him. I could stay here, I have told him. You could go next year, take the children. Asta will be older then, easier. But as I say it I feel sick inside, as though a fist is clasped around my entrails, tearing long strands of me out onto the floor. Go. Don't take the children.

He can't leave me alone with a baby, he says, charring his venison to give it that campfire taste, and anyway he was there last year. He cuts a slice off for Asta while it's cooking, still red inside. She gnaws easily on it with her robust teeth.

'Better tell them she's done that.' Isak laughs, ruffling her hair, her long head normal to us.

'You love her, don't you?'

'Of course I do. She's gorgeous, aren't you?' And he picks her up from her high chair on the patio, holds her on his hip. 'She's getting heavy.'

'I know.'

'Dad-dad-dad,' he says to her.

She smiles. 'Dad-dad-dad.'

'She hasn't said anything else, has she?'

'No, I would tell you if she did. And she doesn't really say that much either. I think she will, she's probably just not ready yet.'

'It's a bit early though, even—you know—for normal it's a bit early. I hate using that term but I don't know what else to say.'

'It's okay, Isak.' I stand on tiptoes to kiss him; baby under one arm.

.

Sometimes I feel as if I am watching her unfold through a fissure in time. It's as if a crack has appeared, shining a ray of light onto her broad, bare feet. We are the first to witness her walking, those first uncertain steps. Knees stiff, feet unfamiliar on the earth, her arms held up to save herself when she does, eventually, fall. A cushion of grass around her feet, toes lifting slightly. The sea breeze shifts her hair, now growing slightly over her ears, fanned across the nape of her neck. I kneel beside her on the grass and she turns to me with her toothy smile and I lift her above my head. Hold her high and laughing. No child can ever come near the wonder of her.

She grows quickly now, with solid food and as she gets more confident on her feet. The months of settling into this place and this child are giving way to a version of normality. A precious window of safety.

.

When she was born, the awe of her existence was fresh and intoxicating. A year later, only a little further south, the spring has been rainy, with only small punctuations of sunshine. I am more in awe of her every day.

On her birthday, we walk in the wind by the estuary, a cold front marking out a line of dark cloud. Across the fluttering water, the peninsula is a dark green mass, high sprigs of the canopy marking itself above the rest at various points. Belvidere is dark and appears wild. Patchy sections of bald sand. It is over there, another space populated with snakes and nocturnal eyes. In summer Isak plans to take a small boat and explore. Drive the LandCruiser across the narrow causeway and over to the beach.

We walk the narrow trails cut between thick stands of reeds, broken by narrow openings to the water. It laps and foams, tannin stained against the muddy ground. The torn leaves of sub-marine grasses suspended within. Stoic river-gums and she-oaks shake in the wind—thick and stunted; they may be hundreds of years old, yet they are squat and hunkered against the elements. Whispering to me.

Asta smiles, broad and toothy, at a crow landing on the water's edge and picking at a small fleshy thing rocking in the waves. Its tatty wings lift at our approach and she waves both arms at it, mimicking its flight. She is not so unlike my other children, who both loved to be outside watching, but she is perhaps more attentive to nature and focuses her big eyes on a single thing for a sustained time. They said they expected her to have more acute vision than we do so I wonder what she sees—what level of detail, what unseen forces. One day soon, perhaps, she can explain but for now we walk, pushing against the westerly wind.

A quick clip of flight and a cormorant distracts her, efficient and purposeful in the business of survival.

TWO

Through the living room window, late in the morning, three twenty-eight parrots walk across the grass, seeking out something, biting then looking up, beaks moving. It is windy and the treetops flail about but the determined little trio, their green feathers wet, hunker into the tufted lawn with its yellow flowers. This time of the day is one of the few regular feeds Asta still has and she is heavy on my lap, fills my arms with her warmth. The time of weaning is bittersweet and we are both unwilling to give up on it entirely. She is latched on, eyes closed. Sometimes she smiles, laughs a little while she suckles. I watch her, occasionally looking up at the birds outside, but drawn back constantly to stare at her, relishing these last days, imprinting the vision of her.

Her skin has grown milky, strong and fair but quite translucent. In the light I can see the sky reflected in her arms and legs, the endless magnitude of it captured within her. Blue—broken by floating clouds, shifting in the breeze. I need no windows with her. I could live in a cell and still bathe in the light, be mesmerised by the heavens as long as she was with me.

Reluctantly she drops my depleted nipple and shifts over to the next. We are instinctive together and don't need to communicate this change. Latching on, she smiles at the rush from the fresh breast. Soon, she drops into a satisfied sleep. I hold her until my arms ache, unwilling to leave this moment. Holding fast to it for as long as I can. Fear and love are tangled around us.

Every night I sleep bare-breasted beside her, Isak relegated to the far side of the bed. He often moves to the couch or the trundle bed in Jake's room if we are too disruptive. Grumbles about the bad habit I have got her into. Occasionally he has picked her up, fast asleep, and lain her in the cot in her room. She will stay there for hours, but I lay watchful, waiting for her call. Soon, I tell him, this will all be over. She will completely wean herself soon. He tells me I'm not trying to help and I know he is right but I argue with him anyway. She's a month past the fourteen months when they told me to wean her but I tell him that's not long enough to worry anyone. I lie to BubBot about it and he scolds me unfairly.

Weeks later, she sleeps through the night in her own bed for the first time and the scent of breastmilk slowly fades.

.

Matilda the chicken is broody. She is a silver-grey Dorking, one of the oldest breeds. We marked her nine eggs with a black X and I scrawled the date on the rafter in the chicken house. Each day when Asta and I dole out cups of seed and kitchen scraps, Matilda rises from her nest and we sneak in, taking only the unmarked eggs. Asta thumps along with her heavy, cautious steps carrying the bucket of scraps, and the chickens mob her, pecking at her fingers as she flings bits of yesterday's meals out into the yard. She laughs at their pecking and the rooster's feeble attempts to ward her off, as he propels himself at her legs. This is part of our daily ritual and Asta has bonded with the birds, wandering around in the pen without shoes, knobs of poo squashed under her flat feet. Then one day, before they are due to hatch, one egg is broken. A tiny form, slick and dark with a visible eye and feathers, surrounded by crushed shell. Asta sits on the straw by the nest.

'Dat,' she points at the mangled chick. I explain to her one of the chickens must have squashed it.

'Uh-oh,' I tell her.

'Uh-oh,' she repeats in her fine, raspy voice.

I take her hand as Matilda comes back from breakfast, ready to puff her feathers over the remaining eggs, and lead her out of the yard. This bit of language development is good information for the BubBot. I don't like to tell them everything but if I don't give them enough of what they want, then I end up with messages or phone calls—which is worse—asking after our wellbeing. Dimitra's visits are now all via video chat every three months. She has not been here yet and I wonder how she would fare among the chickens in her fancy shoes.

Sometimes I am lost in this domestic life, in our daily routines, and I forget the wonder we have created and that we continue to create each day, in each step that she takes upon the earth. Sometimes I forget, but she soon reminds me with a glance of her wide eyes, glittering like prisms in the light outside. I shrink from the world, happy here on this land with her and with them. Until the roar of it becomes audible again.

·

The school sports carnival is on a Friday and, despite it being wet all week, it clears up for the day. So now I am torn, and have no simple excuse. Jake and Emmy are in blue faction and both get up early to anoint themselves in blue zinc and spray their hair blue. I pack them extra snacks, fill bottles of water.

'I can't get off work until midday,' says Isak. 'Most of the main events are over by then. I'd really like you to go, Stacey, it's important to them to have someone watch them.'

'I know.' I've done it before but not last year. I have avoided any kind of relationship with the parents, just a few hellos.

'Please, Mum.'

'Please,' echoes Jake. 'Asta will like it.' And he jumps around in front of her, reciting the blue mantra, making her laugh.

I try to make eye contact with Isak to let him know it's a private conversation but he ignores my signals. Raises his eyebrows and jerks his head towards Emmy. He is rarely so directive but with this I know I must go. Her last year at primary school. She sits quietly, meticulously tying up her shoelaces and listening in to our conversation. Isak packs up the dishes and Emmy takes his chair, sits close.

'I understand, Mum.'

I want to cry.

'I know it's because of Asta and that you're embarrassed of her and don't want the parents asking you questions.'

'I'm not embarrassed of Asta, darling.'

She gives me a look of disbelief. 'I'm not stupid. She's not like us kids. I love her, with all my heart but, gosh, Mum, I know she's a bit weird looking. Not in a mean way though.'

'I know you're not mean to her sweetheart. Asta's not like other kids, she has a genetic condition.' I hate saying it. She is not abnormal by her own measure.

Emmy looks at her with a sweet smile while she sits in her high chair chewing on a mangled apple. 'She doesn't even eat like us.'

'She has to have a special diet, you know that. She has a sensitive stomach.'

Emmy looks up at me, eyes searching mine, 'Do you think it's your fault, Mum? Is that why it upsets you so much?' She melts me with her truth.

'Yes. I do think it's my fault.'

She hugs me tight around the chest, taller and bonier than I'm expecting. 'I'll be okay. Don't worry about me. Why don't you open this?'

A parcel arrived a couple of days ago with a new hat I designed—on the outside it looks like a normal bucket hat, but it has a stretchy mesh liner which grips to Asta's head. I hoped it would make her head fit into a normal hat. Emmy pulls the hat from the packaging and fits it onto Asta.

'Looks good, Mum. You can't even tell she has a melon head.' She laughs and I see the rare seed of a little cruel streak, newly arrived in her.

'That's unkind, Emmy.'

She gives me a matter-of-fact look, 'So are you coming to our carnival? Or do we need to hurry up so we can catch the bus?'

'I'll come. But you two can help me get everything ready.'

She nods and strides off to the bathroom, calling to Jake.

I don't like this attitude but I can only accept it and view it as something I have created. My mother slapped me many times for the cruel streak I cultivated against her when I was just a little older. I will not slap but I lash myself for it instead.

·

I weave the pram through the scrum of early arrival parents, seeking out a corner of shade. Most parents are caught in conversations already, decked out in primary colours, so I set up a folding chair and the pram among them in silence. It is easy to slip through the cracks when they already all know each other. Asta holds a protein bar I made in one hand—a hard, pasty creation of ground nuts and egg with a little maple syrup—grinding it up with the side of her teeth. The bucket hat and her sunglasses hide half her face. She is stocky though, her russet hair very striking, and people do glance at her, despite my icy attitude. Inside I am a growling wolf mother, warding them off.

There is cheering and flags, colour and noise, and Asta is awake and animated, flailing her arms and shouting at the teams of children in their flag race, as mothers and fathers lean across the rope barrier, calling out 'Go-go-go'.

When it is Emmy's team up, she looks over and waves at me so I stand to watch. She runs so hard a spray of sand curls up behind her feet, hammering the flag into the bucket and bolting for the finish line, a tense knot across her face. I clap and she looks over, lifting the blue ribbon off her chest to show me. I raise a hand as she walks past, pump my fist in the air.

When I turn back, an elderly lady is at the pram, engaging Asta in chatter. Hackles rise and I turn to her so quickly she starts.

'Ooh—I was just having a talk to your little girl,' she says.

'Dat,' says Asta pointing to her protein bar on the ground. The lady picks it up and hands it to her. Asta drops it again.

'It's a game.'

'Yes, I know. They all do it at this age.' And she picks up the bar and hands it to Asta. I fold my arms to lock her out but she doesn't get the signal. Maybe I should be pleased to hear that Asta is one of 'they all'.

'What's her name?'

I tell her and the lady is satisfied. The loudspeaker announces a change in the proceedings to leader-ball and she is summoned by a dark-haired woman standing on the sidelines. She cheers at a small grandchild who is distracted and drops the ball. It is hard to remember when I last had a normal conversation with anyone outside our family and LifeBLOOD®. Part of me wants her to come back.

It is noisy, the ball thumps back and forth in the children's hands, the cheering is loud. Asta tolerates the noise, but I have spent so many days listening only to the wind in the trees, the call of birds and her irregular utterances that I feel the rise of anxiety. I push the pram over to the coffee van to get away from them, buy a small plate of homemade slices. Nobody knows me so I don't get waylaid with conversation and it's all too quick. The racket continues, so I wander under the trees sipping my coffee. Asta twists in the pram, trying to get out, looking back at the carnival.

'What is it, darling?' I'm a bit impatient, looking in at her, tightening the straps of the pram.

'Dat.' She points back to the sports, waves of cheering dulling down as the age groups swap over. Rows of children in blue, red, green and gold line up for tunnel-ball in the sun. She moans and arches her back, trying to loosen the straps. Pulls at them. I know it is cruel to hold her in there so tight, but I can't risk letting her wander—her thumping step and unusual gait would surely attract questions. Questions I don't want to answer. So I grab the plate of slices and hand it to her. Asta has not eaten such a thing before—I have kept her to a protein-based diet with vegetables, nuts, fruit—wheat and other grains are off the menu, so is sugar. A piece of chocolate brownie covered in rainbow sprinkles is irresistible to her and she claims it with a firm grip, shoving it into her mouth with gusto and sucking off the icing and coloured dots. It shuts her up but I tremble a little, don't want to hurt her or make her sick. She is quiet, unified with the brownie while I finish my coffee, not with the peace I had wanted though.

Dissatisfied I throw the paper cup in the bin and return to the sports just in time to see Jake's blue team come in last in the wheel relay. He is flushed and looks up at me disappointed, though I clap with as much enthusiasm as I can muster. I stand behind the rope barrier and put the pram in front of me, so Asta can be close to the action and nobody can look in at her. The brownie has left a chocolate smear across her face and her hands are sticky but she waves them around at Emmy, whose senior team is set out for their wheel relay. She looks over at us to make sure we are watching, three ribbons on her T-shirt. I know I have missed events—she has the slightly faraway look that is becoming more frequent lately, the one that worries me because I know she is shifting away. That I have let her down. The siren calls and the crowd starts with the shouting.

'Go Emmy!' I call, hoping she hears. In a flash it is done and they have come in second. She jogs over with her friend to see me, bends down to Asta. I have not met the other child, but I say hello to her and tell her well done.

'You gave her chocolate? Gosh, Mum!' I ignore her reprimand, pass the plate over instead and they jog back to their bay, each stopping to bite into the slice.

'Give some to Jake,' I call after her.

It is almost lunchtime so I return to my folding chair to find people encamped around it so that I can't push in the pram. The grandmother is among them and she waves to me, then gets off her picnic blanket to come over. Isak will be here soon and I want him to see that I have dealt with the sports carnival so I don't turn and leave as I want to.

'Come and sit with us,' she says and picks up the front of the pram so we can carry it over people's picnics. 'Nanny Ray,' she says, plonking it into a small grassy patch in the centre. The sort that doesn't wait for an answer—my mother's generation.

'Hi, I'm Stacey.' She makes space by the pram, gathering plastic lunchboxes into a neat stack.

'Pop your chair in here, love. Sorry we've sprawled out so much.' Her daughter, around my age, reclines on the grass in a large hat engaged in laughing conversation with a blonde pony-tailed woman.

'Thanks,' I tell her. The events have paused, people rush past with washing baskets stacked full with lunch orders for the children. My own included. As I watch them pass, Nanny Ray moves her hands in the pram and I jump inside, stand up and grab the handles. She is wiping Asta's hands and face clean and my heart is pounding. I stop myself from reacting—calm, calm, breathe. She looks up, slightly puzzled.

'Is this okay with you? She's not allergic to wipes or anything is she?'

'No,' I squeak the word through my held breath. Waiting for her to notice who it really is in that pram. But she looks up behind me and smiles. Isak is there, baseball cap on and gleeful with a bag of takeaway.

'I bought us both some lunch,' he says. 'How's it been?'

I give him an account of the races I have watched, leaving out any talk of missing events or feeding Asta chocolate brownie. He crouches by the pram and hands her a few chips. Kisses her on the forehead. A siren sounds and the kids disperse for lunch, gravitating to their parents in tight-knit groups. Emmy and her friend are swift, making space between Nanny Ray and the pram. The friend kisses Nanny Ray, who hands her a lunchbox. Jake joins us with his lunch mostly gone already. I take a bite from the burger Isak brought me but Jake is still hungry so I hand it to him. Soon it is gone.

After lunch, the kids return to their groups, preparing for running events. Isak chats to Nanny Ray about the girls having a sleepover, apologising for not doing it earlier. I try to catch his eye, but he studiously avoids me. The child, Milly, is now staying with us for the night. Parents shift to the sideline of the track now, and Isak pushes the pram over. I don't want to be there and am happy to escape the anxiety and noise.

'I'm going to get a cup of tea, want one?' He nods and I am free for a moment to be alone. The day has made me tired. Chest hard, coiled tight inside and winding ever tighter. I am spring-loaded and ready to launch, the tension of it ringing in my ears, high frequency. I look up at the languid eucalyptus trees and let the lump dissolve into hot tears.

After the presentations and final cheers for the reds, golds, greens and blues, Isak volunteers to help the girls dismantle marquees and return equipment to the sports shed. He chats with another man, a soccer dad apparently. I am eager to get home, though Asta is asleep in her pram and I disrupt her, rushing into the car. Wave a cursory goodbye to Nanny Ray.

Isak is much more comfortable explaining away the 'rare genetic condition'. I feel the lie of it, the words like stone in my mouth, weighing me down. Exposure is what I most dread; what might happen if she is discovered. What might happen if it's my fault for saying the wrong thing. For not deceiving as well as I should. The tearing apart of our lives here, the necessity to move away. Once our burrow is revealed, our safety is compromised. The media will descend and write exposés on the strange family with their prehistoric child. Our faces will be inscribed on the national psyche, forever tarnished. We might change our names and go to ground to no avail. A change of hairstyle or name can't deny the truth. Even if a dingo never took her baby, nobody will ever forget her face or her name. Or the name of her baby. That will be me and Isak and Asta, our children the innocent bystanders whose lives are displayed on screens across the world, shared in social media, like so many wonders of the world. The shifting focus of clicks, which magnetise and drive global thoughts and conversations this way and that, from viral dancing goats to the de-extincted wonders that appear in news feeds. Great auks, the whimsical Atlantic penguin, are returned to the wild, even though all around its once-habitat is in decline. The argument of why swallowed in the Mexican wave of the event. I trail off into our driveway, released at last from being found. My muscles let go of their tension, triggering an impulse to shake.

When she wakes from the car, Asta cries unusually and I carry her inside, rocking her on the couch. She points at her stomach. Jake watches the television, gets himself a snack. She fills her nappy and he looks over at the rumbling sound that comes from her. He pulls a face.

When Isak returns with Emmy and Milly, he has been to the shop and lights his barbecue in good cheer. Asta is still grizzling and in pain but at the sight of the girl in our house I cover her in a bunny-rug and hold her facing my chest.

'You're not, are you?' He slams the fridge door, seeping his irritation.

'No. My milk's gone. I wouldn't try and start her again, Isak.' I'm defensive, clip my words.

'Is she okay?'

'No, she's in pain and sick in the stomach.' I look at him accusingly. 'The chips,' I lie, out of earshot of Emmy.

'Fuck, sorry. Look, I bought some venison sausages for her. That might help.' He shakes his head and wanders out to the patio.

Deeper again, I plunge towards my mother.

I put her to bed, retreat into the garden to feed the chickens and walk out under the trees, where the leschenaultia is in bloom.

On the surface, the ground is still even, but each day, I excavate a little more from the bedrock, hoping it won't become unstable. I hold a teaspoon of the crisp rock in my hand, toss the crumbs into the air and let it spray into the eyes of my children. I save the most jagged pieces to rub into my own eyes, scratching them raw with each spoonful I scour from the depths.

The next day Emmy is pleased that her friend has slept over without a major incident. She rewards Asta by letting her sit between her and Milly on the couch watching kids cartoons while they eat breakfast. They paint her nails and I watch carefully as they hold each finger and toe in turn, examining and discussing her features. I can't hear what they say over the cartoon but I see their exchanged glances, laughing, tickling Asta, whose nails roam everywhere, still wet. They will never guess—I am sure it will not even occur to Milly, and I expect Emmy has said something about her sister. Letting someone into our domestic lives, even a child, feels like a big move to me. Makes me watchful and anxious.

Isak takes them to soccer and netball through all of winter. I had to stop. Sometimes I could watch the soccer from the car but netball means being courtside with Asta and the parents started coming to talk to me. I am sorry they have gone without me. 'I'm worried about you becoming too much of a recluse,' he tells me. I still refuse to go but I miss them.

·

At the end of the school year, Isak buys two kayaks and a canoe from one of the soccer dads who's moving up to a bigger boat. I see his envy about the boat but he hauls the kayaks home on a new trailer, reversing in jagged lines up to the shed. Asta and I watch them scrub out the dry mud and leaves.

'Asta come?' Jake says to her. 'Boat. Go in boat.'

'Don't speak like a baby to her, Jake,' I snap. 'She's two now.'

He is silent and sprays the hose onto a kayak so we have to step away.

'We have to get some life jackets first, mate,' Isak says to him, shooting me a reproach. 'But you're a good swimmer. We can go and test them out first. Make sure they're safe. We'll have plenty of time now it's school holidays.'

They turn their backs to me. Even though we all live together and they are my family, I feel like I am only partly in their lives. It is all changing and I can't quite hold it firm.

THREE

The paths around here curve in wide arcs through low rambles of reed. I am often fixed on the distant view, watching for those eyes that peer into my life. People with dogs. I avoid eye contact. Asta rides slowly on a chunky tricycle we bought her for Christmas, concentrating on the pedals, slow and heavy footed. She meanders a little, tracing her way back to the centre, veering a little to the right then stops suddenly. I walk right into the back of her, attention out there on the horizon. She watches the reeds and points but I see nothing, so I bend over and part the grasses a little. Inside a bobtail goanna is curled and slow moving in the pale sun, filtered through the strands of reed. She stands beside me and looks in at the speckled creature.

'How did you know it was there?'

'Shhh.' And she points to her ears. She bends to touch it, runs her finger lightly over its crenulated back. It turns quickly and opens its mouth wide, hissing, its tongue threatening. She starts back, grasps my hand.

'Goanna.' I crouch down and look into her intense eyes. 'G-g-g. Asta say it.' And I wait, holding her hand. 'G-g-g.' She stares at me, knows I want her to do something.

'Gogog.' She smiles wide, her crispy unused voice surprising her.

'Gogog, yes, Asta. You're so clever.' And I hug her. She rides off down the path, slowly turning and twisting the bike, babbling 'gogog' to herself. I take a video of her and message Isak to tell him. Upload it to BubBot.

.

Autumn rains began so I made a cake on the weekend. Gluten free of course, sugar free with dates and honey to try and treat her. The constant cramps and diarrhoea. Poor little thing. Our natural is her processed and not much I do can remedy it. We stick with goats' milk. Nuts. Eggs from our chickens. Only a little bit of butter triggered her. The crack and moan of her stomach. Curled on the couch under a blanket. I know she hates the humiliation of it but I had to put her in pull-ups. I draw on the skills I learned from my mother and make aromatic tea. She sucks it avidly from a sipper cup.

'We're back, Mumma!' First games of the new season.

Her face lightens. The kids, galumphing through the house, make her laugh.

'We got you a lollipop, Asta.' Jake hands it right to her.

'It's only a little one, she'll be okay if you ration it.' Isak kisses me lightly on the cheek. A little lacking in conviction. I slice cake and boil the kettle.

'The offside rule seems to have a very loose interpretation with some of those linesmen. And he was just a young ref too so he couldn't stand up for himself. Lost two nil. Should have been a shoo-in. They were third on the ladder and us second so now we probably won't make the finals.'

'Jake played well though?'

'Like a hero, eh, number eleven?' Isak bites into the cake with frenzy. 'Oi! Socks, shin pads, strip—in the washing machine. No stinking up the house with your sweaty soccer gear.'

'How was netball?'

'She played like a demon, didn't you, Emmy? Wing attack for three quarters and on the bench for one.'

'They win?'

'Thrashed them. Again.' The tea is scalding and he blows steam across the top of the cup. 'How is she?'

We both look over and there on the couch she holds out the chewed lollipop and a tooth. Silently she lets blood leak down her chin. Looking in amazement at the tooth. A pain in my chest—this already. It's too soon.

'Asta, the tooth fairy's gunna come for you tonight!' Emmy is so gentle with her. Wiping her face with a tissue. 'You can borrow my fairy box and we can draw a picture for her.'

Asta lights up, looks up at her with wide eyes. Total devotion. Following her every move. Emmy takes the tooth from her sticky hand, wipes the blood from it gently with a tissue and places it in the fairy box. Roots down. The girls work together with crayons, heads together and intent.

I have strict instructions for when she loses her teeth so I record it on my phone. Close-up of the tooth, avoiding any association with the lollipop. Send it right away. My phone pings with a now rare BubBot message: *When the 'tooth fairy' comes tonight collect it with sterile tweezers, place it in a sample bag and keep in the refrigerator. We will send a courier.* A week later a posted package arrives with a special envelope for biological substances.

·

Isak wheels the kayaks down our driveway and across the road to the water's edge. We all trail down there. The shallow water is warmed by the sun and circles my legs, fine weed brushes my skin. Asta wades beside me as Emmy paddles out, quickly mastering the pattern of the stroke. Isak squeezes in with Jake and the two of them row quickly out, waiting now and then for Emmy to catch up. They move rapidly further away, birds rising in their path. This part of the estuary is a wide arc where the water terminates against the causeway that connects us to Leschenault Peninsula. It is a still, quiet haven for black swans, who gather here in enormous numbers, some trailing large cygnets still grey with down. Asta waves at the kids but they don't turn to see her.

She holds my hand and we wade through the water, enjoying the thick mud rising between our toes. She smiles, lifts her foot and shakes it in the water to rinse off the grey sludge.

'Poo.'

'Not poo—mud.' She is slower to speak than Emmy or Jake but she is learning. Small, simple words we use all the time are the ones she has mastered. She nods but doesn't repeat 'mud', although I prompt her. A cloud of waterborne dirt and weed is agitated by our footsteps and it slowly settles in our wake, hiding the pockmarked bed of the estuary. Small, sharp mysteries poke occasionally at the sole of my foot. Stones, perhaps, or the abandoned claw of a caught crab. Sometimes the remnant cap from a beer bottle, or a strange shell, long hollowed. Asta bends towards the water and lifts an aged fence post up, releasing a cloud into the water around her. She laughs, squealing a little, and dashes her hand in to lift out a clear prawn, flicking its tail, a spray of water in the sun. I stride to her, the water heavy around my legs.

'Wow, well done, sweetheart. It's a prawn.' Its companions flick against my legs and Asta drops the post with a great splash back into the water. I can see by the residue on it that it was buried in the mud and must have been heavy.

'Are you going to put it back with its friends?'

Asta holds the flicking prawn, looking close at the dark orbs of its eyes, close to the barbs on its face.

'No. Mine.' And she grips it tight in her fist. Flicking against her with all its might, there is no mercy for the prawn and it slows into a stiff arc.

The children have begun to notice her strength. Wrestling things from her grasp is a great challenge for Jake, who is happy to rise to the occasion and tap into his ferocious core. Emmy surrenders, wise enough to know when she is beaten, and wily enough to hide anything precious.

'She's a bit of a brute.' Isak laughs, excusing the offensive connotations he makes with the word. He makes them anyway, renders me silent.

Across the water, they have paddled into the distance and seem determined to make landfall on the peninsula so I turn back towards our driveway, calling Asta to follow.

On the back patio, she drops the prawn into a tub of water but it doesn't move. She flicks her finger at it, mimicking the movement of its tail. It floats on its side, its exoskeleton broken, pale grey flesh popping from the cracks.

'Gone. It's gone, Asta.'

She swirls the water with her hand, producing a current, and the prawn spins in the eddy of it. Stills again as the water rests. 'Gone.' But she doesn't repeat the word, just sits on the patio, staring into the tub.

·

After two years of ever-declining video chat, finally we are getting the promised visit from Dimitra. I didn't expect to be excited to see her, but I am. Despite assertions that she would come to see us, there have been ongoing delays for mysterious reasons. She has never shared her own situation and I am not sure where she lives—sometimes there is a time delay of two hours and sometimes it seems to be evening where she is, despite the fact I have just sent the kids to catch the bus. She has been the only person I can regularly speak to about Asta, even though I am always careful what I say.

I spend several days sorting and tidying, laying out evidence of healthy diet and wholesome family time. Take down the spiderwebs, take the thick layers of curled school notes and merit awards from the fridge. The generosity of LifeBLOOD® has declined further in the past year and we have been left to provide for Asta unaided, told simply that they have already given us a generous boost to our finances by providing a house and a new car. I have since learned to make efficient clothing alterations to suit Asta's proportions and developed an easy pattern for the bucket hat and a more wide-brimmed version. Left alone, I sometimes forget our obligations. My reporting regime becoming less frequent, now monthly and less detailed unless something unusual happens, like the tooth. Sometimes I even lose sight of who she is, however briefly.

In the mid-morning I hear the crackle of wheels on the gravel driveway and pull my hair quickly from its day-old bun. Asta is up in the fig tree that shades the chicken coop, on a platform Isak bolted into the branches. At home she abandons the sunglasses and hat. I call her to come down but at the sight of the car, she retreats higher into the tree.

Dimitra is not alone, but has brought Dr Jeff with her and a young man, dressed in very clean moleskins and untouched workboots. She pulls out a large case on wheels and Jeff carries a file, the three of them looking around like tourists. I know I am a bit of a mess with grotty bare feet so I slip on some shoes lying by the back door. Black cockatoos thrum in the trees, calling back and forth to each other and dropping mangled gumnuts, which crash onto the roof of the shed. The rooster crows and I finally wave to them, directing them to come to the patio. I have cleaned up the table and chairs, disposed of the floating prawn and moved the sticky barbecue into the shed. There is a fresh pot of mint on the table and I have set it with glasses and a tray of freshly cut fruit. Dimitra smiles and extends her hand, with its glossy talons. I shake it firmly, try to exude certainty.

'You look well, Stacey.'

The longer I stay here, the more I devolve into a version of myself that resembles my childhood—the sun has roasted me and even my good clothes are a little tatty.

'Thanks.' I can see their eyes darting about so I pre-empt them, 'Asta was feeding the chickens and she's still in the pen. She likes to play up in the tree.'

Jeff smiles and shakes my hand warmly. 'Good to see you looking so relaxed. This is my assistant, Lucas.' He looks fresh, newly minted from a room somewhere that he has studied in since early childhood.

'Nice to finally meet you. I've heard so much about you and Asta.'

Queasy inside. He has a Scandinavian accent.

I direct them to take a seat while I go and get Asta but Lucas comes with me, striding out in his new boots into the yard.

'You'd better be careful in the pen, there's lots of poo.'

He smiles like he has no clue amid the sharp scent of chickens. The small rooster stands high and crows with such force he seems to stand on the end of his toes. Asta is not on the platform.

'Where are you, sweetie?' I call softly.

'Maybe she's not in here?' he suggests. Looking around at our place, as if he knows what's where.

She has gone, likely out under the trees somewhere, so we walk out to the edge of the tuart stand and I call to her.

'Can she get out?'

'She's not in a paddock or a cage. Of course she can get out, she just doesn't normally run off because she knows not to go out without one of us.'

'Maybe you should call louder?'

'She heard me. I think she's just a bit nervous to come out because you're here.'

I spot her then, in the black heart of a large tree. She hunkers back when she knows she is caught. 'Could you please go back to the house? She might be frightened of you. She doesn't meet many strangers.' Even when the grocery truck comes, or Nanny Ray drops Milly off for a visit, she tucks herself away.

Once he is out of sight, Asta comes out of hiding. Because I see her every day, her difference has become usual and I no longer see her the way others might. I shift my view for a moment, wonder how it might be for them to see her afresh now that she is growing up—her broad features, luminous fair skin and thick rusty hair are certainly unusual but from a distance there is no reason to suspect. It is the closer view, when you see her eyes—especially when she is scared and the pupils widen. They are less human than I would like to think and I imagine when her adult teeth grow in, her mouth will barely contain them.

She looks at me now with dense pupils and I crouch down, hold her tight to my chest and explain that it is only Dimitra come to see us with two of her friends.

'-at?' She pats her head.

'No, sweetie, it's okay with them. They are like family.' Such lies I tell her so she feels safe.

Under the patio, Dimitra has poured them all a glass of water and they sit at the table navigating screens in silence. At the sight of them, Asta holds tight to my leg and buries her face in my dress. Her grip like steel. For a moment they all stare then Dimitra stands and bends over to Asta's height.

'Hello Asta, you have grown so big since I last saw you. I hear you have some lovely chickens.'

Asta burrows closer so I move down to her and pick her up, despite the strain in my back. I move awkwardly to a chair and she sits on my lap, her heavy head facing my chest. Hot breath on my skin. Short and fast.

'I'm sorry but Asta isn't used to strangers visiting and she's a bit nervous.' I could say the same of myself.

'We have time, Stacey, we can wait. It's important we let her warm to us in her own time.'

I offer them some fruit to try and relax things a bit.

'I don't know if you realise it, Stacey,' says Jeff, 'but LifeBLOOD® as we knew it is about to be dissolved. There was a stock market crash last year and we had to sell off our assets to avoid going into receivership. Most of our clinics have been sold and we are now making arrangements for our clients.' He waits for a response but I don't know what to say so I take a grape from the tray. 'I'd like to review our agreement with you so we have some plan in place for Asta.'

I never read the agreement past the first half-page. Isak gave me his abridged version of what it included—education at home, shelter and care for her until she grows up and leaves home. I never really thought about what those things involved. But now I feel ice settling across my skin. What future could I see for that embryo when they implanted it? Embryos come and go and I had lost one before. A child, though, a robust and beautiful child is grafted into me like an organ, not an ephemeral embryo.

Jeff places his hand across a printed document on the table. 'LifeBLOOD®'s client list has gone to another company, Ärva Pharmaceuticals, based in Sweden and they have also taken some of LifeBLOOD®'s staff across, including me, to maintain some continuity for their Australian portfolio.' He waits for my response.

'Can you explain what this means for us, Jeff?'

'Dimitra won't be with us any longer. Lucas will be assisting me to support you but we are working with a lot less staff so the services you have had will be reduced further. We will require only an annual report from you unless you have any particular concerns or an emergency.'

'What about her schooling program?' I have been imagining our lives in the next few years, incorporating some lessons into the rhythm of our days at home.

'I'm sorry but that will be up to you. It's not a priority outcome for the program anymore but the home education packages that had been developed for LifeBLOOD® are available for purchase.'

Money does not flow freely in our house, despite the windfall of this property. Isak is repaying the loan to his mother for our house deposit. I shake my head to decline his offer.

'I do encourage you, though, to work on some fundamental literacy and numeracy. How's her language development?'

'Simple, but improving.' Asta plays with a button on my dress, relaxing a little as the conversation continues around her. Lucas leans in and pulls faces at her to get her attention but she shrinks further to me. I can see his studious gaze taking in her features and response. I don't like his sharp eyes looking at her like an object. He looks greedy for her.

'In some ways, Stacey, at least you will be free to do what you can with her. We won't be able to micromanage this anymore.' The clarity of his words relaxes me a little.

'And in other ways?' Free in some ways, imprisoned in others.

'In other ways, well the Board of Ärva will want some return on their investment in our clients.' He combs his fingers through his silver hair.

'What does that mean? Will they sell our story to the media?'

'We don't know at the moment but we have left the embargo in place on images. Dimitra's and my research has been published but it doesn't identify any of you, or even where she was born.'

They have written about us. 'What if I don't sign it?'

'You have to sign it.' He leans in closer, blue eyes peering into mine. Like a charmer.

'How are you going to make me sign it?'

'There's a clause.' He is matter-of-fact. 'There isn't much choice Stacey.'

'Always the fine print with you people, isn't it?' My anger rises, I wish Isak was here. His cool head and sensible questions always help me feel more certain. If he knew Jeff was coming he would be here. 'So the story is out there?'

'Yes, but not your story per se. It's in scientific terms. The media have reinterpreted it and dumbed it down for the public. They've used artist sketches of our descriptions. We felt it was detrimental to all of us if photos of Asta were leaked. They are protected by high security on our server. It's the best in the business.' He smiles, taps away at his phone. 'There, I sent you one of my articles to read.' He takes a strawberry from the fruit platter and leans towards me, coaxing Asta with the fruit. She peers out for a moment then grips tighter into my chest. Her breath shallow. He gives up and drops it on the table.

'She's shy, sorry.' I stroke her hair to calm her. Dimitra makes eye contact with me for a moment—warning me, I think.

'You need to read the documents, Stacey, and so does your husband. I will leave them here with you. You are welcome to get some legal advice if you wish but the LifeBLOOD® legal team have already been through it and I don't see that there are any loopholes. It's as straightforward as it has always been.' He takes a sip of water and waits a moment for my response. 'You know, there was always a future plan for Asta's living arrangements when she reaches maturity. LifeBLOOD® wasn't financially prepared for the success of this program though. This new company has some big financial backers and they will deliver something better than we could before.'

Dimitra clears her throat and leans in to me. 'Don't stress about it, Stacey. Asta will be fine.'

'She will be fine, but you should remember that you can't keep her here forever,' Jeff says. 'That was never going to happen.' A chill rises through me, my head and face prickle. 'Your other children will leave home too, Stacey. It's no different.'

I can see Emmy with a backpack taking off to travel the globe, or Jake married to a nice girl and living in his own house but Asta is not destined for those futures. 'It is different, Jeff.'

'Only a little. Part of parenting is letting go.'

'I think that's a platitude.'

'It's a truth. I've been through it myself.' He sits back, a forced smile stretching his face. 'Look, just enjoy this time while you can. Like your other children, Asta has a path to follow and we can't necessarily control that.' He leans back, hands behind his head, utterly superior. Makes eye contact with Dimitra, who looks away from him

'She's only three, Stacey, so it's a few years away,' she says. 'Don't worry too much. Just enjoy your life here and give her the best upbringing that you can.'

'Yes, you need to teach her what you think is important. Make sure she knows how to behave around people.' He sits forward again and puts his hand on my knee. Familiar, his grave and magnetic stare. Eyebrows raised. 'But, Stacey,' he says gently, softly, 'there will come a time, as you already know, when she will go on to do the work she was destined for. There are people waiting, sick kids, who will benefit from her genes.'

I am frozen.

He sighs and rubs my knee. 'You need to let go a bit now. For your own sake.'

Numb. Asta twists on my lap, her hot breath on my chest.

'I don't know if I can let go.'

He nods, pats my knee again.

'Don't make it worse for yourself, Stacey. Practise letting go now. Leave her with Isak and go away somewhere. Visit your mother or something. You need to cut the umbilical cord. It will only hurt you and I never wanted that.'

I know I won't visit my mother.

Dimitra taps her talons on the table in a single movement, startling Asta who turns to look at her. 'Okay, I'd like to examine Asta and do some tests. Just routine bloods and so on. Shall we go inside for that?'

I direct her to set up in the living room and take Asta's hand. Several crows are picking at something in the garden bed and I realise they have found the remains of the prawn. They compete for the tiny carcase, savage and ragged in the midday sun. The two men sit on the patio and return to their screens.

Asta sits quietly beside me on the couch, a little less shy than she was with the men. She fidgets with the stray parts of a toy android Jake has left on the couch as Dimitra sets up her equipment—an audiometer, a clip-together contraption built on a floor pad. I don't know this woman at all, yet I will miss her. The thought of not having her as a touchstone, at the other end of the app—wherever that might be—makes me sad and even lonelier. Anxious at her absence, just as I have always been anxious in her presence.

She breaks the silence with her remote tone, a reminder of how truly clinical her approach has been. 'That's a new generation stadiometer, linked straight up to my database so I can get millimetre perfect height and weight measurements for Asta.' She presses a button and it plays a tune. Asta smiles. 'You can stand on it if you'd like.' I stand with her, her dirty feet like speckled fish on the black floor pad. Mine, inside my shoes, are no cleaner. Dimitra's computer logs all the data and she taps at the keys.

This is her last visit with us, so I ask: 'What are you going to do with all this information you've got from Asta? You know, now that you're not part of this anymore?' I wave my hands to encompass Asta and I.

She clears her throat, casts her eyes down a little. Off guard. 'Can I take some hair samples please?' She takes scissors and a sterile container from her bag. I nod and she cuts a small, thick curl. 'Most of my work so far has been to deepen our knowledge of neo-natal and infant development in Neanderthals. I have a new position with another research institute and my study will continue.'

I am nervous to ask where. She is so prim and careful in her choice of words.

I wonder what she has observed and found in her research. 'Can I read what you wrote about us?'

She smiles, flattered perhaps. 'Dr van Tink has sent you one of his studies, so yes, I suppose. You realise it is all carefully de-identified and full of scientific jargon. It's probably quite unreadable to a lay person.'

'Okay, but I will try.' Thinking it through, I don't think I do want to read what she has said about me, Asta and our family. She turns to the test tubes and prepares to take some blood.

She sighs and pauses. 'It has been a privilege to work with you and Asta.' She is a little teary and she takes Asta's hand, rubbing the vein in the crook of her arm. Asta allows her and I explain it will hurt a little, hold her other hand.

'I'm going to miss you.' I tell her, despite my uncertainty that this is entirely true.

She draws blood, Asta turning her face into my chest again. 'It has been a most wonderful journey and I hope it all goes well from here.' She looks at my eyes, 'Just you take care of her.' Her words have weight. What is it she understands that I don't? I go to ask but she shifts her focus to the tourniquet on Asta's arm.

'Everything okay?' I ask her, loading extra meaning in my tone.

She looks out at the patio and nods. 'Just watch them, Stacey. I have concerns this might not be done as well as we could have done it.' Her words drop through me like the melt from a glacier. She is too meticulous to throw such statements around on a whim. 'Ask questions. Just make sure you protect yourselves. I'll say no more.' She draws her lips firm and completes the tests, setting up to do a hearing test on Asta. Quizzes me on her sensitivity to noise. I tell her Asta prefers quiet and gets anxious and with-drawn in noisy environments. Cuts her fingernails into a small jar. We discuss her digestive issues and the need to hold firmly to a Paleolithic-based diet. She reminds me that puberty will come early, without the markers you might expect from human children. I wince at the wording and the thought of puberty when Asta is only three.

'It will sneak up on you, Stacey, earlier than your other daughter, and that's when they'll want her for the gene pool.' She is warning me.

'Do you know where they'll take her?' I will go with her if I have to.

'I did know, but that might change. She will be kept well. She's very valuable and they won't put her life at risk but they'll use her.'

I am barely breathing. She nods at me, close and serious.

She ends with, 'Teach her what you can so she can look after herself when you aren't there to help her.' I feel the portent of the statement like a burst pipe deep beneath the surface. I keep it buried, mindful there will be a moment when it starts to rise.

And then, after all this cold and distant time, she hugs Asta tight into her bony chest. Finally she stands and packs her gear and the three of them crackle back down the gravel driveway to return to the cities where they belong.

.

I am exhausted after the visit and fall asleep on the couch in front of the television. Asta sleeps in a beanbag on the floor beside me. The doors are open so I don't hear the kids come into the house. I wake to the popcorn-maker tocking in the kitchen and the clanking of bowls.

'Do you want some popcorn, Asta?'

'Pop-pop,' and she uncrumples herself from sleep, takes Emmy's hand.

'No butter and no icing sugar.' Jake likes to load his with sugar.

'I know, Mum.' She is impatient. 'I can look after her, you know? You could have a holiday if you wanted to. Dad reckons you need one.' Her statement stuns me after Jeff's suggestion and she gives me a sassy look and sits beside Asta with the popcorn. 'Say *ta Emmy*.' So like my mother.

'Ta, Emmy.' Somehow Emmy can get her to mimic so much more easily than I can. Asta looks at her with steady, wide eyes and takes some popcorn.

'So what makes Dad tell you I need a holiday?' He's been complaining about me, shredding my reputation with the kids.

'It's just what he says when we talk to him about stuff, that's all.' She is getting quite clever with circular conversation. My irritation shifts me to sit up and Jake plops himself beside me with a sugary and buttery mass of popcorn.

'Have you two got some issues we need to talk about?'

'No,' says Jake through a filter of popcorn. In unison, Emmy shouts yes.

'Why can't we go out anywhere all together anymore? Why don't we have birthday parties at home since Asta was born? Why don't you just get over it, Mum, and accept that she's not normal?' I go to respond but she lets loose a tirade, setting the bowl on the floor. 'I think it's you that has the big problem with her because even Milly reckons Asta is cute and whatever disability she has isn't a big deal.' She starts to cry then and I suppress the swelling sadness in my throat, sitting back like I've been shoved.

'And anyway, Mum, she's not the only kid in the world to have a disability and I love her so you shouldn't keep her all to yourself.'

'Have you said all this to Dad?' I can imagine him weathering sadder, longer versions, rationalising with her, blaming my over-protectiveness.

'He said you worry a lot and you need a holiday, like I said. But he also reckons that the thing with Asta has to be kept secret and that's what stresses you out so much.'

I call her to me and she snuggles into me on the couch. 'I'm sorry, I'm sorry'—she cries into my chest.

'I'll try and do better,' I tell her, silent tears dropping down my face.

Jake puts a cartoon on the television and sits on the floor with Asta, finishing the sugary popcorn together.

'Milly can come over anytime you like.' I think a moment, make a rash promise. 'And maybe we can all go on a holiday again, like we did when she was born.'

Emmy curls up beside me for a few minutes, eyes on the television and the emotion slows to a soft pulse.

She sighs. 'They ate it all.' And I go to make her some more, brush the popcorn crumbs from the couch into my hand. A clean house really doesn't last long with them.

When Isak comes home he makes us tea and we sneak outside to the shed. He always wanted a space like this but between work and sport and entertaining the kids it has only been used to store things that don't go in the house: kayaks and bikes. The hard clay mounds of wasp nests punctuate the joins of roof and wall like giant full stops.

'So, who came down?' He pulls out the camping chairs and a plastic crate for our tea. He kisses the top of my head. 'I can see you've been crying.' The sobs start again and he sits near me, takes my hand.

'Jeff,' I eventually get out. 'Told me I have to let go of her.'

He shakes his head and looks down in his lap. I get out something about early puberty.

Isak knots his brow, squeezes my hand. 'It's not just you that needs to let go Stace. What about the kids? And me.'

I tell him about Jeff's idea that I visit my mum.

'Sandra would love it,' he laughs. 'But I really can't see you going over there to see her. Maybe a weekend away; maybe you and Emmy and Jake? I can stay here with Asta. It would be good for you to spend time with the kids. They get enough of me.'

I know I won't leave her, even for a couple of days.

I settle down and describe the trio and Asta's reaction, then the change to LifeBLOOD® as best I can. 'I wished you were there, it was all very well explained, as usual, but I think there must be something in there we need to be careful of because Dimitra warned me.'

Isak has pulled out his phone and looks up Ärva Pharmaceuticals, turns the screen to me.

'Ancient knowledge: Future health' is their caption, with large images scrolling around advertising Poplar Painkillers—golden leaves, sprouting buds on bare limbs, close images of pale bark and finally a simulated image of a child very like Asta chewing on a sprouted twig.

'There,' says Isak, tapping the screen on the child until it swells to fill the glass. 'That's why they've bought up LifeBLOOD®.' Not a real child though, just an artist's interpretation. 'Don't know what you want to do, Stacey? It's not like we can run away from it. We're locked in here.' He raises an eyebrow.

Run, run, run, run, run. 'I want you to read it and see if you can work out what they're going to do with her.'

He nods, swiping around on the phone, digging into the pages.

'And I want to run away with her.'

'Do you really think you can run somewhere and hide, Stace?' He has a told-you-so look. Reminds me of his mother. 'We can't get her out of the country without a passport.'

'There are plenty of places to hide here though.' Deserted wheatbelt places, dug-out mining towns in the Pilbara, struggling schools happy to welcome a new family, no questions asked. 'That was my childhood, remember?'

'Stacey, we signed up for this and whatever they have in store is probably not much different from what the other fuckers had in mind. I'm not running unless it's back home, and she doesn't have a passport so that's not going to work.'

I stand and pace around him. 'That's harsh.' Agitated and sick. In the light from the window, the lines on his forehead are deeper than usual.

'What am I supposed to do?' He twists his mouth, impatiently. 'There are all of us to consider, Stacey.' Implies I only consider Asta. I can't refute this. Inside I am crumpled, curling in on myself, singed in the heat of guilt which ferments inside me each day, of knots combed through, each rip of hair, the sloppy braids, the tears that hatch in Emmy's eyes. A flake of dark ash rises, black scraps caught in our orbit. Crows drone, their pitch declining as their notes lengthen into soliloquy. Feasting on our compost.

He resolves to read the contract before we sign it.

.

Later, while I am in bed, the glow of the screen lights his face. He has their research papers and the contract. Steady and focused, rubbing his head. I turn my back to him and try to sleep.

.

A boardwalk runs through a grove of eucalypts and paperbark and I drop Asta's tricycle onto it in the mid-morning sun. The air moans with flies and the heat has roused crickets. She points at scattering orange butterflies. Tiny, busy things wafting in the long grass.

'Butterfly,' I tell her but she is silent. I don't lean into her, don't force the issue like Emmy does. I think she understands more all the time but her vocabulary is still so small, growing incrementally though her body shoots like spring. She scratches her arm against the dead sticks of struggling basket-bush, rubs it and continues. Her bike clacks like a train on the boards.

Sometimes I long for conversation—those friends we had in Dublin, now scattered in the wind and abandoning social media. I have nobody but Isak and he has peeled away from me like a shed skin but I'm not sure who has shed and who has been shed. I worry that we will never grow back together. My little deceptions have seeped into that thing that sticks us to each other, slowly eroding its hold. Little bit by little bit. I don't even know where it began, or how I might grab hold enough to fix it.

I sit in the picnic shelter and pull out my phone. Asta has settled on the boardwalk, legs hanging over the edge into the dry swamp-bed. I find my mother's listing, scroll past it to Alex and text him. 'Just saying hello.' Awkward. 'Wondered how you're going.' So stiff and unfamiliar. I delete it without sending and rest the phone on the seat.

Large insects are suspended in flight and butcherbirds warble to each other across the treetops. It is an alien world where everything fits together into a glorious pattern of birds and trees, curling shapes and persistent calls, grasses shifting in the breeze. It all fits—magically complementing each part like a network built to withstand almost whatever humanity hurls at it. Whatever overload of carbon and pesticide and population, until it topples. Becomes extinct. And then there is me, creating my own kind of extinction—unable to seek solace from my distant brother and mother. I am already fading, disappearing from the world and my own human identity. Perhaps I am gone already. And Asta, she occupies this space with me—a creation completely outside this time. A person extinct for reasons we don't really know. We are toppling through the abyss, hand in hand. How can I let go of her?

Dry leaves shift and crack on the ground. I stand quickly, grab her hand and pull her onto the tricycle. A prickle of fear veils my back and neck and I walk quickly to the car, barrelling down the road until the safety of our driveway is in view.

FOUR

The samphire beds form a saline marsh, wide and flat, punctuated by the twisted, pale remains of paperbark trees. It is hot, even though it is still early. We do nothing about me going away but I resolve to spend more family time outside our house. We are riding our bikes along the causeway to the peninsula. Jake and Isak have taken the lead. Asta tramps along on her tricycle, having synchronised pedalling and steering after much practice, and Emmy stays with us, slowly weaving across the road. We go without helmets, in solidarity with Asta who will not fit any size. Our heads all equally vulnerable.

The estuary is a cul-de-sac here, fringed with the pink-tinted plants, hard and low and broken by geographical shapes of mud and brown water. To walk through it would be a treacherous and muddy experience, home no doubt to slithering things and sharp crustaceans. Caps of sand show through the water at low tide and stretched-long white egrets stalk with courageous toes. The slow ride allows us to watch the hunt, deliberate steps and long yellow beak deep in the ground, wrangling whatever creatures it extracts.

Emmy is sun-brown and salty-haired, the urban child that she was four years ago has been erased by days outdoors, and her ankles and knees seem to have stretched. I see myself as a young teenager, finding my way into each new town through its beach or river. She is lost in singing, winding a pattern on the road to match the repetitions of the chorus.

When we reach the peninsula, Isak and Jake wait by the picnic area, staking their claim on a bleached table. I lay out a cloth to mask white splats of guano and unpack several containers from our backpack. Emmy pours metal cups of cold water and we sit together, quietly eating. Muscles ticking from the ride.

Each coastal tree that rings this marshy bay is pale and lifeless, crisp with salt and sun. Yet the ibis gather in those desperate branches, moving in a mass from sky to limb to marshy shore in a pattern of feast and frenzy.

Asta doesn't cope well with the summer. Her face flushes and her skin dries and peels like dust. Her energy is low and by mid-morning she retreats inside to the air-conditioning, red and listless. I read her picture books or she pulls out the mixed box of crayons, pens and pencils leftover from each school year. She seems to mimic the other kids, scratching away at the paper with purpose, producing rows of lines and curves like writing, but doesn't form recognisable images like they might have done at the same age. Swirls her fingers through dobs of glitter glue.

She prefers the three-dimensional freedoms of play dough and will shove the pencils off the table edge and open the mixed-up colours of dough, forming them together into brownish lumps and blue-grey. Trouncing them with her heavy fingers, squeezing and churning them, her face lit and focused. 'Egg,' she tells me, wrestling the lump in two, and she grabs a stray apple core from the coffee table and shoves it inside the 'yolk'. 'Baby bir,' she grins at me, holding the lump at my eye level.

'Beautiful egg, Asta.' I kiss her bumped forehead and she lifts herself up, puts the egg under herself and gently lowers herself, careful not to squash it. She mimics the fluffing feathers of the broody hen, still and watching with as much concentration as the real thing.

At four years old, the other two were in kindergarten. I remember the sweet sorrow of those first days, leaving them behind to battle the world of teachers and children and survive as best they could. Proud of their first steps in the world of humanity—their ability to conform and learn the fundamentals of civilisation and education. With her, I cannot forget that we have limited days together. They lay one after the next in my orbit. It is up to me to civilise her and educate her, although it is she who educates me, draws me to conform to her own directives. Sometimes I look back at schoolwork the other two did in the first couple of years, but that dexterity and complexity is some way off for Asta. She is present in the world in ways I try to emulate—immersed in the act of being and experiencing the wonder of life. One day she will be a special kind of wise woman.

Some hot days I seek the air-conditioned freedom of driving and I put her in the front seat beside me, to watch and talk to her, while we venture out into the hills and farmlands and remnant forest. She is too big for a car seat now. Yet another tooth has been lost and the driving lets me think, dream up ways to leave with her. In summer the interior has a tinderbox quality, a dry gum leaf smell, chirping with insects.

Sometimes, while the kids are at school, we have travelled through the hills and out the other side to the wide expanse, dotted with roaming sheep and silent country towns. We just drive until lunchtime and then we stop somewhere for a picnic— at the base of a bridge to hide by a brown river or down a gravel track into shrunken bushland, crackling with reptiles. Secluded places, still without phone reception. I tell her what I know about trees and towns and birds and she sometimes repeats a word or two but there is a lot of silence. I play a game with her to see if we can go all day without speaking to anyone else at all. Even putting fuel in the car can be silent and automated if I choose the right place. Sometimes there is too much silence. And my mind wanders off to the past or the incomprehensible future or imaginings of my life unlived and now impossible. The curled-up foetus of what might have been floats across the windscreen. I test out the stretched distance between me and Emmy, Jake; between me and Isak. Cars are crying places and I drive weeping down escape routes to somewhere I don't know. Dead kangaroos reek and buzz at the side of the road.

On the way home she often sleeps and sometimes I dare to stop and buy some fruit or honey from a farmer's stall by the side of the road. Most have a money tin so no words are exchanged.

On one of those days we travelled far into the dead fields of harvested wheat and I saw a sign—*bichon puppys 4 sale*. I reversed and stared up the narrow gravel track trailing up the hill to a chaotic house surrounded by the shells of dead cars. Looked at Asta—'Dog, would you like a dog?'—she shook her two pigtails as if to say no, so I drove off. But I kept thinking about the dog. That morning I was irritated, unsettled inside because an autumn chill was in the air and they all wanted long pants but Asta's don't fit her anymore. Reminders constantly of her growing bigger. Emmy had done Asta's hair. As we drove, she kept shaking the pigtails from side to side and I started to notice they were touching her face. Back and forth, she flicked them across her cheeks, smiling at the sensation and eventually I realised she didn't say no, so after our picnic lunch, in a silent stand of trees down an old forestry track, I drove quickly back to the sign, stopped and looked again at the crazy house. Braced myself to interact with the puppy owner, to say no perhaps, even after viewing the little dog, raking my mind for reasons why and why not. This was the dog, after all, that Dimitra had recommended I get in some past conversation. Few cars passed this way and I decided to risk the visit so I put Asta's sunglasses on her and dragged her hat over the pigtails, which made her head appear even more peculiar.

The yard was littered with tractor tyres, rusting machinery and large bird cages devoid of birds, and at our approach there was a lot of yapping and a dirty white dog danced on its back feet at the car. The owner, a large, bearded man in a grubby T-shirt, looked a little askew as if he'd just woken.

'We've come about the puppies.' He squinted in the white afternoon sun, reflected off a silver shed, and lumbered to the steps telling me to come in and bring my little one, the dogs were inside with his missus. A trellis weighted with shrunken passionfruit, old roses pushing out orange bells from the dead bloom. A disused harvester.

'Julia!' he yelled, but she was already standing at the flyscreen door, surrounded by white fur leaping up at the shredded wire, which obviously was not going to screen out anything.

I held Asta's hand—not used to strangers, she tucked in tight to me—and we went inside. The air was sticky-sharp with urine and cigarette smoke and four little dogs skittered and slipped amid sodden newspaper.

''Scuse the mess,' she said, but I could see this was a lifestyle—two reclining chairs and a huge screen filled the front room and coffee tables were layered with cups, wrappers, dog treats and a smeary phone. 'You want to cuddle a puppy?' she asked Asta, leaning down to her eye level and scooping up the nearest, smallest one. She placed it in her arms, frowning a little and glancing at me, obviously not sharing the question she wanted to ask.

Asta held the puppy carefully, cradling it as if it were a chicken, and Julia scooped up a second, larger puppy—'One for Mum.' She smiled and dumped the little dog in my hands. It crawled up my chest, laying itself out flat against me, its little head up near my ear and straight away I felt that little gut pull, the knowing feeling that told me it was right. I have not felt that warm happiness that spreads through in a long time so I kept the little dog right where it was, transferred the money on my phone right then, assured by Julia that he was fully immunised.

Despite myself, I could not stop smiling and chatted more to Julia than I had to anyone, except Isak and the kids, in a long time. She told me stories of the mother dog sleeping on her bed and how she eats too much cheese and steals the eggs if she gets into the chookhouse. All the while, Asta got more at ease and sat low on her haunches, puppies hopping up at her, dancing on their hind legs as she ruffled their heads, smiling wide. I could see Julia stealing glances at Asta, eyes lingering, and she passed comment on her good set of choppers and her very special sunnies. As we were leaving she said she had something to give my little girl and disappeared into the back of the house for a few minutes. I took a quick pic of the puppy and sent it to Isak at work—a little proud that I had broken out, done this and hoping for his approval. She returned with a doll and handed it straight to Asta. I recognised the troll doll from some old kid's movie—its faded pink hair and brown body—and I thanked her and went back to the car, the puppy in half a cardboard banana box, lined with a threadbare towel.

The puppy yapped a little on the drive home but fell asleep eventually in the footwell under Asta, curled in the towel. The doll lay on her lap, her wide little hand on its bare belly. A little anger brewed in me about the doll and as I took in its features I saw the reason, driving back through Collie and down the hills of the scarp towards the coast and home. I could see the wide nose and the arched ridges above the eyes—the stocky stature.

'Give me that,' I said to Asta and snatched it, quickly lowering the window and tossing it with all my might into the wide, black road. Impulsive, angry tears rose up and I drove too fast while Asta's face fell and she called out in her rare, wild sadness. Moaning high and loud and slapping her thighs where the doll had lain, slapping and slapping until I pulled over in a truck bay. The puppy cowered at the corner of the box, a wet patch on the towel. Staring out at the horizon, the ocean in the distance, I wept. Spilling out the swallowed frustration and loneliness, my loss and fear and all those life unlived things that driving lets loose. Her wailing fuelled me and I sobbed until my throat was raw. But she did not stop. Her face red and twisted, calling in her high, husky voice—'Babee, babee, babee'.

Her wailing escorted me to my darkness and I realised the depth of my cruelty—the selfishness that drove me to take away her baby, how I have calcified my heart and allowed what I imagine others will think to seep in and break away the love I have told myself I give to my children, especially Asta. My own lost baby, not beating. And I turned the car sharply, spraying stones in my wake which clattered on the metal, wild and reckless up the hill until I spotted the little doll, skewed across a double white line on a wide, hillside curve. I flung the car into the gravel gutter of the road and opened the door into the wind of a passing log-truck, spraying a curse of splinters in its wake, slammed and locked it so she and the puppy couldn't get out. Heat and wind, roaring traffic both ways, the doll shifted in their wake, almost crushed by a dozen hurtling tyres but my raw throat spurred my courage and I ran, inflamed, retrieving the troll. Asta took the doll back quickly into her tight grip, kissed my shaking hand. The puppy climbed up her leg, sniffed the doll and trotted over the transmission stick onto me, climbed up and licked at my face, mopping up the salty tears.

I know this dog is for me and the doll is for Asta.

We drove into the yard a few minutes after the kids had arrived home from school and they were sitting on the back patio, sagging and hot—Emmy on her phone, which she dropped on the table immediately when she saw the puppy. Her face alight with joy, commending me on what a great thing I have done, getting us a dog. Then she stopped.

'Is he Asta's dog?' She contained her emotion, still and controlled.

'No, sweetheart. He's our dog.' And I told her to choose a name, something that Asta could manage. I had not seen this energy in my children for months, except for soccer and netball. Guilt and happiness blended like a murky river. She named him Tayto, after the Irish chips we get sometimes and because his belly is round and white like a potato, and she and Jake set up a playpen for him on the patio, donating some stuffed toys, including an oversized unicorn, which has become his bed. He lays cradled in its rainbow legs now, having chewed its hoof until the fluff came out, tearing chunks off it and making a huge mess. To look at him gives me hope that I might do better in life.

Isak smiled about the dog and said he'd have preferred something bigger but Tayto trails around his feet as he cooks at the barbecue and he is soon won over. He tells me I've done well and draws me into his arms in the smoke of the barbecue. In his smile are newly etched lines. It is so long since he has shown me any affection that I study his face.

'What?' He looks down at me, holding me closer.

'Nothing.' I sigh, the little dog clambering over our feet. Lured by the smell of fresh meat.

'I'm glad you're getting out, Stace. Where did you get him?'

I don't tell him quite how far I have driven out into the landscape. Don't want to tell him what I think of, how I dream up places to hide and ways I might run with her.

I never mention the doll either, but after dinner, when the kids are in bed he asks, 'Where did the troll doll come from?'

'The dog lady,' I tell him, avoiding elaborating. I know he thinks it—that it looks a bit like Asta. We sit together in silence for a few minutes then he pulls out his phone, taps away with his head bowed. I go inside to sort out the dishes, put them on to wash and when I go back out he has uncovered histories of Scandinavian trolls, images of squat figures with wide noses and brow ridges, broad mouths and shaggy hair, dressed in fur.

He cocks his head. 'Looks a bit like her, you know. Don't get upset but I can see similarities.' He flicks to other images and shows me. 'Maybe . . .'

'Maybe what? It's just a stupid legend like fairies and leprechauns, Isak.' I grab his empty beer bottle, clean the table vigorously.

'I'm not saying she's a troll, just that maybe there were some of her folk that survived whatever wiped them out. You don't have to get so fucking defensive.' He combs at his hair with his fingers, it is visibly thinning, and takes a deep breath. 'I'm interested, Stacey, that's all. Asta is not only your business, she's mine too.'

'I don't hear you say that very often.'

'What do you expect from me really? I've given up so much for her, what else do I have to prove?' He pauses but I can't think of what to say. I stand in front of him, sponge in my hand. I blink back tears—the wound still seeping from the drive home.

He waits, his eyes shiny. Mosquitos buzz around the light, swirling like a coming storm.

'I'm trying to do better,' I tell him. I know I've let him down, let the kids down. 'That's why I got the puppy.' I try to sell him on my efforts, explain how I broke out of my comfort zone, took Asta inside their house. He nods and smiles at my description of the house.

He takes my wet hand and we go inside to bed but the puppy cries too much and I let him in, put the unicorn on the floor for him to sleep on. In the night he leaps up on our bed and sleeps by our feet.

•

Whether I like it or not, Emmy is having Milly for a sleepover and her Nanny Ray is dropping them off after netball. I try to overcome my anxiety about it by cleaning and take Asta for a long ride on her bike to, hopefully, tire her out so she sleeps this afternoon. Naps are really not common for her now but she often rests inside in the heat of the day, watching the television. Emmy dressed the troll in some of her doll's clothes and has given Asta a stroller for it and a few other bits and pieces. Asta has taken to dragging it out into the chicken pen and under the trees to the ramshackle of treetop platforms and shelters where the kids play. Isak has hung a swing and rope from the trees for Jake to climb up to a high platform but getting there involves too much agility for Asta, for now at least. She prefers the hollow tree and stays out there with the doll for company. Tayto follows me or sleeps beside Asta if she is inside.

When Nanny Ray comes with Milly and Emmy after school, he yaps incessantly until they are in sight. Emmy leads the way with Milly, dragging an extra bag and pillow for a sleepover. I greet them on the patio, holding the dog to calm him down. The girls both pat him and coo over his cuteness then disappear inside to snack and settle in.

'I made muffins,' I call. Conscious of being judged on my parenting. I feel Nanny Ray's suspicion on me but her gaze is not searching, just besotted with Tayto. I push myself, thinking of Isak telling me not to avoid her; that she's a nice woman who has Emmy to stay with Milly so I shouldn't offend her too much. 'Would you like a cup of tea?'

She smiles. 'I'd love one, Stacey.' And I hand her the dog, who wiggles as she fusses over him, telling him what a cute little potato he is, in low infantile tones. I leave her outside and wait for the kettle, warm a couple of muffins. As it boils, she appears in the kitchen, still with Tayto, who has settled into a cuddle. I had meant for her to stay outside but she is obviously the kind of person to make herself at home. 'Milly loves coming here.

Tells us all the time about your beautiful property. It's good for the kids to have that space.'

My mother always said that when we moved. 'That's nice to hear,' I tell her. 'I grew up in the country and so did Isak.'

'You're lucky,' she says. Her eagle eyes—I wonder what she thinks. Clicking over property values and Isak's ordinary income. She might assume inheritance.

'Shall we go outside?' I take a tray with the tea and muffins and lead the way. 'Asta is resting and I don't want to wake her.'

'She still has a nap?'

'We had a big walk,' I tell her, putting the tray out on the patio. She keeps hold of my dog and starts telling me the girls' excited conversation in the car about the puppy. 'It's good for Emmy, you know. At her age, dogs are the best thing.' I have no idea what she means but her eyes are full of knowing. She continues with a tale of her own daughter, who was obsessed with her little sister and fussed over her to the point of oppression until she, Nanny Ray, got her a dog, and from then on the obsession was transferred off the sister.

'Do you think Emmy is obsessed with her sister?'

She shakes her head. No, no, no, she says.

'Some girls have a natural maternal instinct and I think Em needs to nurture something.'

I can't help but feel a little annoyed at her authoritative knowledge of my daughter. Maybe it's an age thing, or my unfamiliarity with socialising. I try to dismiss the feeling and distract her with the muffin. She comments on how quiet it is here and I tell her there are a lot of birds.

'And chickens,' she says. Asking how many and what kind.

I explain about the Dorkings being an old Roman breed and unwittingly offer her a visit with them. She puts Tayto in his playpen, brings her tea and we wander up the yard to the chooks.

'Do you have a dog?' I ask and relax a little, realising she is just an ordinary woman, sprawled around the middle like most women her age, hair pruned short and close. Practical.

'I have two spaniels—Billy and Bobby.' She smiles and pulls her phone from her pocket, calling up a photo of them at the beach, one wet and the other sitting proud and safe on the sand. 'I walk them every day. Keeps us all fit.'

'You seem pretty fit to me,' I offer, knowing that compliments are often good for relationships.

'Well I should be too; between them and running around after the grandkids.' She laughs. 'Parents these days all work and I don't know how they'd manage without me doing this kind of thing for them. You do a great thing staying home with your children.'

I open the gate and lead her into the pen, roosters and hens rushing to greet us, hugging our ankles like a ruffle. I go straight to the food bin and they flurry at the tossed grains, tapping at the ground like various metronomes. One hen comes close and I pick her up, handing her some extra grains. She pecks from my hand.

Nanny Ray rubs the hen's head but she keeps eating. 'This is Asta's favourite chicken,' I tell her. 'I call her Edna.'

'Sweet,' I hand her the hen and some grain. 'Gee, she's very tame.' Edna empties the hand and stays looking at the other chickens with disdain. 'I bet she gets dragged about all over the garden, does she?'

'Yes, out in the pram and up in the treehouses but she comes home every night.'

Nanny Ray leads us out of the pen and we walk to the trees where the kids play. Toys, cups, bits of rope and rocks, things from the beach are all littered on the ground. Old saucepans and kitchen things, filled with sand and dead flowers, leaves and feathers. I apologise for the mess, but she is dismissive.

'It's good for them,' she tells me. The freedom. 'You'll miss your little one when she goes to school. Such a precious time.' She nods and I feel that little sick that rises when I worry about being discovered. Think of Isak, what he would say—better to say something about her than leave it.

'She won't be at school,' I tell her, tipping the cold bit of tea into the dirt, where it sits like a grey pond. 'She's not up to it. I don't know if Emmy's told you about her sister.' I leave it there, hoping that politeness will allow that space to remain unfilled.

'No, she hasn't.'

I feel her eagle eyes and we turn to the house.

'I did suspect something though, what is it,' she offers, 'some kind of autism spectrum?' She is not too polite.

I am armed and prepared. 'It's a genetic disorder, very rare.' I lie—teetering like first steps. 'You might like to think of it a bit like Down's syndrome but there is no prenatal screening for it, and we don't know yet how much she can and can't do. It's a wait and see kind of thing.' I know it sounds rehearsed.

'She could still go to school,' and she rattles off some examples of local opportunities and institutions. I pretend to listen and lead her to the house.

The girls have woken Asta and they are all sitting in a huddle with dolls and a pile of baby stuff, even though they have long outgrown this kind of play. Asta's doll is centre stage, dressed in a crazy array of accessories, and they are prattling in American accents about fashion. Asta is enchanted, glasses off and watching every move they make when we walk in, Nanny Ray behind me. I feel that sharp fright like a bolt through me and turn quickly, ushering her outside. I feel myself flush, concocting a quick excuse about not wanting to disturb their game.

'Milly! I'll just say goodbye then.' She looks suspicious and a little offended, takes the girl out onto the patio and hugs her close, obviously speaking low and soft to make sure it's all okay. 'I'll pick her up Sunday,' she tells me, sending her back into the house and I walk her to the car. She closes the door, winds down the window and tells me it was lovely to chat with me, then pauses, clears her throat and looks at my house. 'I can see that you're ashamed of your little Asta,' she says, avoiding my eyes. 'I can assure you I am not judgemental and if you need to talk to someone about it you are welcome to give me a call.' She looks up to me, the setting sun shining right in her eyes. I could stand to shield her eyes but I don't. Something in that cruelty makes me feel free.

'Thanks.' I am not ashamed of Asta. I could say it but I don't—I am ashamed, but of myself, not Asta.

FIVE

Early in the morning, Isak starts his chainsaw. It whines for hours, creating a constant sonorous anxiety for Asta, which I try to break for a while by taking him a cold drink. She will not come outside because of the noise and she has hidden herself in a play tent in her room, fussing over her doll, Tayto asleep on her bed.

Isak puts the savage thing down on the ground, its teeth spattered with the red core of the tree, and drinks, face murky with sweat and sawdust but delighted at the massive task. He has felled a dead tree, slicing through the pale grey skeleton into the dark rosy interior to create large discs and a pile of skewed branches which he heaps up to burn. He and Jake roll the discs into the play area and make a circle of picnic seats then return to cutting up the tree.

Some of the trees just die—leaves losing their colour quickly until they drop, textured bark giving way to a pale, smooth core of bare branches, twisting into desperate shapes beckoning the sky for rain. And when it comes, the long-awaited downpour of large drops arrives like inkblots. The weight of them marks the ground and pools on the surface, slowly soaking into it. Within days, the dormant earth is green and seeking more. Sometimes it comes and the grass grows tall, requires slashing. We talk of getting a few sheep, then don't bother because it's too much work. Sometimes the sky returns to a blinding blue and the first sprouts of grass wither back into the sand without dropping seed. I wonder, when this happens, how many false starts it will take before no seed remains and the greening doesn't begin. How many of our trees will die and how many will sprout? It's a fine balance and it seems to be leaning askew. Death triumphant.

It is late autumn so we are permitted to burn. In the evening, Isak pours petrol on the branches and throws in a match. It booms and flashes blue, then takes hold on the wood. Asta and Emmy wrap potatoes in foil and, after the initial rage of the fire, we place them in the orange coals and roast them for dinner. Isak threads thick sausages onto a curved piece of wire hanging over the glowing remains, smiling widely and telling the kids how his uncle always cooks on campfires back home. The picture is his idyll, tinged with love and melancholy. Afterwards, he is quiet and the fat of the sausages falls and hisses.

'You could go if you want to,' I tell him, knowing well enough that he is afraid to leave me alone. 'Take Emmy and Jake.' Though, if they went with him, perhaps he would feel so liberated of me he would not return at all.

'No, Stace, it's not fair. I can't leave you here on your own.' He pokes at the sausages with a knife, checking on their readiness and avoids eye contact. He is a good man.

'You want to.' I sit Asta on my lap, smoke drifting over us. I love the smell of wood-smoke and she is warm, tucked close. 'We'd be fine—Tayto can look after us.'

He laughs. 'I don't think that furball can help.' I watch his longing as he pokes at the fire, beer in one hand and eyes focused on the flames, which quiver with memories for him. I want to tell him I'm sorry but the words don't come, instead he drifts to his own places and I cling to Asta, who is now too heavy to sit on my lap. My legs ache but I suffer it anyway. When the sausages and potatoes are ready, she springs off me, excited by the food and the fire.

In the morning it is all reduced to a circle of white ash, still smoking slightly. The burned patch doesn't generate any grass and Asta often returns to it to dig in the ash. Weeks later, she still comes into the house smelling of smoke.

.

Occasionally I return to the new-look website of Ärva-LifeBLOOD® to seek out some guidance but there is really nothing new there. Even though Dimitra was cold, she offered some support, but I'm afraid of this new, detached company even more than I was of the one that patrolled our lives for the first year. I record Asta's milestones, her height and weight, send it every half year via email to Jeff. There is something frightening about the way they have left us. Though I'm not sure I would like it better if they hadn't. Then he emails me to arrange a video chat—tonight with Isak when the kids have gone to bed.

By eight-thirty Jake is busy with a game and Emmy has disappeared to her room. Asta is asleep and Isak sends Jeff a message to say we are available. Immediately the call comes. He barely asks how we are and says he will get 'straight to the point'. Anxiety prickles my skin all over, I can barely breathe.

'Can the two of you bring Asta up here next week to the transplant clinic? Are there any commitments that might get in the way of that?'

Isak shakes his head for us. Looks grave.

'I need you to leave her with us for a day so we can harvest some cells from her for a patient. Young girl born with a congenital heart problem. You see it's rather urgent and this is one of the last resorts.' He looks at us then, trying to elicit some empathy, I think.

'What does that involve exactly?' Isak holds my hand, sits closer. Knows the pound of my heart.

'Well we have some of the girl's sister's heart cells and we're going to sequence them alongside Asta's to give her a stronger organ. We'll grow the heart and get it functioning then do the transplant. It's ground-breaking stuff.' He shifts and sniffs. 'Asta will be under anaesthetic and we'll go in and harvest some cells from her heart under CT scan. Very low risk, non-invasive.'

I am cold and hot, panic rises.

Jeff can see me in the webcam. 'Don't worry, Stacey. I have substantial investment in her wellbeing too.' Turns from me. 'Isak, you will need a day off work. Better make it two just in case. We've booked you a hotel in the city and you can bring the kids. Make it a holiday.' He smiles, his sparkle-eyed smile. He charmed me once but now it's strange and cruel.

'It's no holiday, mate,' says Isak. 'Look at her, she's already crazy with worry.'

I jab him with my elbow and whisper, 'Don't say that.'

Jeff laughs a little, raises his eyebrows.

'You need a holiday, Stacey, I said that last time I saw you. Please, please—don't worry. She'll be fine. The parents have raised money to have this done privately. The girl's life depends on it and it means a lot for the company and our project. The costs to create children like Asta have been huge and there have been very few returns yet.' This is a return—a piece of her heart.

Soon, the call ends and he is gone.

Isak gets us both a glass of red wine from the kitchen. I lay on the bed and cry.

'I could go if you would prefer that.' He sits beside me, handing me the glass so I sit up. 'You can stay here with Emmy and Jake.' The wine is rich and soothing. 'We'll go and come back and you don't need to put yourself through it.'

'I'm sure you care about her less than I do,' I snap at him.

He raises a hand as if to stop me. 'Don't go there, please. You know well enough that I love her but I think I'm more balanced about it and what she means to our family.' I feel ready to explode but what I might say would be too toxic. I take the wine and walk silently into the garden. The ground is damp with dew and I walk into the unlit places under the trees and sit alone in the circle of cut logs. Wish myself into the rich dark, above the trees and away.

·

In the end he takes her there alone. Firm and aggressive with me, he draws up a shield. Leaves with her in the front seat as I do when I go driving.

I tidy the shed while he's away; assess the condition of the camping gear and fill the gas bottle. It's always good for an emergency or an escape.

A humid storm weights the air and rampant squawks of cockatoos in the distance draw closer. They gather in the treetops late in the day, dropping green sprays of leaves and mangled gumnuts. More come and, instead of the squawks and echoes across the treetops, they synchronise into a thrum, which contracts the thick air with its rhythm. I stand under the trees, watching small teams of red-tails as they shift from one branch to another, walking up the limbs and being out-ranked by others. I start to count them and stop at about sixty, though there are more camouflaged amid the trees. In the dense evening, their chorus like a unified breath. I long for that unity, that Asta and I could be part of something that chants with one voice, one purpose. At an invisible cue, several groups depart at different angles and head inland.

Isak's car pulls up in the driveway and Asta jumps out, runs across the yard to me. She clings to me, points to a tiny plaster on her chest.

'See, she's fine. Just a tiny stitch.' He looks in my eyes, seeking some sign of things being well between us.

Curses pass through my thoughts—authoritarian, bully—but I stop myself. Asta pulls at my hand and we return to the house as more large raindrops resonate on the patio roof, beating ever faster into a crescendo. Stop just as suddenly as they began. He seems pleased that I tidied up the camping gear and takes it as a sign of forgiveness.

.

One day when he comes home from work, Isak stares at me with fresh eyes and holds me close to him so that I wonder what has happened in his time away that day. He kisses me carefully and runs his fingers through the grey hair gathering at my temples, looks sad.

'I do love you, I'm sorry I upset you.'

There are, surely, women at the plant where he works—women who are younger and more attentive to their appearance, have more interesting lives and witty things to say.

'I understand.' Perhaps I do partly. 'It's tough love.' Something my mother said when I complained about her enforcements.

I never imagined it would be like this. My reclusive life takes me further from the world where he dwells, where Emmy and Jake will step further away with each passing year. Where Asta will be taken from me.

SIX

After a full, red moon last night, the tide has receded bringing to the surface all manner of tangled weed. Sandbars permeate the skin of the estuary like bands of scar tissue. This revelation brings out the stalking egrets, solitary hunters on divergent paths working their way through the sea grasses, sifting out tiny fish. There are more than I have ever seen but they are a scattered community, slow and spare across the expanse. In patches the water is so still it is reflective, smooth as glass, in others it is yellow with the proximity of sand. The stubs of fence posts mark out a submarine boundary, their dark wood soft with rot and slowly falling away. The egrets prefer the ruffled surface where fine underwater foliage shifts with the movement of the water.

I have driven to the long jetty, a remnant of industrial shame, when toxic sludge was piped out into the dunes, settling and poisoning the peninsula. The structure has been reworked into a long rocky walkway, piercing into the middle of the water, and now provides a haven for cormorants, its wake moulding a sheltered bay. Tayto pulls on his lead, desperate to bring on the exodus of the birds but he is no match for Asta, whose firm grip is immovable. He pulls and gasps but I tell her to keep him at her side, focusing her attention on training him, telling him to 'heel'. The cormorants twist their heads, agile as darts, do their best to ignore us, but their well-trained eyes don't allow us too close. They rise and shift as we pass.

At the end of the jetty is a well-used deck spattered with white guano and I reward Asta with a rest and a drink, sitting with her on the grey wood and laying out a picnic snack. A cormorant is perched at the opposite corner, eyeing a seagull, which draws slowly closer, and we watch the stand-off between the two, competing for the high perch. It's like the sleeping chickens, I tell Asta. Whichever one sleeps at the highest spot is the boss chook. The cormorant holds its ground against the seagull, which veers off with the breeze.

The air is ripe with brine and weed and all the living and dead brought to the surface at ebb tide. The dog holds his nose high and twitching. He and Asta both stop and watch the cormorant's head twist, its wings held aloft, their raggedy black edges moving in the wind. There is a hold in the air and all of them are poised, waiting, while I seem to be missing out. The dark webs of the cormorant's feet bend around the wood of the jetty, its eyes wild. Then with the current of air, it lifts and dashes into the water, narrowed as a needle. Tayto and Asta jerk around in unison, watching it emerge again, water beading off its black neck. A visible lump in its throat. I wonder what she sees—what level of detail, of movement and heat beyond my vision.

'Duck,' she says when I ask her. 'Col-duck' when I press further and she narrows her hand into a point, darting it down like the cormorant piercing the water. There is nothing dart-like or narrow about her hand. It is more like a mitt. If she had the opportunity to play sport she would be a good catcher with her sharp eye and big hands. I pack our picnic and lead the dog back along the jetty. He is slower now, tired from pulling and the thrill of birds, and lopes along at a steady beat. Asta skips ahead with the wind in her hair, stooping sometimes to collect feathers, which she holds in the breeze, letting them go and watching their journey in the air, their drop into the water. Halfway back to the car she stops and looks north towards home.

'Ma!' She points out into the water. I peer out and see nothing, walking closer to her side. 'Fish, Mumma.'

'Where?' And we wait, silent and watching the surface.

'Dere,' she points. And seconds later, they appear in the distance—two dolphins trailing each other. I think she saw them through the water. As they come closer, she smiles widely and grabs my hand but the dolphins soon alter their course back to deeper water. She watches the place where they were long after they have gone and I explain to her that they are not fish, but dolphins. Dol-fins. Waiting for her to repeat. Her lips are red and wet in the wind and her mouth open, showing the monuments of new teeth. I touch her shoulder—'Dol-fins, Asta.' And she looks around at me.

'Dol-fin,' she parrots. And I feel a small victory. 'Not fish,' she adds. Reminding me she has been listening. I kiss her hand and lead her back to the car, past an elderly couple walking their dog.

Time is slow as tar some days, dripping through each day in stretched moments of silence. It is only when I look at Jake's lengthening feet, growing knobbly with the approach of his teens, or hang young-girl bras on the line that I am reminded of its relentless progress. Sometimes things seem changeless as if it will just go on and on and sometimes it seems to dart by me, over before it began. Even Asta is changing before my eyes, leaving behind the cute little toddler that she was and becoming someone of her own. Since the heart cell donation, one nerve of her has been extracted from my flesh. It is me that gave the cells.

.

On Saturday Isak sets his alarm and takes Jake to play cricket down in Busselton. I have never seen one of the matches but Isak sits in the car or under a tree for several hours watching the boys in a slow and concentrated stand-off with the other team. He makes breakfast for Asta and I stay in bed a while. When I wake she is having a second breakfast with Emmy, who is laughing at something on her screen. I make tea and sit with them on the couch.

'Dad left you a note,' Emmy tells me, pulling a folded paper out from under Asta's plate.

Your mum rang!! Told her you'd call back. I fold the note, sigh and Emmy looks at me. 'I haven't seen her since I was eight you know.'

I nod, acknowledging that it's a long time.

'And she's never met Asta.' She eyes me with her knowing look. Accusing.

'I have invited her over here,' I lie. 'She always has something on, she's very busy.' I tidy the dishes, busy myself in the kitchen to avoid the call. Emmy lurks around with a tea towel, helping a little but her presence is force. I send her to feed the chickens with Asta and find the number while they are outside. Hands damp.

She answers quickly, her hello unusually soft. 'Did Isak tell you the news?' Her style, always a little dramatic; she cried wolf to me so often I can no longer tell—'It's Marco, darling, he's gone.' On the quiet line I can hear the chatter of caged birds.

'I'm sorry to hear that, Mum,' I concede to her. 'How are you?'

'Obviously not good, love.' Despite myself, tears come as she details his long struggle, the remission and the different treatments she sought for him.

'He was a good man,' I tell her, meaning every word. 'He was good to me, when we were always fighting.' He cooked, calm and rocking his hips in the breezy kitchen, smells of fresh basil and home-grown tomatoes. Peaches from his garden remain the best fruit I have ever had. Despite her wandering, she always returned to him—his was her only fixed address.

As I'm ending the call the girls come back inside and Emmy catches me in time to take the phone. She wanders into her bedroom, talking in low tones, probably about me. Perhaps I should have offered to go to Mum's but I don't know how I'd leave Asta. I know Isak pines for his mother but I never had that kind of bond.

When Emmy finally hands the phone back to me she announces, 'I invited her over,' turns and walks back to her room. Despite not having spent much time with my mother, she has somehow adopted this habit of drop-turn-run with information and it incites me to follow, a pattern worn into the soles of my shoes since childhood. I resist and concede, as I have done so many times before. Find her sorting schoolwork on her bed, unsurprised when I arrive.

'She's coming?' I wait, knowing Emmy has the power.

'Maybe.' She tells me something about money coming to my mother from Marco's estate.

·

Two weeks later, Isak is driving to Perth to collect her from the airport and Emmy takes the day off school to go with him. I spend the day weeding both the vegetable garden, and the soft plastics and pharmaceutical medicines from our house. Hiding the evidence, he reminds me, lifting his eyebrows with a mischief I rarely see now. His crooked smile appearing again through layers of silt.

They return home in the depth of night, Emmy staggering straight to bed, a wide cloth bag of presents under her wing. I am thankful to greet Mum with Asta asleep. To get those moments in first—the long hug, soft and oil-scented. I breathe it deep. 'Rose and sandalwood, for grief,' she whispers, stepping back to look at me, her smile a little more folded into her face than it was. I wonder how she was such an overpowering figure. Just a little lady, her long hair growing fine and pale, still trailing down her back. Her dress a little more draped and layered than it was once.

Isak ferries in several bags and lodges her in my sewing room, which I have transformed for her stay. I make chamomile tea in my best cups and sit beside her on the couch, our slow and soft conversation filling in the details of Marco's sickness and her journey through alternative treatments. Photos of their long holiday during his remission then him slowly withering. There is no doubt she has suffered and it has worn down her fire. She has inherited his lovely cottage in the mountains, so he will keep her in one spot now, she jokes, even from beyond the grave. Despite myself, I am softening to her presence, becalmed with sadness. In the early hours of morning, I show her to her bed, which I have covered in a beautiful batik bedspread she sent me years ago.

'I have something for you from him,' she says, opening a small suitcase and extracting a wooden jewellery box. 'He left this to you. He said you loved it when you were a kid and because he hasn't got any kids that he knows of, he wanted you to pass it down in our family.' I know what it is immediately and I sting with tears. I take it, thanking her. She looks intensely at me as if trying to read my reaction, wanting me to love him, to show her the signs of forgiveness. I am grateful she is here, so I crack the lid. Inside is a bronze bowl, very old. And a couple of dark bones, that might be from a finger or a toe. His mother had brought it here on the ship from Italy in the sixties. Marco told me his grandfather and uncles were digging the foundations of a house and dug up a very ancient grave—they were amazed at the size of the bones and thought the person must have been very strong. Now, the small knobbly bones take on a whole new meaning and I wonder how ancient they really are. My own hands tingle as I hold them again, stroking one of the fingerbone's gentle curve as I did when I was younger.

.

I wake a little late. In the living room, Mum is on the couch in a silk dressing-gown with Asta under one arm and Emmy snuggled into her on the other side. A jolt of fear, anxiety. I force it down, try to normalise—offer to make tea—but her look pierces me. She holds my gaze and strokes Asta's head, who smiles up at her and calls, 'Ma! Nanna come.' And grins with her huge teeth, eyes liquid and wide. As she grows, she looks so different it is impossible to pretend that she is a normal child. She lobs herself onto the floor, picking up two felt fairies and a rainbow unicorn. 'Mine babees,' she says, pushing them out at me. 'Nanna give dem me.' She looks back to my mother. There is no fear in Asta and the two of them gaze at each other with a strange intensity, holding it for too long.

'Where's Dad?'

'Shed,' says Jake, 'cleaning up the kayaks and stuff so we can take Nanna out.' I retreat to the kitchen and she follows me quickly.

'So . . .' She pauses dramatically waiting for my response. But I put the kettle on and avoid her eyes, accidentally look at the droop of her breast in the low-cut nightie. 'Why didn't you tell me? I wondered why I only got photos where I couldn't see her properly.'

'I didn't know what to tell you.' I try to stop the anxiety but my hands are shaky and I can't keep all the tea leaves on the spoon. She takes over, making a pot and rinsing cups, shaking her head and telling me that I can share anything with her and I know very well how open-minded she is. Nobody in the world would be less judgemental.

'I know,' I tell her over and over, unexpected tears spiking in my sinuses. But I don't think she'd understand if I told her the truth and I don't know what the consequences would be. Perhaps there is nothing worse than what is to come anyway? Either way I will lose her.

'I could have helped you. All this time and I could have been here for you.' Her dressing-gown gapes, showing her sun-ravaged skin.

'You were with Marco,' I excuse her but she insists that I have always been her priority, though for me this has never been evidenced in her behaviour.

'He needed you more.'

'Look, sweetheart, I know I've been absent for you a lot but this is big life stuff to deal with, having a child with a disability. What exactly is wrong with her?'

I bumble around, over-complicating the genetic disorder thing, that it's not a disability and not giving her any clear answer. I know I sound like I don't know what I'm talking about. 'Ask Isak to explain it,' I conclude.

We take the tea to the table, where we can see the girls—Emmy's head in Asta's lap as they watch television. The comparison is not hard to draw—Asta's face is completely different from Emmy's.

'Whatever it is,' she sips her tea, 'she's absolutely beautiful. Those eyes.' She smiles and we fall into silence. I can hear her swallow, the crack of it retracing my steps to those mornings where she made me wait for her attention. How I longed for her sustained gaze, her encouraging words and curlicue philosophy but she kept me hungry. I am returning from far away, toes stretching towards the path we once trod, where I often trailed at arm's-length, while she was busy with other people. She casts me a steady stare and I can feel the pulse in the arch of my foot.

'So—' she raises her brows and whispers, 'whose is she?'

I jolt at her words, shake a little then breathe; breathe and remember her now in the harsh glare of reality, instead of the humbled replica I hoped she might be. She is not so different from the woman she was, happy to expose my raw childhood self and watch me squirm.

'Come on, be honest. The truth sets you free.' A favourite platitude. She wiggles her eyebrows up and down.

'She's ours, of course.' But I know this is not entirely true and I know she reads me like nobody else. She nods but I see in the curl of her lips she is not satisfied.

'This genetic thing is not in our family, so it must be in Isak's then. Have you asked them about it?'

When his mother's number appeared on my phone I never responded and now she only calls him, usually on weekends, their conversations in Afrikaans to exclude me. I mumble something about not seeing them for so long.

'I would have gone to the wedding, if you'd given me enough warning. I always wanted an excuse to go to the Kalahari.'

'It was very small. I didn't need you to worry about being there, Mum. It's expensive to fly there.'

'I would have gone anyway. I could have walked you down the aisle.'

'I didn't need you to give me away.' I wasn't hers to give but I don't think that's what she means.

'It's a stupid tradition anyway,' she says. A little hurt.

'Mum, it's years ago now and it doesn't matter.' But the concept isn't so obsolete.

'You met them all though, so you must have noticed if any of them are like Asta.'

I feel irritated by her persistence in driving me into conversations I never want to have and I want to walk away but I know that will only lead to more avid pursuit. I start to feel quite sick, leaving the tea to slowly chill while she sniffs around my raw wounds. I have to give her something, some scrap to distract her from the truth. Tayto comes to sit at my feet and the children feel a shift in the mood, scattering from their languid places on the couch.

'She wasn't conceived naturally, Mum.'

She sits back and waits for the rest of the story, lips parted. I'm not quite sure where I am headed after this first sentence so I relive the horrific miscarriage in detail, including the weeks of waiting for the natural onset of premature birth, when I knew there was no heartbeat. What that did to me and how it left me desolate and broken. How we tried to have another one but it just didn't happen. At the end of it I am in tears and she is too. I know her hunt will resume later, she will not be sated by my tears.

·

Isak often takes Jake and Emmy in the canoe or kayaks to the wide river which spills out into the estuary and they explore the narrow tributaries or skirt around the banks of the peninsula. I have taken Asta in the canoe a couple of times but she can get quite restless if she's confined for too long and her heavy step can easily unsteady the small craft. She has less sense of balance. It's stressful, even in the shallow water near our house, so I find excuses, none of which are satisfying to Isak. He just sighs and goes without us, a little crestfallen. Over the past year, since the heart cells, his enthusiasm has waned even more and the boats have gathered spiders in the shed. It is yet another site of erosion between us.

I have packed an extensive picnic and planned to wait on the shore if it all goes horribly wrong. Asked him to launch in a nice, quiet place with plenty of trees; I know he will read between my words and hear deserted, places to hide.

Now that she's a little older, Asta has a range of conventional sunglasses and several hats to choose from. I have mastered a wide-brimmed pattern and Emmy has braided her hair into two thick red ropes. Her solid legs make it difficult to wear shorts or pants that are not excessively long, so I have sewn some for her in rainbow colours, which she likes best. I have come to realise that her view of the colour spectrum is more nuanced than my own and that her love of rainbows is built on a vision that I can't imagine. Whenever they appear, she is transfixed by them. I have taught her the name of the colours to try and prompt her to tell me exactly what she sees but neither of us seem to have the words to share her insights—'more lellow, more pink'—the line between us is sketched in inexpressible tones.

Mum takes a special curiosity in Asta and sits beside her in the back of the car. Asta likes the attention from her 'Nanna' and does her best to hold a conversation and show her the treasures she collects, which she stores in various bags. I am watchful and wary but there is a part of me that has accepted the inevitability of exposure to my mother and I am relieved at the thought of sharing this, of unburdening all of my worries. The guilt and fear and grief. She is just too good at digging out the truth from me.

'Aren't you glad I invited her now?' In the passenger seat, Emmy is in tiny shorts and a bikini top. The outfit more revealing than Isak would normally allow.

'Yes, thanks Em.' And she is pleased that she has one up on me.

'I can see. You seem really cheered up, Mum.' I take her hand, long and bony like my own and hold it to my lips. Her eyes shine with tears. 'Love you, Mum,' she says.

'I love you too, Emmy darling.' And now I cry too. She has broken away from me, turned into an adult too young—just like I did. Unwittingly, I have recreated some of the distance I felt with my own mother and now it is too late. Too late to pull her back to childhood, to look after her. She has had to look after herself, and Jake, and sometimes me, evidently.

Isak pulls into a gravel track along the riverbank and I drive behind, down through braided paperbarks and thick reeds to a grassed picnic area, shaded with very old river-gums and she-oaks. This wide river trails down from the hills where I got Tayto and spills out into the estuary. It is slow and dark, slopping gently into clumps of reeds and small beaches. A few people fish along the bank, so we veer left to avoid them. I park under a tree and Isak reverses the trailer close to the water to launch the boats. He and Jake work together to untie and launch the canoe and two kayaks—both talking and laughing.

'They're so alike.' Mum catches me watching them and I nod, seeing in Jake the shadow of his father when we fell in love. It all seems so long ago now, almost a dream. Isak strides over to the car in an oversized T-shirt and board shorts, a zebra embroidered on his cap. One of his few remaining souvenirs of South Africa. I wonder that she sees any resemblance at all—he has changed so much. In him I see what I have done. He is in ruin, ruddy and fractured by stress and isolation. His rare smile seems desperate.

Taking Asta's hand, he says, 'Come on, sweetheart,' and whispers to her. She grins widely, lets him lead her to the canoe. Jake holds it stable and Isak supports Asta while she lobs herself over the side and perches on the front seat, one hand on each side. The boat rocks but she grips tightly, lips firmly pressed over her big teeth. It is not often I watch her so, and I notice the angle of her chin, tucked right back. She is so distinct now, and with her hair pulled into braids, the angle of her face is very unusual. The brow ridges firm and solid, hollowing into her large eyes, growing ever more faceted. They have shifted lately to a darker shade of blue, rimmed now with a darker line. Even the whites have a slight blue tint. She has a few freckles. I stand under a tree and watch her, while Mum and Emmy carry the picnic to the boats.

Isak smiles at my mother, holds out a hand to her and escorts her onto the canoe. 'Here you go, Sandra.' He passes her a paddle and she laughs, a little flirty. Emmy and I take the two-person kayak and Jake takes the other on his own, while Isak and my mother row the canoe and we head upriver, against the current. I am not used to paddling and Emmy laughs at my efforts to coordinate with her, passing comments on our meandering course. Isak slows to wait for us and I can see Mum has handed her paddle over to Asta, who pulls it deep through the water, wrenching it back and splashing Mum. The canoe rocks with her movements and Isak compensates, watching her closely.

Eventually Emmy and I find a rhythm. It feels good to do something with her, imagine how our relationship might have been as we paddle together, angling the kayak, pointing out a grey heron taking flight from a low paperbark tree hanging over the water. A tiny sandpiper drills into the riverbed. As we round a bend, Jake appears waiting at a fork in the river but Isak calls him back, heads for a wooden jetty on the other bank.

We lay out our picnic on the wide jetty. The kids sit in a row, legs hanging over the side to the water, eating and talking. Mum sits alongside, watching them, seems to drink them in as if they might disappear. I feel a little guilty for distancing us so much, she might have been good for them. I lay beside Isak in the shade and reach for his hand. He peers at me from under his cap, a little surprised.

'You okay?' he whispers. 'Out here.'

I nod, smile at him, and he squeezes my hand. He gestures towards my mother, 'She's mellowed.'

'I'm not so sure about that,' I whisper, thinking of our conversation over breakfast. I tell him that she thinks I had an affair because Asta looks so different.

He laughs. 'She would. Judging you by her own standards.'

I roll onto my side and look down at him. 'I want to tell her the truth.'

He lifts his cap and stares at me. 'You aren't allowed to.' We are silent and I lie flat again, watch the play of light in the dark, drooping needles of she-oak. The whip of a songbird, wide and pure, curls back and back until it fades. 'Why?' he asks into the air.

'I need someone else to talk to.' I tear up a little at the thought of my loneliness. So many long days of isolation. 'And she seems better. She's their grandmother, after all. If not her, then who?'

'I don't know what they'll do if they find out.'

'I don't give a fuck.'

'You say that now, but . . .' He sits up and so do I, watch the four of them perched on the other end of the jetty. Jake now holds a fishing line in the water. 'Things could get worse, Stacey.' His tone is ominous and he reaches for a slice of watermelon, spits the seeds at Emmy's bare back. She turns and scolds him. They laugh. So close. So bonded. I can't help but feel jealous. He is never playful with me anymore.

We row back down the river, faster now as the current helps us. Asta has begun to master the paddling and the canoe forges out, far ahead of us.

'She's like a little machine,' says Emmy as we struggle to keep up. I am exhausted and we lag further behind.

They wait in the distance, pulling the canoe up near the sun-bleached branches of a dead tree. Isak is pointing up at the top of it and as we get closer I can see a large nest, made of thick old wood. In the top, the head of a bird, its curved beak silhouetted against the sky. A brown and white sea eagle glides overhead, wings barely moving. It seems to soar, motionless, yet steers itself deftly to the nest, where it stands on the edge, the baby eagle looking up at it. Mum holds Asta's hand and they stand on the riverbank, both focused on the nest. It's a beautiful bird, but it's clearly nervous at the approach of our boats, its head rotating surveillance. Isak pushes the canoe back into the water and we follow his lead back to the car.

On the drive home we pass the long walkway where Asta and I have watched the cormorants. 'Dol-fin,' she calls, remembering that we have seen them here. 'Not fish, Nanna.'

I pull into the car park to show Mum and message Isak, who continues home. We sit in the car for a moment, windows down, and I spot the sea eagle, high above. Point. We are all transfixed as it glides on the air currents, barely moving. Then a flutter, quick and sharp it dives into the water, two thick sprays as the big bird plunges in, catches something and heads away, back towards the nest. So certain.

·

Mum borrows my car and goes down south to visit some of her old friends for a couple of days. Not Dad she tells me, she 'doesn't want to see that prick as long as I live'. On that we can agree. I do her washing, peg her long dresses on our line. They fly wide and spin in the wind. Asta sits on the grass, staring at the coloured dresses. 'Nanna gone,' she says when I ask her what she's doing. Tayto lies beside her and they stare at the airborne colours. The other kids are at school, Isak is at work and in the wake of their presence we both lapse into quiet sadness.

When Mum returns, the boot of my car is packed with gourmet produce and boxes of fresh fruit from orchards along the way. A case of red wine, several bottles of olive oil and a T-shirt for each of the kids. She has judged the sizes well, even Asta's, who walks about proudly in hers, even if it's a little long, and clasps Mum's hand with her vice-grip. They carry it all inside and I make us tea, wonder at her newfound affluence. Finally, she's free of living off the government, she tells me.

'All these years I've dodged them and played them, got caught and dodged again.' She had an alias when we were children and we were never allowed to mention it. Mail arrived to post offices for our fake mother. I used to be ashamed of it, knowing she was duping the government, that we lived on undeserved funds. *Your father never paid child support*, was always her justification. 'Now I'm independent, just in time to be an old woman.' A house, Marco's superannuation. These must be life-changing for her.

'It must be nice,' I encourage her.

'Well this place must have cost a packet.' She casts her arms from the patio around to include everything in our boundary. 'What happened? You two were always on the bones of your arses in that suburban hellhole. If you were so cashed up, you could at least have come to see me.'

273

My instinct is to lie, or try to evade her as much as possible, but I am silenced and I know I must tell her. She is the only one I can tell and I must tell somebody, even without Isak's approval.

I wonder how to approach such a monstrous revelation, how to slip it into casual conversation. I know that if I try too hard, like I have before, I will bumble it and sound awkward. But I can rely on my mother to pursue the secret she knows I am keeping and I have, after all, started the conversation. She is still sniffing the trail, seeking a truth unimaginable to any sensible person. I have long since abandoned any claim to be one of those.

'The property was compensation.' My hands are hot and I put the cup on the table, wipe them on my skirt. 'After Asta was born.' No way back now.

'Something went wrong then. What the fuck are you two doing going for IVF anyway? You never had fertility problems before. If you were meant to have another child it would happen eventually anyway.' She hooks me with her eyes. Tea in hand, she clasps it tight as victory.

'It was a medical trial.'

Her face visibly shocked. 'Oh, stupid girl.' She puts her tea down, starts to wind up, hands like birds. 'Drugs or genetics or something else? Genetics, I'd say. I knew she wasn't Isak's.' And she goes on, telling me off for not learning the lessons she taught, not being wary enough of institutions, the medical profession.

'She is ours, conceived in vitro and altered.' I am glad Asta is having her afternoon rest, curled up with Tayto in front of the television, and doesn't hear my explanation, doesn't hear me say Neanderthal—how I hate that word now, like all the poisonous, derogatory and racist crap uttered by our forebears. It is yet another way of oppressing, controlling and exploiting. Poor Asta doesn't realise her difference yet—that she is not the same kind of human as we are—but soon she will. She is getting wise enough to compare herself to Emmy.

Once the truth is out, Mum is silent. Staring out at the slow-moving trees, their tops rustling like crushed paper.

'Why?' she asks.

It's an albatross question. It travels long, wheels around my head sometimes and rarely makes landfall, unless shot. But she will have the truth, despite my shame and naivety, the tenuous logic I used to convince myself, and my poor, poor Isak. Even to me, nothing I say satisfies that question.

'You two are broken,' she tells me. 'I see it.' And I don't disagree, but how do I resolve things, how do I rebuild it now it is torn apart? She has no solution.

The truly difficult question rests at the edge of us. I hear it whisper, growing more distorted for the lack of light it is given. Like all horror, it grows in the darkness and still we do not open the trapdoor on it. The children's steps are on the driveway and Tayto barks, tail whipping him into a twister.

Our family feels doomed, poisoned from within, by my own rash behaviour. Yet, how can I regret her when she stands there with her purity, her sweet and curious face? She is my own, more than any child ever could be. She is my creation, my will. Mum sits Asta on her lap, watching her face with fresh awe.

She cooks dinner, has the children eating large quantities of spinach and we share a bottle of red wine. She is quiet, just processing it all, she tells me. It's a lot to process. She touches Isak on the shoulder as she puts the glass in front of him, and they make eye contact. He looks from her to me and back again and I nod. He rakes his fingers through his hair and takes a big gulp. Despite our brokenness, at least we can read each other. Some bonds are locked. He stands and hugs her for a long time. 'Never, never, never tell a soul, Sandra. They'll take her now if they find out.' I feel released of the pressure of silence. As if, finally, she can be the mother I need.

Sleepy from wine, I reach out in the dark and feel his warm chest under my hand. His voice vibrates deep with concern, but I distract him, unprotected by contraceptives just like we did when we were young and careless. The thrill and hope of it will buy us time, at least for a while.

'Another one wouldn't be so bad.'

He pats my shoulder, 'Just be happy, my love, be happy in the now, because things will change. They will all grow up.' Sweet and bitter are locked together like hard fruit.

.

My mother makes no move to leave, but seems to immerse herself into our lives. She cooks things I haven't eaten for years, laden with vegetables, much to Isak's disdain. Every time he suggests a barbecue her menu becomes more elaborate and we soon finish the case of wine—the only way he can take the curse off all those vegies, he says. In years past, I would have found her presence invasive and been chilly towards her, she would quickly read the signals and find reasons to move on. But now, with this secret held at three corners, it has changed the shape of our relationship. Isak blames her mellowing and need to care for someone now that Marco is gone, but I think it is her concern. She has always been drawn to a good tragedy waiting to happen.

I take her walking by the estuary, share with her the wondrous life of the birds here, where they gather in a rare landscape.

.

One afternoon during Asta's siesta, I log on to Ärva–LifeBLOOD®'s website and take her through some of the PregCam™ records. I tell her all about Dimitra and her close study of Asta as a baby. How they have left us to it for a while, told us to just try to keep things normal and healthy. Told her the story of the heart cells, shown her a glimpse of what lurks in the future. She is quiet with the realisation of what awaits Asta once she has 'grown up', even though the truth of it is very murky.

She has mixed with a lot of conspiracy theorists and people prepping for the apocalypse so she interprets it all through her own paranoid lens. Some of it, though, makes perfect sense and touches on my own fears. The things I push down into the darkness. They probably still have you under surveillance, she says. We have to disconnect ourselves.

'When you're ready, you let me know—and I'll help you get the hell out of here. I know how to escape.' It's true. She had us packed and unpacked so often, leaving a bundle of mail at some country post office to eventually be tossed in the bin. She kept us offline for years, unless we were living with Marco. Eventually he convinced her to let us be part of the world.

I never wanted that for my children—all that instability, changing home and school so you never have any real friends. Isak would agree.

'Think of Asta though, what the fuck do you think they're going to do to her?' She is near hysteria, eyes wild and wet. I am afraid of her like this, and wonder why I have told her the whole truth. What she will do with it if I don't run, or if I do. I think of Isak's words.

I tell her about my long drives, the paths I have traced out into the wheatbelt. She knows someone out there on a station from years ago. Someone else across the border into South Australia. Very remote, on the fringe of an Indigenous community.

'Wait, Mum, just wait until she's older.' Things will change, they will all grow up. Asta is a lot younger, the other two don't need to be disrupted. We can't all run off and live an itinerant life like I did when I was a kid. 'Let them all be normal for as long as they can.'

I want to keep our normal. I'm not ready to let it unravel.

·

It is overcast when she leaves, warm with humidity, and Isak packs her expanded bags into his car. She lingers over breakfast, sitting between the girls on the couch, drinking them in.

'This is what happens when people own houses,' she tells me, 'they're not free to come and go as they please.' She holds me for a long time. 'Don't let this place keep you from doing what's right.'

The kids stand in a row and she holds each of them in her arms. The wind has picked up and a thunderstorm is coming.

Isak has started the car but she runs back to me, the door of the car open. She holds my face in her hands and looks intensely into my eyes.

'I'm here for you. Just say when.' Squeezes me tight.

Despite myself, I cry and they drive out of our gate and the car fades into the distance.

For days, we all quietly ache for her presence.

SEVEN

A storm rolls in across the peninsula and strong winds toss the heads of the trees. It roars in the night, estuary waters surging high and covering parts of the low road. In its wake, the high-water line is marked with fragments of reed and broken sea grasses along the bitumen. Early in the morning, Asta and I survey the yard, noting the dropped branches and the anxious, ruffled chickens. Tayto is barking in a high pitch under the trees where she plays and as we get closer there is a dense pile of small sticks. It might be a nest, so I pick him up and turn it carefully. It is empty but there is a small magpie, fully feathered and damp with rain, slumped on the ground nearby. Above us, the whip of the air tells me the mother is swooping. I duck, throw my jacket over Asta's bright hair.

I hand her the dog, who twists to try and get to the bird. 'Run back to the patio,' my voice bleeds out into the wind. The baby is cold, but she moves a little at my touch and her oversized beak shifts. I collect her gently. Grains of sand cling to her feathers, her cold feet on my hand, and I place her back in the cup of the nest. She is almost big enough, but her flight feathers have not grown out yet, her wings are still too short to fly. On the kitchen table, we both look at the small bird, Asta with curiosity and me concern.

'Baby magpie,' I say to Asta. 'It's cold, we have to warm it up so it doesn't die.'

'Baybee pie,' she says, gently stroking its head.

I put a hot water bottle under the nest. Tucked among the sticks are bits of string and thread from our clothing and a long strand of red electrical wire. Asta gathers earthworms for it, chops them up herself and it soon fluffs up, starts responding to her care. I try to teach her, but we are learning together.

Soon, Pie is walking around on the patio and eating the dog's food. The mother stays close by, warbling and talking, encouraging the baby bird. Eventually it flies away with her, but they both come back each day to eat the dog's leftovers. Asta digs in the compost heap and leaves out plates of macerated worms.

.

She is rarely sick, but in the winter the children bring home a terrible flu that passes on to all of us. I try to treat the symptoms with essential oils and hot herbal drinks but it is very persistent and Isak takes Jake to the doctor. Asta is listless with fever and lies around on the couch while I minister to her, despite being sick myself. I ring my mother for new ideas on treatments but she reiterates the things I have already tried. One night, Asta's face is hot and she pulls at her ears, moans, eyes half shut and in a delirium. I sit beside her bed, cooling her with a damp flannel and trying to steam out the sickness with infused eucalyptus.

'She needs to see a doctor.' Isak stands in the doorway, his pyjama pants sagging. He confuses me sometimes; knows that we can't take her to a doctor. 'Maybe give her some of Jake's antibiotics.'

I can't do that.

'We could ask them.'

I fear Ärva-LifeBLOOD®, like a terminator, like Nazis or torturers—what they might do. What they will do. But there is nobody else to ask.

'I'll get the screen, you want to do it here?' He is worn down with nights of sickness himself and leaves me to deal with it.

My hands shake as I call up the address and submit the request for a video chat. There is a quick response. A young woman answers and I ask for Dr van Tink—it's an emergency, I tell her. But he is unavailable, so I ask for Lucas who soon appears on the screen in a clean office. I explain the sickness, her long fever and turn the screen so he can see Asta, then turn it back. 'She has an earache,' I tell him.

He is animated, face like a sharp little dog. 'Otitis media. The research points to it as a major health problem for the Neanderthals.' The word fills me with tension. He smiles but his nose wrinkles like a sneer.

'We have developed a new penicillin, made from a type of moss that grows in the Iberian pine forests.' He grins and rubs his fingers. 'It's what they had so I think it will be safe. We have tested it on a child already.' I assume it is a child like her but I know he won't say if I ask.

'You think it will be safe?' I try to extract more detail.

'Just keep up a probiotic diet just in case. The other child recovered in a couple of days.' He looks over the screen and turns off the sound, gesticulating to someone else. His long hands chop this way and that with ample words, generous punctuation. A silent movie. Then he touches the screen, 'I've had some couriered to you, just follow the prescribed dose.' He pauses, waiting for me to respond. 'Everything else okay?'

'Where's Jeff? Is he still working there?'

He pushes his flopping fringe off his face and smiles unconvincingly. 'Of course, just doing some field research. I'll let him know, so he will be in touch just to see how she is.' After a cursory goodbye, he ends the call.

That night I barely sleep, between Asta's fever and my thoughts, which skittle through the conversation again and range back into the past ones, resting every so often on the suggestion of my mother. It really is a big country and there must be remote places we could go. After Emmy and Jake leave school. And if she were sick like this, I would have nobody to help me. Nobody could spare her suffering.

The following afternoon, a white car delivers a blank white package and inside are three boxes of Ärva-LifeBLOOD® medicines. The antibiotics in a plain box, dosage printed on top and two boxes of Poplar Painkillers from their website, New Children's Formula. I wonder if the children are the new part, or the formula.

Asta is still listless and heavy-eyed so I crush the tablets and mix them into some sweetened yoghurt. A day later, she is fine and a message comes from Jeff. No side-effects, I tell him, she's getting better.

'See you soon,' he responds.

It hangs like a threat, and I'm uneasy, unsure of what to do with this promise, this curse.

After the interruption to our lives, everything returns to our kind of normal. Emmy has a lot of work to catch up on. Since Mum's visit, I regularly switch off our connectivity so I feel safer and she studies at Milly's house after school. Isak always drives to pick her up, Nanny Ray communicating directly with him to arrange things. I wonder if she perhaps sees it as a charity to my daughter, who I expect complains about the problems I cause her. Sometimes I send eggs to compensate for them feeding her so often, taking her to netball. Isak drives around for their sports and I am home with Asta day after day.

.

The sky is heavy. November looms and claws of heat stretch out for days, broken by quick bursts of rain. Asta has her seventh birthday on an overcast day, squawking with birds rearranging themselves for the shift in season. Isak has made her some robust play equipment, a swing seat hanging from a big old peppermint tree, a rope ladder up to the high fort, which Jake abandoned some time ago, and a smooth monkey bar. She loves them and spends most of the day playing there, hiding in the hollow tree when it rains. Mum sent a parcel with a colourful hand-knitted jacket and a matching rag doll. In there was another parcel for me marked 'private'—she sent her old map book, marked with places we stayed when I was a kid and inside a handwritten list: 'what to take'. I tuck it deep into a box in the laundry where Isak never goes.

In the evening, the weather has cleared a little so I set up a picnic for her under the trees and we all have dinner there to celebrate. I ordered a portable aquarium for her online, to store the creatures she catches in the estuary or under the trees and hopefully delay their death. Emmy has bought her something special, she says, wrapped up in rainbow paper. It's a girl thing, she says, and sends Jake and her father back to the house for the tomato sauce. Asta tears the paper, excited and holds up child-sized bras, laughing and putting them on her chest. I lurch inside, glare at Emmy.

'Really, Mum?' she asks. 'You didn't notice?'

Asta pulls the bras off the hanger and over her head, squeezing them over her shirt.

'They fit?' Emmy kisses her head.

I can't stop the tears that spike at me but they are busy fitting the bras under Asta's T-shirt, exposing her enlarged nipples for a moment. When she raises her arm, a small patch of dark hair. Too early. This is all too early. And so quick I didn't see it arrive.

Emmy sits back beside me, serving up potato salad and chatting happily about Asta being a big girl, and what it was like for her to be a tween. She doesn't say that she was eleven or twelve, not seven, though she surely must know that. I want to slap her, but I hold myself and walk into the house to get something.

Serviettes, I think I said. My head is thick and pulsing and I hide in the bathroom, try to gather together some calm. It doesn't come and I cry and cry, for I don't know how long.

'You okay?' Isak calls. I don't answer and he stands outside the door. 'Stacey?' I am silent and he opens the door anyway. 'The bras?' I nod, cry more. He kneels down by the toilet and wraps his thick arms around me. We can't stop it, he says and strokes my hair. 'It's bound to happen.'

'I'm not ready yet.' I never will be.

'She's still only seven,' he says. 'And they don't need to know. She's not grown up yet.'

'It's a sign, Isak. You know what "grown up" means, don't you?'

He nods and hugs me tighter. 'I know how you feel, they're all growing up.'

'It's different though, you know that. When she starts to bleed, that's what they mean and this is the start of puberty. At seven.' She is too young.

He's never really understood the depth of my bond with Asta. She's not like the other children. The other two have grown into their own people but she is still little. What I gave for her is not what I gave for them. I gave them up for her.

Days later, the bras go into the washing basket. I bury them under the leschenaultia. Asta looks for them but I tell her they are lost. Emmy is busy and doesn't try to find them. My mother calls and I thank her for the gift. I'll be here for you, she reminds me.

Isak has a long conversation with his uncle about his mother's difficulties living on the farm. He is volatile afterwards and hurls accusations at me. The kids scatter, Emmy taking Asta's hand.

'I can't go and see my family but you don't hear me moaning about it.' Though he moans about it now. 'I've lost you for who knows how long and the kids feel like you love her more than them. I rush to your defence all the time and never tell them that it's true, even though I believe it is.' His words are arrows and I return once more to that open wound.

I would understand, I tell him. 'Go if you want to—I mean it. I'll be okay.' I don't say it—please don't take the children. It sits there unuttered, the only thing that anchors me. I worry that once they are gone they will realise how awful it is to live with me, how I am holed up here in a siege of my own creation.

'It's not that simple.' He resolves to send them some money so she can hire help for a while.

•

I fall into a grey place, each day feeling the darkness of it spread and deepen. I walk with her along our usual paths; she collects small fish, which live and die and we stop to watch kangaroos under the trees in a nearby paddock. Their twitching faces and knitting claws seem to tie it all together, winding around my thoughts, which spin and spin and spin.

EIGHT

I have insisted Isak go and see his mother. It has been eight years and, after many refusals, he has booked tickets for the winter holidays for himself, Jake and Emmy. I could bear the guilt of it no longer. His outbursts of anger. Since my mother's visit I have felt the hostility build—envy, although my relationship with her has always been fraught with drama. He sees me reconnect with her and the way the kids mention her in conversation. I have sent her a birthday card. If he goes now, I tell him, things are stable. I will be fine. I can speak to Mum anytime and if I'm desperate I can always call on Milly's family for help. I'd have to be really desperate. 'Don't worry.' Even as I say it, something sulphuric and volatile rises up in me. I know he detects it, but his need to see his family is greater than his instinct and he does not heed that toxic energy, doesn't feel the burn of it. I kiss them all goodbye and can't meet his eyes.

I have studied Mum's list and as soon as they leave I go to the shed and find some white electrical tape, blank out part of the B on his numberplate so it reads as P, turn the 44 into 11; I remember her doing this, all those years ago. Escaping domestic violence, she said. I feel I have abused Isak, he is not to blame for this. It is me that has broken our lives.

I clear out all of the takeaway rubbish, and wet weather gear from soccer. I leave it all in a big heap in the middle of the shed, don't try to hide it, and drive the car close to the house. I can do this, I know I can.

On the second day, while Asta is asleep, I drag out the spare double mattress and force it through the back doors of Isak's LandCruiser, cover it in the batik bedspread and set it up like a gypsy caravan. It looks cosy, long-term cosy, and I sit for a moment in the back of the car, checking her list.

I spend some time cooking in the middle of the night, pack it all in the portable fridge and collect together some of the camping equipment, a first-aid kit, some things for the dog, clothes, Asta's troll and rag doll. Fold Jake's socks into rolls. Inhale the smell of the shin-pads. The clean clothes in a pile. I leave our bed made and, when I am done, I drop into Emmy's bed and cry, cry, cry.

When I wake I have second thoughts. Spend the day waiting. I set Asta up with glue and scissors and let her stick paper all over the coffee table. Tayto watches me as if he knows and the house feels poised and empty as a cave. Ready to expel me. I wander through it looking at all of their things—their strewn clothes and schoolbags. I smell Isak's shirts. He messages me that they have arrived safely and they are tired. 'Glad to hear it.' I wonder what he will say to me if I do this. I have neglected Asta and she lies on the floor beside the gluing, asleep with her arms above her head. The armpit hair grown bushier in the past few months. There will only be regret, each choice has its own and I have chosen her now, as I did from the start, when she was just a gathering of cells.

In the morning I wash the dog and our hair, shave her armpits and clasp the mammoth hair necklace around my neck. I make a big breakfast. 'We're going on a holiday too,' I tell her. 'Taking Tayto with us.' I am so anxious my hands are shaking.

She looks at me, not really understanding what it means. 'Go in car?'

'Yes, sweetie, in the car. Like the day we got Tayto but to sleep over too.'

She waits, looking at me intensely and touches my cheek. She has grown tall for her age, almost to my shoulder. I know that she will be a small adult, so it is all the more difficult for me to see her grow.

'Ma, Emmy come back soon.' There is a rip in me, one that has frayed and can't be repaired. It lashes back and forth in the wind, threads of it leave welts on my skin. I am unravelling into warp and weft and knotted strands—soon nothing will hold me together but her cells, her solidity and strength. I am tatty and soiled and there's not much of me left, yet I gather together the pieces for her, to shield her.

I fold her warm, strong hand in my own, reduced to bones and sinew, and lead her to the car. Tayto comes at the jangle of his lead and hops up on her lap. I am too tired to drive but I start the car.

'Ma, feed-a chooks,' she calls, urgently. I had forgotten them, shame again—so I pour out the whole food bin onto the floor of their house, fill three buckets of water and leave the gate of the pen open so they can free range. He will be back in two weeks and I'm sure there is enough foraging around for them.

Impatient now, I barrel down the driveway too fast, throw a spray of gravel at the end as I corner onto the road and tear through the cathedral of twisted paperbark trees, slowly dying and desiccating. Each year they have declined, it seems unstoppable. This is my home, what little of me is left belongs here, yet I flee like a fugitive and plot a course east through narrow roads into the hills. I fill the tank and a jerry can with fuel, buy as much water as I can and leave my card in the service station as a final clue. It would have been easier with cash but those days are gone. We will go far on this anyway, but I don't know how far is enough.

Within an hour, we have crossed the scarp, which divides the coastal plain and its remnant forest and pastures from the great inland. Descending from the hills, a sigh of relief spreads through me. It is so sparse here, with rare towns and wide expanses of paddock, some arid with salinity and others revegetated, garnished with crops and olive trees, huddles of sheep like mounds of stone. The landscape and the towns are in advanced states of decay, many abandoned, and nature is slowly reclaiming them. There are strongholds, resplendent towns down on their luck but still breathing. Facades of federation pubs, churches and civic buildings are sometimes fine and sometimes not. Loosened from civilisation, I am buoyed by the hope that we can hide somewhere and I sing to Asta, who hums along but can never remember the words.

Soon the earth turns to red and wide pink lakes of salt, rimmed by tufts of grey-green plants, shimmer on the horizon. The forest has lowered, shifted to curling salmon-tinted eucalypts. It smells different from the coast, with a drier, less pungent atmosphere. Still, life is abundant, despite its reputation as the middle-of-nowhere.

I am tired and start to drift so Asta and I pull into Lake Grace for a lunch stop and look for a park or some trees. The long, straight railway line passes directly through town and we pull up beside the old train station to use the toilet. A green patch of lawn looks like a nice place to sit for a picnic but when we get closer I realise it is synthetic grass. There are wide, empty streets and few signs of life. I keep driving and we eat our lunch, wary of being spotted along the way. I imagine my face out on social media—missing with red-haired child, who shall remain unphotographed, unidentified. We just keep going, although my eyes are heavy. Tayto sleeps in the footwell and Asta is cross-legged on the front seat, watching the landscape. Quiet, as she often is when we do our day-drives.

'Home, Ma?' she asks, as the day fades. I tell her okay and follow my mother's directions up a slight side road, which narrows to gravel, stretching long and straight between gold crops. Out among it, high on a hill, is a living farmhouse. Often, I know, an older and decrepit one on the same property will be empty, cast aside in times of plenty, so I drive on.

The sun is a golden ball, lowering on the horizon when I spot the rusted tin and dropped weatherboards that I had hoped to find where she said it would be. The farm gate is hooked with rusty wire, which I prise off carefully, scraping the gate across the gravel in a wide arc. The sprawling branches of an abandoned fig tree fill the front yard and three very large palm trees droop dead fronds onto the driveway. I park amid them, camouflaged, and survey the house. It is clear that the property is sown with canola crops all the way up to the house and the marks of last year's harvest show on the pushed-over pickets of the fence.

Tayto is desperate to get out so I lead him up to the back door, hanging askew. The flyscreen judders backwards and I push the door, which opens easily, rustling across the grit of rodents. The dog pulls on his lead, nose wet with glee. Asta stays on the faded concrete porch, peering around the corner with large and fearful eyes. Through the wet area at the back are rusted stains on the lino, and it leads into a kitchen devoid of everything except an old gas stove, door gone, and a sink. I try but can't remember being in this house, though it may have been one where we rested on a journey years ago. Smells of animals and glue. Particle board cupboards hang at odd angles, doors jammed shut or open onto sagging shelves, one shoved full with old spray cans.

I enter the hallway, hoping to find something less trashed, Tayto sniffing wildly and Asta now shuffling up to grab my hand. The door is closed on the left and I force it free. A grey floral carpet and wide old fireplace show the former opulence of the house. Long spiderwebs hang from the ceiling, thick with red dust. This will be fine for the night. It has been kept closed and sealed, for people such as we, I think.

Asta helps me carry in the mattress and our things and we lock in there for the night—dog, child and me curled up together. I barely sleep, just rise and fall with her breath and the dog's scratching. Things roil about in my head—where to go and how to get there, my plans veer off like shrapnel, each ending in a corner, where I can't escape. Tayto whines at the door and I take him out on his lead. This wide sky is glorious, despite the frenzy inside me.

We ventured into the interior landscape when I was young and my mother came to help a friend who had married a much older man and was stuck out there, somewhere. I don't know exactly where, perhaps in the Pilbara. Her kids ripped around the property all day on dirt bikes, marking a deep ellipse surrounding the house. They had a pet joey, but nobody answered when I asked what happened to its mother. These things emerge from calcified parts of me, places where I have never returned. I sleep.

In the distance, a gunshot. Isak, Isak—the thought of his return makes my breath short. I wake with a fast pulse. The urge to turn around and pretend this never happened.

In the night, things claw at the windows, closing in on us as they circle around and test out all the openings. In the morning I tidy a place for breakfast. I am too tired and I don't think I can drive a full day so I test my ability to shrink into the landscape. We stay for two nights. Asta is wide-eyed and jumpy, sits on the bed and whispers to the dog, who licks her fingers, her face. He is glued to her. She will not leave the room without me and runs through the kitchen as if it were haunted, to wee under the wild lemon tree in the backyard. 'Ma,' she says to me, 'go home.' But she doesn't know that I do this for her. Only for her.

They will be there now, reuniting with their oma. She will barely recognise them after so long. Emmy won't know how to occupy herself on the farm but Jake will take to it like his birthright.

A slow white ute drives past early on the second morning, turns around again and leaves a cloud of red dirt in its wake. I panic, try to slow myself but pack up anyway and return to the highway. The choice is in front of me—left is home and I have fuel enough to just get there; right is the Eyre Highway and the huge expanse of country where, without money or a phone, we could easily dry out by the roadside like crushed wildlife. Blow away into the desert. She looks each way with me, her esoteric eyes looking into mine for a moment, darkened by worry. I turn right.

By the time we reach Norseman I have built up my courage to continue and pull into the wide roadhouse on the edge of town, inching up to the fuel tank and fill it right to the top, clicking it several times. I lock Asta and Tayto in the car, windows slightly opened and rush inside, frantic without even trying. I tell the squat woman behind the pie warmer, 'Someone stole my handbag off the back seat and I don't have a phone or cards.'

'Cops are in town, love, you can drive around there.'

I nod, of course I will go there next.

Outside, my car is in the sun. 'Could I please just use your phone, my kid is in the sun? I'll get a credit card number to pay for that fuel.' She nods. I order coffee too and she hands over the handset, printed with oily fingers and deals with the next customer. I stand with my back against the cool glass refrigerators and call her number from memory.

'Thanks for the birthday card. I wondered if you would really go through with it,' is all she says and she reads the numbers to the woman who hands the phone back to me when the transaction goes through. I add some water and chocolate, two plastic-wrapped rolls onto the counter.

'I'll probably call you tomorrow, same again.'

She laughs, tells me she'll get a safe house ready, to look after that beautiful child and I hand the phone back, thanking the squat woman effusively.

Asta is red and hot, silent tears leaking from her. The dog pants like mad, eyes dark. I pull the car forward a little and crank up the air-conditioning. There are long trucks parked up in the broad grounds of the service station. With a bit of food we all cheer up—I pull the meat from my roll for the dog and pour water into a bowl on the ground by the car. The thrill of the plan lifts me and I play some music as we drive through the highway intersection and out of town, in the opposite direction to the police station.

The road descends into a long plain, surprisingly green with low savannah trees and mounds of grey grasses, a few early flowers. There are no farms here. We round a bend and come to the ninety-mile straight. I finish the cold dreg of coffee and pull over for a moment on the shoulder of the road. Asta and Tayto and I walk a few minutes, the dog pulls desperately on his lead. She wears her hat.

'Ma, go home.' I can see the tension in her; body stiff, brow desperate.

'We're going to see Nanna.' Her face lightens, the tension releases a little. 'You love Nanna. Dad took the other kids to see his mum and I'm taking you to see my mum.' I don't think I'd really decided this for sure until the call and a little peace comes to me. It feels right. We return to the drive. Great black eagles swirl overhead, hunch over dead kangaroos, tearing ragged flesh. The landscape is low and there is little variation except the grey mounds on the roadside, their angled legs skewed strangely, long tails flat against the bitumen. She soon sleeps beside me, her stomach groaning from the bread. The earth changes from rust to peach. It goes on and on until it bends a little. Signs remind me to watch for kangaroos, camels, emus, wombats but I see no life at all except the eagles and the scrappy crows cleaning up what they have not.

I drive through skin-and-bone towns, just truck stops with funny names—Caiguna, Cocklebiddy—places low and spiky but busy with passing traffic. I weave the car around two oversized trucks carrying dusty yellow haul packs headed for the mines, spray stones through the shoulder of the road. I am busy with this but sometimes I forage through my own raw flesh, unpicking and reliving time that is spent. Conversations with Emmy; watching her with Asta and knowing what I am taking away with me. Slippery fragments of closeness with Jake. Moments of silence and blame. Spare towns, low trees interspersed with wide expanses of tufty grasses and lakebeds devoid of moisture.

When she wakes, I pull into the next wide parking bay, high and picturesque. There are people there—a dirty white campervan in the sun, folding chairs visible at the edge. A man with a shaved head capturing his image on a phone, speaking loudly. I drive through and back onto the highway. 'Poo,' she tells me and I drive a little more until the shoulder of the road is wide enough and I can pull into the bush, crushing clumps of grasses. I walk Tayto while she stays close to the car. His nose is wild with scents, and spangles of rubbish glitter between the bushes.

At Madura we stop for fuel, pass a long queue of road trains and I brace myself for the encore phone call. It is not difficult to summon the feeling of panic and I am convincing, because it is my truth. I return to the car with a range of hot roadhouse food and more coffee. Mum said to be careful at the border and I want to sleep before we get there, in case we can't pass. We drive on into the red landscape, becoming even more sparse.

As evening lowers, I pull in to a rest stop. A road train and some campervans are also stopped here but I find a spare place away from them and reverse in so we can lay with the back doors open. Asta and Tayto walk among the grasses. The sun sets and we curl up together to sleep. It is very cold but she doesn't suffer it like I do so I snuggle close to her, draw the cloud of dog close to my feet, his fur and claw a damp comfort of home. Outside, the clink of bottles, voices, laughter. He wakes and growls. The glow of fire then silence. Though I am exhausted, I sleep cautiously.

At dawn the truck starts, crackling on the gravelly ground, a kettle whistles. I tie the dog to the tow ball of the car with his breakfast and set up a picnic on the bed. Brush her rusty hair and think of my Emmy. The grief is a veil, its surface like worked wax; solid as stone though it appears to flow.

Soon we reach the border—a large sign, warning about quarantine, permits for importing fauna. My skin prickles. A short queue of cars and a line of trucks wait for inspection. I get out the leftover fruit and prepare a bag to hand over. It might be enough to deter them from looking further at us. My chest purrs. A woman in an orange fluoro vest takes the bag, peers into the car at Asta, who is in her hat and glasses. She looks straight ahead silently, picking up on my terror. Tayto bounds up to the window and she pats his head.

'He needs to be restrained, can you please strap him into the back seat before you keep driving?' I agree and get out to do it while she walks around the car, opens the back door and taps details into a screen. My heart pounds. She leans over to inspect the numberplate. Dark hair in a ponytail.

'Um, 'scuse me.'

I look up at Asta, still stiff with terror.

'You've got an issue here with the plates.'

Tears prick at my eyes and I crouch down out of Asta's sight, sobbing. She hands me a tissue and the dusty boots of another inspector joins her.

She ducks down. 'Would you like to tell me why you're driving with your plates taped?'

I sniff, work fast. 'My husband, he's abusive, I was just so fucking scared.' I go with it. It's instinctive, from years of listening to my mother. Bawling now. 'I had to, I was worried about her. She's special needs, you see, and he can't deal with her.'

She pats my back, tells me it's all right.

None of this is all right though, especially the twinge of pain with the word husband. He would hate me. He will. I sob more.

The other guard speaks, 'Come on, love, up you get, let's get the next car in here.' He shakes the bag of fruit, 'Is this all you have to declare?'

'Yes,' I manage. Except my daughter, large-eyed and scared, not on the list yet. Both of us endangered species.

He hands me the white tape. 'Sorry but we can't let you through with fake plates. Good luck though.' He opens my door and we drive forward, stop the other side of the quarantine so I can blow my nose.

Asta takes off her glasses and hat, 'Ma, see Nanna.' She smiles at me, wipes my tears with her hand. I kiss her beautiful forehead. Sometimes it feels that the world gapes wide, revealing its slavering threats to me. I am sure I will drop into it, into the vast misery that awaits me. That I deserve. Then she rescues me, touches my face. Calms me with her innocence and love.

We drive. Signposts and wide roads lead to various mine-sites along the way. The landscape inland being ravaged and transported, emptied of all that is worth money. All that remains is worthless. The sadness of it resonates with my own emptiness and I stare up those long avenues, wondering what it is they are extracting. What they are leaving behind. A few tatty threads.

At Kimba there are grain silos and a railway line, though no crops are growing. The road slices through hills, tall faces of rock either side. Towns grow larger and we stop again for fuel. My mother like a bee in a jar, anxious for our safe arrival, tells me of a campsite on the river where we can stop. The highway continues with its pale eucalypts and sparsely covered earth.

Late in the day I spot the road which skirts along the river and we draw into a side track, find a quiet tree in the evening. There's a public toilet here so Asta and I clean ourselves up a bit. Eat the last pieces of banana bread and sleep in the back of the car. Tayto barks in the night at the crush of wheels on gravel nearby. I tense.

Winding up to the mountains, pale doubles of my young days stride out from the mist of early evening. The winters bring a sharp frost here, the air so chilled it is as though the world were breathless. The safe house has a 'For Sale' sign at the front and old paint yellowed from years of tenants. I park across the street and walk down the side. Tayto lifts his leg on the house stumps. The earth is dark, cold and exposed and we step across broken pavers to an outside toilet, where the key is hidden under a coil of garden hose. Through the back door it smells of mouldy carpet but, finally, I release the tension I have held in myself and put my handbag and keys on the laminex bench in the kitchen. The power is off but there is a box on the counter full of candles, matches and some food for us and the dog. The fireplace is set and I only have to strike a match for it to roar to life. My mother has really taken care of us and I can't wait to see her, a feeling so rare that tears come to me, the tiny seeds from her biscuits stuck in the cracks between my teeth. I wonder if they will lodge in my oesophagus, seek out suitable ground for germination. I have raised the stakes between us and I feel it penetrate into my heart. She holds us in her nest, from where I have fled once already.

Late in the night, she knocks gently on the door and holds us both to her, tight against the simple engine of her body. I sob and Asta pats me on the back gently.

'I am not keen on that car parked out front with your number-plates showing for all to see.' Shakes her head. 'I'd be moving that somewhere. We can get it burned out in the bush.'

I retract at the thought. I can't. I can't burn his car.

'Leads them straight here. It has to go. First thing.'

I am so tired I can scarcely speak and Asta just wants to touch her. Mum brushes the knots from her hair and braids it into thick ropes. Runs her fingers across the ridges of her brows and looks at me. 'She's grown a lot since I saw her.' The grief of this statement pours in gulps, which I fail to swallow. Asta curls, staring at the fire and falls asleep.

'You are right to worry.' She hands me a glass of red wine. 'But you can't hide from it, darl, she's nearly grown up. Poor kids. Nobody will escape the pain of this Stacey, but you know I'll do all I can to help all of you get through this.' We both know this is the first place they'll look for us. 'Emmy will understand, in time. So will Isak and Jake.'

'I needed to see you, Mum.' Just saying those words to her and really feeling them has knitted us back together.

We drink the bottle and I sleep in her lap. Feel her lift soft blankets over the two of us and leave quietly. Her perfumed oils linger in the air.

At dawn, there is a knock on the window and Isak's shadowed face stares at me, eyes blank and hollow. My heart belts and I roll into a ball around Asta, who stirs and shouts 'Dad' when the door opens and he takes her away. Behind him, in dark glasses, is Lucas, bony arms folded across his chest.

'Ma go see Nanna,' Asta says to Isak.

'Great work, Stacey,' he growls, voice husky. Does not look me in the eye. It burns in me. A hot coal sinking through from top to bottom, melting all in its wake. I have died at my own hand.

He takes her to Lucas and they speak. I am broken. Still.

.

We arrive home after days of silent driving. The yard is scattered with feathers and all the chickens are dead. The children aren't there. I walk in the back door and go to bed. I can hear him speaking to Asta and the skittering claws of the dog running through the empty house. I lie awake until he comes to me.

He stands at the side of the bed, tells me to sit up and looks at me now, his face ragged and drawn by deep grey shadows.

'How could you?'

Silence draws out between us. The television burbles in the background. I touch his hand but he draws it away.

'I had to,' my voice is croaky. 'I had to try, Isak.'

'You should have talked to me.'

'You would have talked me out of it.'

'Yes. So how did you think it would work?' Tears well up in his eyes. 'And while I was at home,' sobs—'fuck. After all this time I haven't seen my family and you do this. Now.'

I cry, try to touch his arm, and just repeat sorry, sorry, sorry but it is empty and meaningless and it can't possibly make any amends for what I've done to him.

'Look, I understand why, Stacey, but why now?' His voice cracks again. 'Why do this to me?'

'I love you, Isak.'

He turns away from my eyes.

'This is not an act of love—you don't do this to someone you love.'

I breathe deep and accept that all he says is true, but it was an act of love for her. I remind him of this and he nods, settles a moment.

'Go back to South Africa.' I promise to stay here. I won't try it again. He will have to, he tells me, because the kids are still there. He rushed back on his own when he got the call.

'There's no point in you trying it again. They'll find you. She has a tracker, but you knew that. You were there.' He shakes his head but I am confused and don't remember or know what he's talking about. 'They injected a micro-tracker. In her arm. Dimitra did it when she was a baby. When we moved down here.'

'I don't remember.' Those visits were a blur and sometimes I left Dimitra alone with the baby. Just for a few minutes.

'You and I signed off on it.'

I don't remember. I never read all the documents and fine print. It was overwhelming.

'You were there.'

I was there but I was not and I cover my face with my hands, search inside myself for the truth. I find a scrap. I was in the shower, heard her crying. Blood and syringes and a red lump on her upper arm but it wasn't clear to me then. When I look up, he is gone.

·

I tiptoe outside in the night. He is asleep on the couch and the car is unpacked. The dog trails behind me. In the moonlight the white and grey feathers glow and shiver on the long blades of grass around the yard. It is silent.

Barefoot in the pen, the nest is filled with eggs. It smells. Several dead chickens have been pecked to the bone. Ribs emerging from their flesh, feathers hard with blood. It settles inside me like ash.

I collect the chickens in a wheelbarrow and bury them near the leschenaultia. Tayto follows me around excitedly, helping sniff out the corpses. It is an awful contrast to the strewn hens. I count them but they are not all there and I hope that perhaps the missing ones have found a safe place to hide. When I am finished I sit on the grass and watch the day break. I can't imagine what it will bring.

·

Isak brews coffee and speaks in Afrikaans, walking away from me with his phone. He looks thinner and his bare feet shuffle on the floor. Asta is still curled in sleep and I sit by her bedside, watching her. It must have frightened her. I have done this to her too. I run fingers along the inside of her left arm and she stirs.

I find no sign of a lump now, or a device. I want to ask where it is. I would try to cut it out if I could feel it.

He finds me there and calls me out to him, 'I'm going.' He keeps walking and I follow along behind him as he carts his bag out to the car. The dog follows him too. 'Flying back.' He turns at the back of the car, 'You have to stay here. If you don't they'll take her off you right now so just fucking stay here. Don't even go for a walk.' His voice is flat and low.

'Okay.' I feel like dropping to my knees, *please, please forgive me.* 'When will you be back?'

'I can't tell you, Stacey. I need some time.' He throws the bag in his car.

'What about the kids and school?'

His back is to me. He doesn't answer my question but walks to the driver-side door and opens it.

'I've spoken to your mother. She'll be down here tomorrow afternoon.' He leans down and scratches the dog's ear. 'You gave it a good try. And I'm grateful at least that she helped you. Who knows what might have happened to the two of you if she wasn't there.'

He slams the door and drives away, doesn't look at me. Even now, he tries to make me forgive myself. The love he has for me is so much more honourable than my own. My shame is black as crows, it hovers at my back.

My mother stayed for months. Long months where I cried and slept and sat dumbly on the patio staring out at the trees.

Isak came back and went, and Emmy threw her arms around me, hot and sobbing. Jake held my bony hand as though I were an invalid and they left, tracking past me with bags and boxes. Moving. Back into our old house. Mum scented the rooms with rose and sandalwood. Bought some chickens for Asta and showed her things to cook.

In that time, she had no siblings and was not a little sister to anyone. She grew and became quieter. One day a stream of blood flowed down her leg in the shower and I wailed so loudly the walls quivered and grew thin. Transparent. My fingertips dissolved in the air and the sound trailed out across the water, blasting back the sea.

I have lost my children.

We were soothed by the ministrations of my mother, who strode through it all like a winged victory. 'The day would come,' she said, 'no point in crumpling yourself up and trying to hide from it.' She swept the floor and told me the things I most dread would still come to pass whether I faced it or not. 'You signed up for this and you will eventually have to honour the contract.'

'Even you,' I told her, 'even you betray me.' It was fortunate for us all that she ignored my accusations and remained stoic, caring for me as I tore at my flesh with my own teeth, locked in the bedroom.

It was the dog scratching at the door who brought me home to myself, his mournful eyes reminded me to hold her in my arms while I could, to give the rest of myself to her so she remembers that she is loved. I came back for Asta.

.

A sea eagle hangs in the sky, its wings still but it shifts like a kite in the current. Higher it soars, then with a screech disappears. Leaves no trace. I'm unsure whether its soaring takes it down to prey or up into the broad expanse. There is no sign of which way it went.

The sand is churning in the waves, suspended in the water as it belts and roars against the coast. Curling and white, punctuated by wandering seagulls or a small, dark mass rising and falling on its journey to the shore. Four freighters are indistinct on the misty horizon and clouds, dense as felt, hunker over Bunbury as it scrambles out to a point in the sea.

We have driven across the causeway to rock-craggy Buffalo Beach, an unlikely landing place for early settlers, with buffalo and palm trees, a haven for long-departed hippies. It is a front line to the lashing waves of the Indian Ocean, endlessly swiping back layers of sand and serving up the leftovers of life. Sand and wind, sand and wind.

She scuttles off, wary of the violent surf, printing her wide step into the beach. We walk towards the great mass of lumps in the distance. They quickly form themselves into a crop of stones as we draw nearer. Amid the wracks of weed, Asta gathers hard balls of sea grass, tumbled along the seabed and glued with grit, and keeps them in her cloth bag. Shells and sponges, floral-like shapes long and tufted, spread like fingers, gathered like bouquets. She arranges shells into a group on the sand—three smooth forms like creamy snails, a stick running beside them. She picks it up and drags a long line in the sand towards the fizzing backwash then runs backward, laughing as a wave washes her line smooth. At the rocky mounds she crouches down, laughing at the collected variations of sea-smooth stones and keeps a few in her bag. I sit on a high point covered in fossilised tree roots, encased in limestone. This place is ancient and quiet today. There is nobody but us—no fishermen or dogs or other children. Just the seagulls and the soaring eagles. Asta's bag is weighty with her collection but she rambles along, stuffing it full.

Then she nears something soft and pink, a lump of flesh. I run. Breath short. Signalling with my hand for her not to touch it.

'Dat,' she shouts in the wind, hair lashing and stiff with salt.

We stand together in the pelt of the waves. It quivers in the wind but it is not real flesh—something made to resemble it. I kick it with the tip of my thong and it rolls over and then I see it is a rubbery torso, an adult's toy. I catch Asta's hand, quickly turning her from the poisoned remains. I have never seen such a thing but the imprint is a stain—its image rocking in the wind. Washing in the sea.

We walk swiftly, slowing as we put more ground between us and that. I am glad for the violent sea. Its force a match for any man, washing clean but sending it back—our conscience. Asta finds a large carcase, turns the pelvis, sand blowing up at her with a vile fishy stink. She rubs her eyes and I wipe her teary face with my skirt.

Clouds are shifting ever closer and the hunting eagles are gone. I put some speed in my walk, imagine the cocoon of the car. Battle the bile which rises. Torn hunks of foam skate across our path. The tide is closing in, working its way swiftly up the sand. I take Asta's weighty bag for her. A dead fish, its fearful eye and wide-spread mouth gaping with the horror of being cast ashore. Scattered cuttlefish like discarded sanitary pads tossed across the sand, crushed by the tyre tracks of four-wheel drives. And above the patchy dunes a light bird fights off two predators. The black pair hover above the car park. Crows. The rescue helicopter patrols the coast, its thrumming blade extinguishing the belt of the sea against the beach. I want to get home—angry that our beautiful walk has been eclipsed.

It awaits, I know it and the hard reminder terrifies me.

As we drive around the head of the estuary towards home, a hundred black swans hang in the water, like questions aimed at the heavens.

There is a white car in the driveway.

ACKNOWLEDGEMENTS

This story is set in Wardandi and Whadjuk Noongar country and I respectfully acknowledge their elders, past and present.

This novel began as a short story called 'The Exhibit', published in *Westerly Magazine*, and I am grateful to the editors for their encouragement. I have enjoyed two residencies to Varuna, the National Writers' House in 2018 and 2019 and this was invaluable for the development of *Fauna*, as was the collegiality and encouragement of the writers I met there.

I am hugely thankful to my agent, Gaby Naher, publisher, Jane Palfreyman, the editors who polished this work, Ali Lavau and Deonie Fiford, and the people at Allen & Unwin, who have helped the novel find its way.

Edith Cowan University has supported me to research and write this novel with a period of study leave from teaching. I am grateful to my colleagues and the postgraduate group at the South West campus for their support during my absence, and my presence.

This story would not be what it is without those who support me in so many ways I can't list them. I would not know what it's like to be a parent without my beloved, Graham Parton, who also made sure I regularly visited the rivers, estuary and sea featured in this novel. Thank you Allegra, Florinda and Frank for teaching me to be a parent and to my own parents, John and Margaret, who are fantastic examples.

Thanks to my fellow writer, Robyn Mundy, who sent me encouraging messages and read early drafts, to Sarah Mills for my author photo with the chook and also to my sister-in-law, Hanriette, for details of Isak's South Africa. I am grateful for the support of my early readers, Jo, Maria and Narrelle, and the mentorship of the wonderful Richard Rossiter. Thanks also to Carmela, Ghislaine, Dave, Anne, Paul and Hannas for various acts of love and kindness, and special mention must be made of Louis, who inspired Tayto.

My research on Neanderthal people was informed by the work of Dimitra Papagianni and Michael A. Morse, whose book *The Neanderthals Rediscovered* provided me with many insights. I drew my understanding of de-extinction from Beth Shapiro's *How to Clone a Mammoth*, which makes the science behind this quite accessible.